SEA RAIDER
OF THE GREEN SUN

"The Sea-Zhantil," I said.

"Aye. It is a proud title. It is one I cherish. A certain man once carried that title upon the Eye of the World. A great corsair of the inner sea. A Krozair——a Krozair of Zy. He was the Lord of Strombor."

"I have heard of him," I said. But my heart thumped.

"Yes," Gafard said. "He disappeared from the inner sea before you were born, I imagine. The greatest Krozair of his time, this Dray Prescot."

"So you, a follower of Grodno, relish using the title of a Krozair of Zy?"

He boomed a laugh and gripped his longsword hilt. "A title lost by the Zairians! A title won by the Grodnims! I glory in it! And, for another reason, another reason far too precious. . . ."

"Hai! Largodont! Your dinner is this way!"

RENEGADE
OF
KREGEN

by
ALAN BURT AKERS

Illustrated by Jack Gaughan.

DAW BOOKS, INC.
DONALD A. WOLLHEIM, PUBLISHER

1301 Avenue of the Americas
New York, N. Y.   10019

Published by
THE NEW AMERICAN LIBRARY
OF CANADA LIMITED

Copyright ©, 1976, by DAW Books, Inc.

All Rights Reserved

Cover art by Michael Whelan

First Printing, December 1976

1 2 3 4 5 6 7 8 9

PRINTED IN CANADA
COVER PRINTED IN U.S.A.

TABLE OF CONTENTS

List of Illustrations

A NOTE ON DRAY PRESCOT

Dray Prescot is a man above medium height with brown hair and brown eyes that are level and dominating. His shoulders are immensely wide and he carries himself with an abrasive honesty and a fearless courage. He moves like a great hunting cat, quiet and deadly. Born in 1775 and educated in the inhumanly harsh conditions of the late eighteenth century English Navy, he presents a picture of himself that, the more we learn of him, grows no less enigmatic.

Through the machinations of the Savanti nal Aprasöe—mortal but superhuman men dedicated to the aid of humanity—and of the Star Lords, the Everoinye, he has been taken to Kregen many times. On that savage and exotic world he rose to become Zorcander of the Clansmen of Segesthes, and Lord of Strombor in Zenicce, and a member of the mystic and martial Order of Krozairs of Zy.

Against all odds Prescot won his highest desire and in that immortal battle at The Dragon's Bones claimed his Delia, Delia of Delphond, Delia of the Blue Mountains. And Delia claimed him in the face of her father the dread emperor of Vallia. Amid the rolling thunder of the acclamations of Hai Jikai! Prescot became Prince Majister of Vallia and wed his Delia, the Princess Majestrix. They are blessed with two pairs of twins, Drak and Lela, and Segnik and Velia. One of their favourite homes is Esser Rarioch in Valkanium, capital of the island of Valka, a part of Vallia, an island of which Prescot is Strom.

In the continent of Havilfar Prescot fought as a hyrkaidur in the arena of the Jikhorkdun of Huringa. He became king of Djanduin idolised by his ferocious four-armed warrior Djangs. In the Battle of Jholaix the ambitions of the Empress Thyllis of Hamal were thwarted leading to an uneasy peace between the empires of Hamal and Vallia.

Then Prescot was banished to Earth for twenty one miserable years. His joyful return to Kregen was marred by his ejection from the Order of Krozairs of Zy. Now he is determined to forget the Krozairs of the inner sea and return home to Valka and Delia and the children . . .

Alan Burt Akers

Chapter One

We ride into Magdag

We rode, Duhrra of the Days and I, into Magdag, Magdag, the city of the megaliths, the chief city of the Grodnims, those devoted followers of Grodno the Green, stank in our nostrils, us followers of the true path of Zair.

"This place is a cesspit of vileness." Duhrra spat, juicily, into the dust of the roadway. "It should be smashed like my hand and cauterized like my stump."

"Amen to that, Duhrra. You know I am taking ship here for Vallia. You are gladly welcome to join me. If you wish to smash and cauterize Magdag kindly give me time to go aboard and weigh."

He gazed at me, his big moonface sweating, his foolish-seeming mouth gaping.

"Duh—you're a hard man, Dak."

"Aye—and I should be harder. Now shut your black-fanged wine-spout. Here is a pack of Magdag devils in person."

We slumped in our saddles and half closed our eyes and let our heads droop on our breasts as we rode past a body of Magdaggian sectrixmen riding toward the west. I did not even bother to fleer them a searching glance as we lumbered by. Ahead lay the fortress city of Magdag, a place of great power and great evil, and I wished only to take myself as speedily as possible aboard a galleon from Vallia and tell her captain to sail me home as fast as his vessel could sail, home to Vallia and Valka.

Home—back to Esser Rarioch, my high fortress overlooking the bay and Valkanium, home to Delia and the twins!

The dusty road led straight to the western gate, an imposing structure of many levels, battlemented, loopholed, a tough nut to crack in any siege. The road itself thronged with people coming and going, for as a large and prosperous city Magdag demanded the unremitting toil of many hands to keep its belly fed. Here, on the Green northern shore of the inner sea, those working hands would be slave.

Shadows of the gate dropped about us. The smells began in earnest. I intended to talk to no one. Straight to the harbor—the nearest of the numerous harbors of Magdag— and there seek information on the first ship of Vallia; yes, that was the plan. If I had to wait a sennight or so I felt I could just support the extra torment, for I had suffered much of late. The twin Suns of Scorpio streamed their mingled light upon the walls and battlements of the city, giving the evil place a spurious grandeur and glory. All the light and color of two worlds cannot in the end disguise true evil. So I thought then and, by Zair, so I think now.

The stupid sectrixes with their six legs and their blunt stubborn heads sensed the ending of their day's labors and a comfortable stall and food, and they speeded up their lumbering trot. Maybe they were not so stupid after all. Jogging awkwardly up and down we passed the lofty pointed arch of the gateway beneath the hard, incurious stares of Magdaggian soldiery, hired mercenaries mostly, with a few Homo sapiens among them, and turned sharp right-handed for the harbor area.

The eternal sounds of a great city rose about us, mingling with the stinks. The shadows clustered.

"And remember, Duhrra. You wear the green. Think like a Grodnim. Look like a Grodnim. Act like a Grodnim."

"Aye, Dak my master. Uh—Think, look, and act like a devil."

"Aye."

He shifted the stump of his right arm, severed at the wrist, and folded swathing rags more securely to conceal his hook.

"I do not forget I wear the red beneath all this green."

"That is well. Do not forget and strip off and reveal all to everyone. In all else—forget."

He caught the tone of my voice and hawked and spat again and we cantered through the deepening twilight toward a certain sailors' tavern where news was to be had. The shadows lengthened.

A line of beggars along the decaying inner wall cried out and held up pitiful mutilations, rattling their wooden begging bowls. These were men who had been used by the overlords of Magdag in war, and being wounded or rendered unfit for further duty, had been cast off. They were not even of use as slaves.

Somewhere a few good days' ride back to the west lay the corpses of half a dozen devils of Magdag. The gold and silver oars that had once jingled in their purses made the same bright sounds in ours. Money has no cares over its owners. I drew out a handful of copper obs, that almost universal single-value copper coin of Kregen, and threw them, one by one, at the beggars as we passed. The act gave me no pleasure.

"Grodno bless you, gernu!" "May the delights of Gyphimedes be yours tonight, gernu!" The babbling cries lifted as we rode past. The gutter ran with slime here. "May you sup with Shagash, gernu!" "The sweet Greenness of Grodno upon you, gernu!"

I kept my ugly old face iron-hard as we passed. There was every chance, had this scene been enacted fifty years ago here, that some of those men might have come by their afflictions at the end of my longsword. Duhrra's sectrix pushed close.

"Waste of obs," he said.

"Aye."

My thoughts pained me. In Holy Sanurkazz, the chief city of the Zairians of the southern shore of the inner sea, sights like this, of maimed and blinded men piteously begging, were almost unknown. The various orders of chivalry of Zair saw to that. That was one of their prime functions besides the greatest function of all, which was their sacred duty, the destruction of everything of the Green and of Grodno upon the Eye of the World. My thoughts should not pain me. Once I had been a Krozair of Zy, a member of the Krozair Order held in highest repute. I had been ejected, ignominiously thrown out, declared Apushniad, my longsword broken. Of all the fancy titles I held on Kregen, only being a Krozair of Zy had meant much to me. Now I must push all thoughts of the Krzy away. I was for home, for Vallia and Valka. And, too, I do my wonderful four-armed warrior Djangs a grave injustice if I say I did not hold being their king as of high importance and meaning in my life.

The names of places that have special significances to me ring and resound in my head. At that time apart from Felschraung and Longuelm, which were not places but the names of my wild Clansmen of Segesthes, a number of names could move me.

Strombor. Valka. Djanduin.

Yes, and Felteraz, too, here in the Eye of the World where I had been cruel to Mayfwy, widow of my oar-comrade Zorg. I can remember my thoughts, triggered by that pitiful line of broken men, mulling and jangling in my skull and giving me not so much a headache as an infernal feeling of wishing to get home to my Delia and finding some sense in this beautiful and horrific world of Kregen. I was just thinking that, too, under my alias of Hamun ham Farthytu, Paline Valley in Hamal had meaning for me, when I caught the suppressed breathing from the shadows of the next archway, the incautious chink of steel.

The reins tautened under my fingers and I slowed the eager sectrix. Duhrra reined in alongside me.

"I came here in order to take a ship and sail away. I did not seek trouble." My right hand crossed my body and fastened on the hilt of the longsword scabbarded at my waist. "But sink me! If any cramph wants to make trouble I will accommodate him!"

Duhrra's long exhalation of breath sounded like a bene-diction. His big face gleamed in the erratic light of a distant torch bracketed to a slimy wall. "I knew there could only be trouble in vile Magdag. By Zair! Right happy this will make me—"

"You take the left-hand rasts, Duhrra."

"Aye, master."

Duhrra could swing a longsword with his left hand. I knew.

We rode another half a dozen yards and the tall pointed archway rose over our heads carrying either a cross street or a house above the harbor road we followed. The shadows blacked out the forms of the men waiting. I did not think they would be stikitches—professional assassins—but more likely would be desperate men ready to kill for money, and men of that stamp are to be found wherever men congregate together.

Well aware they could see me, I did not draw.

Surprise is a useful weapon. So is a longsword. Even the sword I bore, taken from the body of that Grodnim Jiktar who had attempted to stop me opening the caissons of the gate of the Dam of Days and so destroying a convoy of foemen's ships. I held the hilt that was almost the hilt of a true Krozair longsword. The blade bore the device of a lair-godont, a most ferocious carnivorous risslaca, surmounted by a rayed sun. That device denoted a Green Brotherhood devoted to Grodno. The sword had served me well since we had left the Dam of Days and the Grand Canal at the extreme western end of the inner sea. Now it would serve again.

The lesten-hide grip over wood and iron ridged firmly into my hand. This thing would have to be quick—quick and deadly. I saw the shadows move.

The thieves made the mistake of shouting. No doubt they sought to frighten us. As they leaped so they screeched.

"Gashil! Gashil! To Sicce with you!"

Duhrra bellowed a fruity oath and his sword blurred up and down. My blade leaped for the throat of the first attacker. He staggered back, trying to scream, with the black blood spouting. Twice more I struck as the leems of the sewers leaped. One reeled back, sightless, faceless, dying. The other, a Rapa, skewed his sword across and partially deflected the blow so that the blade sliced through the crest atop his gray vulturine face. He stopped screeching "Gashil," the legendary patron of bandits, and screamed out a string of Rapa oaths. But, for all that, his sword lunged in again. I leaned out and over, looped the weapon in a shadowy blur, lifted it, and so slashed down. The Rapa dropped his sword. He took a step from the shadows into the pink moonlight, his hands to his head. He had been cleft down to the bridge of that big vulturine beak. Only then did he fall. Rapas are fierce opponents and worthy to be called warriors, even if they do stink in the nostrils of apims like me.

Duhrra's sectrix backed and collided with mine. I swung a swift glance toward him. The one-handed man's sword skittered up into the air, spinning, catching the slanting rays of pink and golden moonlight. I saw beyond his sectrix the lithe vicious shape of a numim closing in for the kill.

"Look out!" I yelled, trying to kick my beast into action and so close. I would be too late.

The numim, his goldenlion-face a single blaze of ferocious pleasure in the moonlight, which slanted narrowly above the eastern roofs, leaped for Duhrra, a longsword upraised. I felt that my comrade was doomed. I reversed the sword ready to throw, and—

A bar of steel twinkled cleanly in the moonlight. It thrust straight at the numim. The lion-man's leap ended in a shriek and a gurgle. He slumped to the ground. He tried to rise and run, and collapsed, and lay, groaning and cursing.

Duhrra turned his big face toward me. He looked more like an idiot than ever.

"The rasts," he said. He lifted his right arm.

Where he usually wore his hook, fitted for him by the doctors attached to the Akhram by the Grand Canal, now a brand of steel flamed black and gold in the moonlight. I knew why he had carried what I supposed was his hook concealed in rags, for we had wished to prevent news of a one-handed man being bandied about. Now I realized he had concealed more than a mere hook.

He waved the blade at me, socketed into leather and wood over his stump, and his great idiot face showed pleasurable delight in a new toy.

"They did not expect this, Dak. They didn't like it."

He slid a leg over his saddle and jumped to the ground. I was very conscious of the shadows about us, the darkness of the pointed archway in which the ambush had taken place, the comparative brilliance beyond as She of the Veils rose higher and cast down her light. Eyes could be watching us; but that was a thing I could do nothing about.

The wounded numim lay gasping on the ground. He had rolled over and so lay on his back, gasping and cursing, and glaring up at us. Blood stained his golden mane. I had known a numim who had been a great man and a good friend, even if he had been a citizen of hostile Hamal. I stopped as Duhrra bent.

"You, rast," said Duhrra of the Days, "May receive a boon at my hands. You may go to roister with Gashil, to sit on the right hand of Grodno in the radiance of Genodras. You are equally doomed, cramph. For Grodno is the true devil."

And Duhrra sliced the cripple-blade across the numim's throat and so slew him.

He stood back and turned to me.

"He had seen my hook—or, rather, the blade. He would have talked. I do not think you would care for that, Dak, my master."

All I could say was, "No."

Methodically, Duhrra cleaned the cripple-blade and its tang which fixed into the socket of the stump, turning with a cunning twist to lock. He unlocked it and cleaned the tang and the socket as we rode on, for we did not wish to tarry with the street cumbered with dead bodies. Magdag has a force of hired mercenaries to fight with her own people, and she had the night watch, who delight in catching thieves and ne'er-do-wells, for each one gains them a bounty when sent to slave at the oar benches of the galleys.

Presently Duhrra, his stump once more concealed, said, "You seem to know this devil's nest passing well, master."

"Aye. I once lived here for a space—in good times and evil. And must I keep on telling you I am not your master?"

"No, master."

"What does that mean?"

A hurrying group from an alehouse passed, men and women of a number of different racial stocks, all swathed in dirty green garments, with link-slaves to light their way. They passed the sectrixes like a flood, opening out before and closing aft. I twisted in the awkward wooden saddle to stare after them. The torchlights scattered red and orange reflections. The shadows grew darker and swooped down, writhing. Silently, with only a rush of sandaled feet, those people passed us.

"Are they phantoms?" Duhrra's face showed no shock, but I saw the coverings over his stump moving.

"No, you great fambly! They are workpeople going to their hovels after drinking as the suns set. They go in a group with torches because—"

"Yes. Well, there is one little lot who will not disturb them this night, by Za—"

"Onker!" I bellowed.

I had no need to say more. But Duhrra, who looked like a great muscle-bound idiot, could play games, also.

"By Grodno the Green!" he said loudly. "You call me onker, master!"

I glared at him. Neither of us would smile. The moment was amusing. I shook the reins and we cantered past the alehouse with its sign of a broken pot—broken by skylarking children, I shouldn't wonder—and so turned into the Alley of Weights which would take us to the main waterfront of Foreigners' Pool. The alley lay in darkness, but from the waterfront the sounds of rollicking and roistering lured us on. I had no real fear of another attempt on us so close to the clustered taverns of the waterfront, but we rode with swords in our hands, just in case. As to the carousing —the sounds rose thin and few. I had fancied the Pool would be jumping; perhaps it was too early.

She of the Veils had risen clear of the roofs now and as we reached the end of the Alley of Weights and saw the dark water before us a jaggedly rippling ribbon of pinkly golden light stretched, as though to welcome us back to the sea. Lights shone from the taverns and alehouses, for sailors' work is thirsty work. Again I fancied business was slack. The tavern I wanted, known to be the favorite of the Vallian seamen who had sailed here all the weary way across the Outer Oceans, was called *The Net and Trident*. I knew little of it, for, as you know, my former residence in Magdag had been once in the slave warrens and once in the Emerald Eye Palace.

In those old days I had spied out a deal of Magdag, as I have mentioned, with a true Krozair's eye for weaknesses in the defense against the great day when the call rang out and we of Zair went up against the hated men of Grodno.

Well, the call had gone out, and I had failed to answer the Azhurad, and so had been ejected, was no longer a Krzy, was Apushniad. I'd been on Earth at the time, banished for twenty-one terrible years; but how to explain that to a man of Kregen?

A couple of drunks staggered past. Our sectrixes let a silly snort escape their nostrils, and I kicked the flank of mine to remind him his work was not yet done. The third sectrix with our dunnage strapped to his back tailed along in the rear.

There were damned few ships tied up. I saw an argenter, one of those broad, stubby comfortable ships, probably from Menaham, although her flags were not visible in the harbor. Beyond her lay three of the broad ships of the inner sea, dwarfed by the argenter. Seeing both types of ship so close together gave me a true idea of the impressiveness of the ships of the Outer Oceans. The little merchant ships of the Eye of the World would never brave the terrors outside the inner sea.

There was no galleon from Vallia moored up.

I looked hard as we reined up outside *The Net and Trident*. No. No, it was sure. I could not see a single Vallian ship.

Well, I was annoyed. It meant I must wait until one sailed in from the Outer Oceans, sailing in through the Grand Canal and along to Magdag. I would wait. There was nothing else to do.

We tied the sectrixes to the rail, at which they showed their spite. Later, when I had asked the questions boiling in me, we could stable them properly. We pushed into the tavern and stood for a moment adjusting to heat and light and noise.

The place was not overly full, and the patrons were

mostly sailors of the inner sea, with a mercenary guard or two, and at a table beneath the balcony of the upper floor a group of men who might be merchants in a small way of business.

A few serving wenches—I dislike the name of *shif* commonly given to these girls—moved among the tables and benches. We moved farther into the room, letting the door swing shut at our backs. My right hand hung at my side, ready. The sawdust on the floor showed itself to be old and in urgent need of replacement. The odors of old grease and burned fat and sour wine clung about the room.

Nodding to a table in a corner where no one was likely to get at our backs, I went over and Duhrra followed. His right arm was buried in his green cloak. We wore the mesh mail beneath our green robes, but we had removed our coifs earlier. We sat down and stared about, rather as two hungry and thirsty travelers might do. And, in truth, that was what we were.

One of the girls hurried over, plastering a smile on her face. She was apim, and not happy, worn out and tired already even though the night's drinking had barely begun.

Duhrra began an argument about the wine she might serve, and he went dangerously near perilous ground by asking if they had any Zairian wine recently come in from a prize. She tossed her hair back tiredly and said they had none, and she could recommend the local Blood of Dag which, she said, as a wine was, as was proper, a bright and beautiful green. Duhrra's face did not express his distaste. But he started to speak.

"Excellent!" I said loudly. "And a rasher or two of vosk with a few loloo's eggs. And pie to follow—malsidge, if possible, or squish."

"Malsidge?" said Duhrra, not too pleased. "Make mine squish."

"We are taking a long sea voyage," I said. "Malsidge."

"Malsidge is off," said the girl. She wiped her mouth and smeared the red stuff over her cheeks. "Huliper pie today."

"Very well." I put my hand in one of the pockets of the robe beneath the cloak. I made a habit of carrying money spread out over my person. I let a little silver chink show through my fingers. Her brown eyes fixed on the silver as a ponsho fixes his eyes on a risslaca's eyes.

"Tell me, doma, what is the news of the ships from Vallia?"

She would know all the gossip, I guessed. Whether she willed it or not her life would be bound up with the men of the inner sea and their vessels. She would hear them talking.

"Vallia, gernu?"

Her tone had changed markedly since the gleam of silver between my fingers.

"Ships from Vallia sail into Foreigners' Pool. When is the next one due? Has she been signaled yet?"

She shook her head. She looked frightened. Still she had not taken her eyes away from that gleam of silver.

"No, gernu. Not for a long time. The ships from Vallia no longer sail to Magdag."

Chapter Two

The flash of a Ghittawrer blade

As I have said before, there is nothing intrinsically wrong with the color green. It is a charming, restful color. Our green vegetation makes of our Earth a marvelous place. I know that if green suddenly vanished from the spectrum we would all be immeasurably the poorer for that. But as I sat there, in that squalid tavern on the waterfront of Foreigners' Pool in Magdag, so overwhelming, so bitter, so malefic a hatred for all things Green overcame me that I shut my eyes and gripped onto the inferior earthenware pot that it smashed into shards and the bilious green wine ran and spread over the table.

"Gernu!" cried this poor serving wench.

Then sanity reasserted itself. Of course! She did not mean that Vallian ships never came to Magdag. The inner sea lies at the western center of the continent of Turismond. It is separated from Eastern Turismond by a devilish cleft in the ground from which spurt noxious and hallucinatory vapors, and also by The Stratemsk, so monstrous a range of mountains that men believe their summits reach up to the twin glories of Zim and Genodras, the red and green suns of Antares. There was no way, as all men knew, across The Stratemsk on foot. And—there were no airboats in the inner sea. Equally, it needed a ship of the Outer Oceans to navigate in those stormy seas, all the way from the Dam of Days in the west, south and so past Donengil, and then north up the Cyphren Sea, sailing with the Zim Stream and so passing the northern extremity of the continent of Loh, and so at last due east for Vallia.

No. No, this girl did not mean the galleons from Vallia no longer sailed to Magdag.

She meant the seamen from the galleons no longer came
to her tavern, *The Net and Trident.*

I told her this, in a gentle voice, but still she flinched
back.

"Indeed, no, gernu. I speak sooth. Since King Genod, may
his name be revered, told them not to sail here, they have
not come back."

"He did *what?*"

"Gernu . . ." Her voice sounded faint.

The door opened and on a gust of fishy, fresher air, men
bulked in, apims, diffs, laughing and talking, scraping chairs
and tables, bellowing for wine.

The girl cast one last longing look at the silver between
my fingers, and fled.

I sat like a loon.

Of course, I could take passage in an argenter. Sail to
Pandahem. But—but there was no other answer. That is
what I would have to do. I did not like it. There was no
other way.

Pandahem, the large island to the south of Vallia, had always been in trade and military rivalry with the empire of
Vallia. Pandahem was divided into a number of different
nations. I had friends—rather, I used to have friends—in
Tomboram. This new and evil king Genod Gannius here in
Magdag had arranged a treaty with my enemies in Menaham
in Pandahem. He wanted to buy airboats from Hamal and
use the Menaheem to transport them to Magdag and so
gain an invincible sky force to crush the Zairians. I had put
paid to that scheme, at least for now. No doubt he would
try again. By then I would be well out of the Eye of the
World, back home in Valka, my island off the coast of
Vallia. But . . . in order to sail home I would have to ship
in an argenter from Menaham.

By Vox! How the Bloody Menaham would crow if ever
they discovered they had the Prince Majister of Vallia in
their hands!

Duhrra was looking at me.

He put that moonface of his on one side, and a frown
dinted in the smooth skin of his forehead. His scalp was
bald and gleaming, with that small pigtail dangling down
his back.

"You show nothing on your face, Dak. Yet is not this
news bad? It is not what you expected."

"No. It is not."

"Then you cannot return to your home in Vallia. You

will have to return with me to Sanurkazz—or Crazmoz, which is my home—and we will have fine adventures on the way."

I could not answer.

This Duhrra, whom I had dubbed Duhrra of the Days, did not know all there was to know of me, even here in the Eye of the World, where years and years ago I had been a Krozair Brother and the foremost swifter captain of the inner sea. Those cramphs of Magdag had trembled at my name. I knew it to be true. Nursing mothers lost their milk, strong men blanched, maidens screamed, if they thought themselves in danger from me, from Pur Dray, Krzy.

Duhrra called me Dak, for that was a name I had adopted in all honor, even though I believed he had heard me addressed by my real name. He never referred to it. The Krozairs are a remote and exotic breed of men, even among their own countrymen who have not aspired to the honor and glory of becoming Krozairs.

The serving girl bustled about seeing to the ribald and vociferous demands of the newcomers. They were mercenaries, and even seated at table they swaggered and boasted. Presently she brought our vosk and loloo's eggs, and the huliper pie, together with a fresh jug of that ghastly green wine, the Blood of Dag.

I flipped the silver oar up. It glittered in the lamplight. "You forget this."

She bobbed a quick curtsy, the same kind of submissive dipping of the head and bending of the knee as one saw on Earth, and caught the silver coin and dropped it safely down her blouse.

"Thank you, gernu. May Grodno smile on you."

Another man might have thought, *Zair certainly is not.* But I thought only of a scheme to return to Vallia and Valka and once more clasp my Delia in my arms, my Delia of the Blue Mountains, my Delia of Delphond.

"Eat," said Duhrra. "Eat, my master, and afterward you will feel better."

He was partially right, of course. I ate. The stuff tasted foul. I took up a handful of palines, for they are usually—although not always—to be found in a dish on every tavern table, and I munched moodily. Palines are sovereign cures for a headache, cherrylike fruits of exquisite taste, sweet firm flesh, and are an item sadly lacking on this Earth, this Earth of my birth four hundred light-years from Kregen under Antares.

This disastrous news had shattered me.

I had been through horrific experiences before, many times. But this feeling of being trapped numbed me. I had been trapped when the Star Lords had banished me to Earth for twenty-one years. Then there had been no possible way for me to do something and return to Kregen. I had made attempts and had scared up some response from the strange woman who called herself Madam Ivanovana on Earth and Zena Iztar on Kregen. But now I was actually on Kregen, my duties for the Star Lords for the moment discharged, and willing and able to travel at once to the only woman who means anything to me—and I was prevented by mere geography. Distance and time separated me, as I then thought.

So be it. I remember I sat up and found myself looking at one of the mercenaries at the adjoining table. I would make my way back to my Delia, as I had before, and I would do so come hell or high water.

With that decision made and already plans for that damned Menahem argenter forming in my mind, I was aware of the mercenary rising from the table.

Duhrra sucked in his breath.

The mercenary was a Fristle. His powerful humanlike body was clad in the mesh mail. His catlike head, with the striped fur and the slit eyes and the bristling whiskers, lowered on me most evilly. He advanced from his table and he loosened his scimitar, which all Fristles use no matter what other weapons they chance to be issued with.

"You are looking at me, dom," said this Fristle, very menacingly. He was vicious and tough, that was evident. "I do not think I like that."

I knew what had happened. So wrapped up in my thoughts had I been I had allowed some of my anguish and my anger to show on that iron-hard face of mine, thereby destroying any illusion I might cherish of being an iron-hard man. The Fristle had seen this and with his quick catlike temper had taken this as a deliberate affront, a challenge.

I sighed.

"You are mistaken, dom," I began. "I was not—"

That was a mistake, to start with.

"You are calling me a liar?"

"Not at all." I searched around for words. This situation was not quite unparalleled. I had acted the coward and the ninny as Hamun ham Farthytu in Ruathytu, the capital of Hamal. Now I wanted to avoid trouble. For Duhrra's sake as much as mine, I wished no brawling here. "No, dom. I would not call you a liar—unless you were, of course."

"Cramph!" he said. Even in the simple word *cramph* he insinuated a cat's hiss into his voice. Then, splendidly, hissing out into the tavern room and bringing everyone's attention to center on us: "Rast!"

A rast is a six-legged rodent disgustingly infesting dunghills. I have used the word a few times in my life.

I stood up. I stood up slowly.

"I was not looking at you with intent. In that you lie. You call me a cramph. You lie. You call me a rast. You lie." My right hand slowly crossed my waist toward the sword hilt. "It seems, dom, you are a chronic liar."

"By Odifor, apim! His scimitar flamed. "I must teach you your place!"

His comrades lolled back in their chairs, laughing, mocking, catcalling, telling this mercenary, whom they called Cryfon the Sudden, to be gentle with me and only knock one eye out and not to stick more than two fingers' breadth of steel into me and so on.

He had no fear of my longsword. In these confined quarters with tables and chairs to entangle legs, the quick and deadly scimitar would do its work wonderfully well. His Magdaggian longsword, no doubt with the initials *G.G.M.* etched into the blade, hung disregarded, scabbarded from a baldric.

I moved to one side so as to give myself room and whipped out the longsword. The lamps cast their glow upon the blade, for it had been newly cleaned and it shone lustrously.

The mercenaries at the table suddenly fell silent.

The Fristle, who a moment before brandished his scimitar with every intent of giving me a good thrashing, short of slaying me, stopped stock still. His breath hissed between that catlike mouth.

"By the Green!" he said.

Duhrra moved at my back and I guessed he was swathing up his stump again.

"Gernu!" said this Fristle mercenary, Cryfon the Sudden. "I did not know—I had no idea. Your pardon, gernu, a thousand thousand pardons."

Where before he had been calling me rast and cramph, as well as dom, which is a friendly salutation, now he called me gernu, which is the Grodnim way of saying *jernu* or lord.

One takes one's chances on Kregen.

"I was not staring at you with intent."

"Indeed not, gernu. In that I lied. I lied most foully, as Odifor is my witness."

One of the mercenaries, a bulky numim whose golden fur glowed gloriously in the samphron oil lamp's gleam, called, "You always could pick the wrong 'un, Cryfon." The numim rose, bowing to me. "Gernu—you will pardon the poor onker and take a sup of wine with us?"

He was a Deldar, and the leader and spokesman of this little gang. I turned to face him and realized I still held the looted Grodnim longsword. I swished it in a little salute and sheathed it. Its flash was scabbarded. But in that movement I caught at some of the meanings here. The device! The lairgodont and the rayed-sun emblem. At the time I'd picked it up on the Dam of Days, with its headless late owner sprawled by the valve wheels, I had considered the problems of that device. I'd chipped out the emeralds and given the device a rub with a rough stone, but the quick eyes of these men had picked it out, and recognized it—and, too, no doubt, they had seen the condition, the lack of jewels, and had drawn conclusions from that consonant with a Green Brother patronizing a low-class drinking tavern like *The Net and Trident.*

Even a Green Brother, a Ghittawrer of Grodno, down on his luck was a man not to be trifled with. And, too, it was not only because of the longsword, which they now knew would have chopped the Fristle mercenary, Cryfon the Sudden, very surely, scimitar or no scimitar, close quarters or no close quarters. Also, there was in these men's shocked deference to a Ghittawrer Brother the subservience to power and authority vested in mystic disciplines, the force of religion, the aura of invincibility.

I had seen similar, although not so violent, reactions in Sanurkazz when an unthinking carouser came face to face with a Krozair Brother. But the Zairians are a ruffianly lot anyway, and they tend to joke more and to make rough good humor out of the mystic disciplines—making very sure first that no Krozair is within earshot. These Grodnims, in line with their religious character, took a more narrow view. They believed more fanatically. They were more fervent in their observances. For them the Green was all.

Was this, I wondered, one reason why now the Green rose in ascendancy over the Red?

"I thank you, Deldar," I said, speaking stiffly, as a Ghittawrer Brother would. Truth to tell, I had been speaking as a Krozair might, and that seemed to serve. "You are kind. But I must go about my business."

He nodded at once, quickly. "I understand, gernu. May the blessed light of Grodno go with you."

"And with you."

Well, if he meant it—so did I!

We threw down coins to pay for our meal and wine and went out. Duhrra took a tremendous breath once outside, under the stars, with She of the Veils rising up into the night sky.

"A po-faced lot, these Grodnims!"

"Aye. And you had best be, too."

He rumbled and moved his wing, but he remained silent.

We had come out of that well. But I determined to get rid of the device. I would not care to part with the weapon, for it was the finest I was likely to get my hands on for some time.

Those mercenaries in there came from the galleys in the adjoining harbor. No doubt they found *The Net and Trident* more hospitable since the withdrawal of Vallian ships. There would be more room and better service, and a discount, too, I shouldn't wonder. But they were hard, tough men. I had fought their like on the Eye of the World. How long would it take them to arrive at the truth? That the insolent apim who had fronted down their comrade, Cryfon the Sudden, had merely found the Ghittawrer sword? Stolen it, most likely, with a knife in the back of the Brother in Grodno.

Even if they reached that conclusion I fancied they would not be too anxious to rush out and test it.

The power of the Green Brotherhoods is long and terrible, in ways quite foreign to the powers of the Krozairs.

Then I thrust all this petty business away.

Here I was, aching to return home, and stranded in the inner sea, thousands of miles from Valka.

The thoughts tortured me. We mounted up. I had no real idea what to do now, for all my plans had envisaged my going aboard a Vallian galleon this night. I had not even seriously considered the alternative I had thought on, that I would have to wait a sennight or so.

Now, no galleon would come at all. . . .

We rode past the argenter.

I said, "It seems, Duhrra of the Days, that we shall have to take passage in her."

"I will still sail with you, Dak."

"Aye." Duhrra had been earning a living as a wrestler when I first met him. I had a good idea he was no stranger to the sea. "It may well be I shall have to pay passage money."

"That seems just. Use the money you would have paid the Vallian captain."

I humped along on the sectrix for a space, avoiding all the usual impedimenta of a waterfront. Then: "There will not be enough for a captain of Pandahem." I could not explain that as the Prince Majister of Vallia all I needed to have done was convince the Vallian master that I was who I was. I could do that, all right.

"It would seem, master, that the Pandaheem are more greedy than the Vallians."

That was a reasonable assumption on the facts.

"Probably. Let us find an inn and get some rest. I will talk with the master of the argenter in the morning."

"We must slit a few throats and gain ourselves some gold."

"Let us talk to the master first, and discover his price."

"As you say, master."

I reined in and Duhrra's sectrix snorted and shied away. Both animals we rode and the pack animal were annoyed they had not been fed and watered, rubbed down, and bedded for the night.

"Listen to me, Duhrra of the Days. You act the part of a Grodnim here in Magdag. You understand that reason well enough."

"Aye. They'd draw out our tripes if they discovered—"

"When we go aboard the Menaham argenter, forget all mention of the word Vallia, except to give the place a round curse every now and then. Menaham and Vallia do not get on."

His heavy-lidded eyes regarded me in the flaring torchlight from over a nearby dopa den.

"I see. That makes the problem a little clearer."

"Just remember—it's my neck as well as yours."

We slept that night at the hostelry of *The Missal Tree* just off the waterfront but still in the harbor area. We were merely two weary travelers seeking a bed. The sectrixes were seen to by a lame Relt, one of that race of diffs who are cousins to the Rapas. The Rapas seem to have taken all the ferocity, the Relts all the gentleness. We turned in and, as I say, we slept. Old campaigners both, this Duhrra of the Days, and me, Dak.

Duhrra's stump was well concealed, and the Ghittawrer emblem likewise was covered with a flap of green cloth.

The argenter captain did not ask our business or why we wished to sail out of the Eye of the World, for which I was grateful, for I had been cudgeling what brains I have to find a reason that would stand inspection. He stroked a hand through his broad black beard and stared at us with sober calculation showing on his heavy, seamed face. He wore a gold ring in each ear, which offended my aesthetic sense. He was a hard man, as he would have need of being, and he drove a hard bargain.

When we left him amid the bustle of his ship's company preparing for sea, with the seabirds calling, those ill Magbirds of Magdag, with the mixture of stink of tar and oil and seaweed in our nostrils, and went down the gangplank, Duhrra favored me with a look that spoke volumes.

On the quayside and heading for the tavern three along from *The Net and Trident*, Durrha said, "A large sum, Dak."

"We will find it."

"Oh, aye, I never doubted that."

We found the money, and a couple of overlords of Magdag awoke with thick heads and a garbled tale of assault in the night as they rode beneath an archway, so I guessed, for I had not cared to slay them, realizing the furor that would cause. With their gold we bought passage, for they had been staggering home well loaded after a night's gambling. Their luck was now our luck. The link-slaves had run, screaming, at the first sight of sword-twinkle.

A fair northeasterly breeze bore us on bravely after the towing boats had cast us off. With all plain sail set—and the argenters had only plain sail—we creamed along, leaning over only a little on the starboard tack. Our cabin was as well-appointed as one might expect. It was, to tell the truth, luxurious by many of the sea-standards I have known. The twin suns shone, the sky lifted high and blue above us, the seabirds were dropped astern, and ahead of us lay only the Grand Canal, the Dam of Days, and then the long haul south and east and north, to Pandahem. From thence I would find a way to reach Vallia.

When the first of the black clouds appeared, boiling on the southern horizon, I felt the sudden gripping sensation at my heart. When I had been living in the inner sea before and had attempted to sail to Sanurkazz and to Felteraz, the Star Lords had sent a most violent rashoon. Rashoons, those sudden and tumultuous gales of the inner sea, are known and accepted as part of life. What the Star Lords sent was greater and more vicious, huge black clouds swirling, winds that tore canvas to ribbons, that smashed a ship over onto her beam ends.

The hands took the canvas in smartly enough. We snugged down. I recalled that the woman—so marvelous in her scarlet and ruby and gold clothing, astride a white zhyan, the woman whose use-name was Zena Iztar—had promised me I would not leave the Eye of the World just yet. She had said I would be prevented, and when I had asked if the Star Lords would prevent me, she had answered no. I stared at those ominous clouds, hanging dark and angry, and I cursed.

The master, Captain Andapon, appeared confident. His beard lifted arrogantly.

"It is only a rashoon. That is a mere nothing to a sailor who has sailed the Outer Oceans."

He was right, if it was only a rashoon, a local storm.

"It will pass, never fear."

And he *was* right. The black clouds rose a hand's breadth into the sky above the horizon. The light shone strangely over there. I stared. The clouds were dwindling, were thinning, were withdrawing. I stared harder. A white speck appeared, diving down on the argenter. The ship wallowed. Captain Andapon bellowed and his men swarmed aloft to cast loose the canvas. The air felt still and warm, the breeze dying. Still that white speck flitted nearer. No one else aboard appeared to have seen it.

The suns shone on that flying dot. And as I looked up so I recognized the white dove of the Savanti. Long and long had I seen this white dove, the Savanti's counterpart to the bird of prey sent by the Star Lords to be their messenger and spy. I gripped the rail. I could not look away.

The white dove hovered. I knew the Savanti, those mysterious men, mortal but superhuman, of the Swinging City of Aphrasöe, were once more taking an interest in me. They were the ones who had first brought me to Kregen. They had wanted to make of me a Savapim, an agent to work for the humanization of the world. I had failed them because I had cured my Delia; her baptism in the Sacred Pool of Baptism of the River Zelph in Aphrasöe not only cured her crippled leg but conferred on her, as it had on me, a thousand years of life.

What could they want of me now? Why did the Star Lords stand aloof? Was this what Zena Iztar had meant?

The argenter, *Chavonth of Mem*, wallowed and rolled in the windless sea. The sky cleared. The suns blazed forth and no speck of cloud obscured that wide expanse.

"This will not last for long," said Captain Andapon. I had to admire his hard grittiness, even though he was a member of the country I familiarly knew as the Bloody Menahem, those people who had allied themselves with Hamal against Vallia.

The watches changed and the bells rang and the lookout screeched from the maintop.

"Sails!"

"They bring a wind, Pandrite be praised!"

We all stared up uselessly at the lookout. He pointed to the south. His voice reached us, hoarse with yelling. "Swifters!"

Captain Andapon stamped upon his own deck, and swore.

"May the vile Armipand take 'em! Swifters!"

He meant they would be pulling, using their banks of oars, sailing independently of the wind. We were still becalmed.

The men of Menaham had no fear of the bitter struggle between the Red and the Green, for they were neutrals. Swifters flying the red or green flags would treat them merely as passing strangers upon the sea.

Soon the swifters hove into view over the horizon. As they neared it became clear they had seen us and were bearing down to investigate this lone ship. That made sense. Captain Andapon bellowed and the Menaham flag rose up not only to the mizzen, but also to the main and foremasts. I looked at the colors: four blue diagonals and four green diagonals from right to left, divided by thin white borders. I thought back to the Battle of Jholaix when the yellow saltire on the red ground, the colors of the empire of Vallia, had borne down and trampled the colors of Menaham along with those of Hamal.

Now those colors would protect me from the Red and the Green; for to the Greens I was a hated enemy Krozair, and to the Reds I was Apushniad, an unfrocked Krozair.

The lookout bellowed again.

Captain Andapon leaped nimbly, for all his bulk, grasped the larboard shrouds, and climbed a dozen ratlines. He shaded his eyes and peered at the swifters. Before he descended to the deck he looked down at us, all standing there and looking up at him. His voice cracked, flat and brutally.

"They showed neither red nor green. They are small craft, less than ten oars a side. You all know what they are." His voice smashed at us. "Beat to quarters! Stand to arms! They won't take us without a fight."

So I knew, too.

Renders, pirates, sea-wolves of the Eye of the World. They took and looted and burned Zairian or Grodnim; it was all one. This fine fat ship of Menaham, all becalmed and idle, would be served up to them, like ponsho on a plate!

Chapter Three

Ringed by renders

If it was not the Star Lords, then the hand of the Savanti lay in this. This contrivance was not beyond them. Superhuman, their powers. They possessed powers I had not thought about overmuch and perhaps I had neglected a duty in that. If the Star Lords—of whose powers I knew so little it amounted to nothing apart from their capacity to hurl me like a yo-yo from Earth to Kregen and back—could hurl a sudden thunderstorm upon a ship, then surely the Savanti could attract a pack of sea-wolves to a becalmed ship. It would take very little to do that.

The renders pulled on. Now they were clearly visible. Four big, open pulling boats they were, scarcely swifters at all. The swifter is your true galley, lean and deadly; these boats, although slender of build, hauled their single bank of oars over the gunwales, in closed rowlocks of rope and thole pins, and they possessed neither ram nor beak that I could see.

"You look a fighting-man," said Captain Andapon. "But your man—?"

Duhrra was standing near. "He is not my man," I said. "He is my comrade."

"Can he fight—with one arm?"

"I will fight with one arm," said Duhrra of the Days.

How anyone could ever imagine him an idiot—even with that idiot's face—amazed me then.

The master nodded briskly and went off shouting to his crew. The Bloody Menahem are accustomed to fighting. Thinking about that statement makes me realize that most nations of Kregen are accustomed to fighting, and there are many fighting-men; but not all men fight, as you

31

know. Perhaps there is a greater proportion of warriors on Kregen than on this Earth in these latter days.

This would be a bloody affray. If Captain Andapon struck without a fight the renders would probably butcher us all. There was the chance they might offer us the choice. If we fought I did not think we would win, for they outnumbered us. But from the tenor of the crew's voices, and the way they handled their weapons, I knew they would fight.

The men were talking among themselves and I overheard the way they called on the Gross Armipand to blight, wither, and destroy these rasts of renders. The name of Opaz was called on, also, with pleas for a successful outcome. How strange it is that a man can feel fellow feelings for men who are supposed to be his mortal foes! I did not like the Bloody Menahem. But I felt a surge of spirit as these Menaheem prepared for battle. If we were all slain we would all go down to the Ice Floes of Sicce together—blade comrades. Odd—odd and unsettling, those feelings that would not be denied.

The four boats pulled up and then separated out of varter range to take us on the two quarters and bows. The crews of the varters were busily engaged in greasing and winding and coddling, and selecting their best chunks of rock, their straightest darts. A kind of ballista, the varter, with great penetrative and smashing power, hurling a dart of iron, or a rock, in a hard, flat trajectory. *Chavonth of Mem* was not equipped with catapults. Their higher trajectory and longer range might have been useful; I could see artillery in the boats and so the varters would have to be adequate until the renders closed and boarded.

Then it would be cold steel.

I had no bow.

Standing higher out of the water, *Chavonth of Mem* could shoot her varters earlier than the boats might. With that thrilling screeching clang the first varter loosed. The rock plunged into the sea alongside the first boat, raising a water spout. The other three followed, and the rocks flew. Very quickly the varters in the boats opened up and scored. A rock flew to thud most messily onto our deck, smashing two men and a boy into red ruin. How this brought back the memories!

There were no grand concussions as the great guns fired, no leaping rumble through the decks, no swathing clouds of gunsmoke. But in all else—oh, yes, I had not been a sailor in Nelson's navy for nothing!

The boats came on. One drifted away, her larboard bank of oars ripped and idle, water slopping inboard, men tumbling out and swimming desperately for the nearest boat. A Deldar of the top spun about, there on the deck, clapped a hand to what was left of his face, trying to scream and only gurgling. Lines parted aloft and blocks spattered down. A bowman fell from the maintop screeching like a leem pierced through with a lance. Blood stank on the air, bright in the sunshine over the deck.

"Prepare to receive boarders!" bellowed Andapon. He swaggered aft to his poop-ladder, clambered up, and so pushed through the afterguard clustered there to the starboard quarter. He wore a back and breast, and a huge helmet adorned with a mass of blue and green feathers. He swirled his rapier widely. I followed him, for the first boat to touch us was almost here.

Duhrra said in my ear, "It is said, sometimes, it is wiser not to wear mail when fighting at sea."

"So it is said. But you wear the mesh mail, as do I."

"I think, if I fall into the sea, it is too far to swim in any case."

"You must do as you think fit."

"Aye, I will—master."

His big, sweaty idiot moonface loomed above me. I turned back to face what might come. He had never once remarked that I had upended him and dumped him down flat on his back and thereby won myself a gold coin when I'd been starving. He'd had two hands, then. . . .

So deeply had I been thinking about the Savanti and the Star Lords, and giving a part of my mind to Duhrra, and, as I have indicated, doing some not inconsiderable boasting to myself, I had neglected what was staring me in the face. I had simply thought of this affray as just another fight. I had given it no thought. When Andapon yelled in baffled fury and his party with the huge rock perched over the quarter ready to drop on the boat yelled also, I woke up.

I raced forward along the poop, leaped down the ladder, belted for the break of the quarterdeck, yelling and waving that damned Ghittawrer longsword above my head. I was almost too late. A torrent of yells and shrieks burst from forward and the men posted there on the forecastle tumbled back in ruin. There were no gangways so I ran along the deck, leaping onto the hatches and jumping down, taking the starboard side. Now more men appeared over the

forecastle. If I knew the ways of renders they'd be in
through the foreports, into the forecastle.

Men rallied with me. We charged forward and met the
pirates face to face, hand to hand. They were wild, hairy
men, clad in remnants of armor, some bare-chested, swirling
their weapons with a will. Gold and silver glittered about
them. Immense lace-knots and feathers flaunted above them.
There were women among them, fighting alongside their
men. That was unfortunate. The struggle broke free as our
impetuous rush, reinforced by a clamor from our rear telling that Captain Andapon had realized how nearly he had
been fooled, carried us on. We smashed them and drove
them back, over the beakhead, down and into the sea.

A man crawled up onto the foot of the bowsprit, yelling.
He backed up, his face filled with horror. Six arrows struck
him simultaneously and with a pitiful howl he fell off to
splash into his watery grave.

"Below!" I bellowed.

Swinging about to lead a rush down the forward hatch-
way I realized Duhrra was no longer with me. He'd followed
me good and hard, breathing hotly down my neck. In the
press we had been parted. By Vox! If these miserable renders
had done for Duhrra of the Days I'd do woe unto them.

Captain Andapon bellowed a group of his men about him.
He saw that I was prepared to take a hand below. His second in command had been killed. A rock flew low over the
deck, parting lines, but, thankfully, missing everyone. One of
the render boats had resumed shooting then. Andapon
would deal with the fellow trying to get aboard over the
quarter. One boat had been sunk. So that left one to be
accounted for.

"Where away that other Pandrite-forsaken boat!" I
yelled. The Menaheem jumped. One shouted back from the
waist. I did not think the pirates would attempt to board
from there and the man pointed forward on the larboard
side. In the next instant an arrow took him through the
throat and, silently, he toppled back.

"Come on, lads!" I yelled, quite like old times, and went
bashing below.

In the dimness shot through with vivid streaks of sunlight through the scuttles—and also through a rock-
smashed hole—the outlines of men appeared, struggling,
flaming with the wink and glitter of steel.

"Chavonths!" I shouted as we ran forward. I had no wish
to slay a Menahem or to be slain by one in the confusion.

Truth to tell, for I was most annoyed by this time, the latter consideration far outweighed the former.

At that instant a gleam of sunlight speared through an opening where a man leaped down onto the deck. The light glanced off a gleaming, sweaty bald skull, highlighted a dangling scalp lock of hair.

"Duhrra!"

"You're just in time! They're breaking in like leems!"

The last boat's crew poured in to help those of their fellows who had smashed in during the attack we had repulsed up on the forecastle. Now we faced them in the semigloom and, by Krun, there were a lot of them.

In among the rough furnishings of the forecastle we struggled hand to hand. It was all a dimly seen business of cut and thrust, of muffled chokes and gasping grunts, of men abruptly shrieking as the steel bit red.

They were sure of themselves, these renders of the inner sea.

My stolen Ghittawrer blade flamed. Men leaped and shrieked and died.

Men were falling about me as the sea-wolves cut their way through. Duhrra and I stood together and presently we were back to back, our blades dripping red.

I'd fought with Viridia the Render, up along the Hoboling Islands of the Outer Oceans. She and her crew of cutthroats would have been at home here. So we fought. Step by step we were forced back, back to the low wooden door leading from the forecastle into the waist. I swirled Duhrra around so that I faced the pirates.

"Dak!"

"Get outside and chop the first cramph who follows me."

He ducked through without another word.

I leaped, slashed three quicktimes, left, right, left, dropped three of the screeching hellions, then turned and bolted for the door. As I shot through so Duhrra's bulky shadow blotted the suns.

"Hold, Duhrra!"

"Aye! Do you think I'd take off your head?"

And down, swish, thwack, squelch, came his longsword, neatly decapitating the first render incautious enough to thrust his head and shoulders through after me.

The door could not be shut.

Other renders leaped through, swirling their blades, shrilling in triumph.

I fancied that familiar victory yell would die in their throats now we had room to swing a blade.

Duhrra and a few of the mercenaries of the ship—Rapas, Brokelsh, Womoxes—bashed in again. We held the pirates for the moment. The wind hung breathless. The suns burned down. The deck became slippery with spilled blood. And still our brands flamed and cut and thrust and kept that vengeful seeking steel from our own throats and guts.

For a short space the pirates drew back.

Duhrra appeared a gleaming mass of crimson.

"I think it will not be long now, Dak.".

"We'll have 'em yet! Look at their hangdog faces!"

" 'Ware shafts!" The cry went up from the mercenaries. Arrows flew.

I spread my fists on the Ghittawrer blade as best I could, ready to ward off the arrows. Three I batted away and then the fresh howls shrieked to the brilliance of Zim and Genodras at our backs. I risked a quick glance aft.

Captain Andapon and the remnants of his crew were being bundled forward, struggling and laying about them. But the renders had broken through aft. Now the crew of the argenter was trapped between the two render parties, and, as Duhrra had said, it would not be long now.

"By the Black Chunkrah!" I said. "We'll take a fine crew of 'em to sail with us across the Ice Floes of Sicce!"

We were ringed in.

Now the renders ceased loosing shafts for fear of hitting their own men. I sized up the men opposite me, selected a likely looking Kataki with his steel-armed tail, his low-browed face fierce and leering upon us.

I sprang.

"Hai! Jikai!" I bellowed.

He swung his blade up and I sidestepped, caught the vicious stab of his tail in my left hand, pulled. He staggered. I took the time to slash right-handed at a fellow who tried to cut me down from the side and then brought the long-sword blurring around to chop through the mailed junction of the Kataki's neck and shoulder. He dropped. I dropped his tail, cut savagely left and right, and so leaped back to the ranks of the crew.

If I was going to take that last trip to the Ice Floes of Sicce, then this little affray was going to be a true Jikai. I'd see to that. I dislike using that great word *Jikai* except when the fight is a Jikai—if this was mere pirate's brawl on the inner sea, all well and good. If it meant the end of me, then it was damn well going to be a high Jikai.

The renders hesitated, hanging back.

The crew around me, no doubt heartened or depressed by that flashy show-off charge of mine, prepared to go down fighting. The renders yelled—deep wolfish howls and shrill wolfish howls; they were all one in the bedlam—and charged.

We met them fiercely. Blurred, scarlet impressions flashed before me: of smiting and hacking, of thrusting and ducking. Against mail a good solid meaty blow is necessary. I gave plenty of those. Now one or two strokes slid in from directions where a comrade should have been standing. I felt a smash against my left side and before the Brokelsh could recover my blade lopped his arm. I had to leap wildly thereafter to keep off a Rapa who insisted on engulfing my blade with his throat. He fell. Another took his place. The deck slipped and slimed in blood.

"Hai, Jikai!" someone was yelling.

"Fight, you cramphs!" I bellowed.

Captain Andapon was down, still shouting, weakly trying to flail his sword up against two men who would have taken his head had Duhrra and I not stepped across and spitted them both.

There were precious few of Menaham left.

A squawking shrill lofted. The renders, still struggling, fell back. No one, for the moment, understood the meaning of the hail. Then a woman, high on the poop, shrilled and pointed.

We all looked. For the moment the fighting stopped and we all gaped out to sea like loons.

Smothered in green flags a swifter pulled in toward the argenter, white water smashing away from her ram. Armed men crowded the narrow deck aft of her arrogant prow and the beak was lifted, ready to be dropped and run out. The three banks of oars rose and fell, rose and fell like the wings of a great bird of prey.

"Swifter!" yelled a render. And then, immediately, "Magdag!"

Thereafter we could watch the educational sight of the renders madly rushing from the sinking argenter, clambering down to jump and sprawl into their three boats, and to push off frantically. The crew began to row. Their oars worked in a frenzied manner, hauling the three away in different directions.

"Saved!" said Duhrra. "And by Magdag."

"Thank the good Pandrite they came up when they did," said Captain Andapon. He had staggered up and now, gripping his wounded side, stared hungrily at the swifter.

What followed was even more educational than seeing renders fleeing a sinking ship.

Whoever commanded the swifter knew his business.

Every oar blade rose and feathered together, every oar in unison. We could hear the double roll of the drum-Deldar as he banged out the rhythm. White water creamed away from the long, low bronze ram, that cruel rostrum that could degut a ship and leave her shattered and sinking. Now the Magdaggian swifter captain swerved his ship as though on tracks, lined up on the first render boat. We all saw the ram hit, saw the planks fly up, bodies go pitching into the water.

The swifter did not halt. One bank of oars backwatered and the other pulled ahead. The swifter spun. Like a great leem pouncing on lesser predators she smashed the second boat. The third knew it could not escape. The oars faltered and came to a clumsy halt. Men were standing up in the boat, waving rags. The swifter did not hesitate.

Straight over the boat ran the galley, her sharp bronze ram crunching timber and flesh, strewing the sea past her lean flanks with wreckage.

We heard the yells and then the peculiar double *rat-tat* of the drum. Whistles blew. Every oar dug in and held. The swifter came to a stop in an incredibly short space. A boat lowered. Another boat swayed out from her center deck space. One boat went to pick up the half-drowned wretches of readers, the other pulled for the sinking argenter.

The argenter's crew, or what was left, babbled with near-hysterical relief. Men were running below to bring up their possessions. Captain Andapon had quite forgotten he had just been saved from death, had near enough forgotten his wound. He raved on like a maniac.

"My ship! My beautiful *Chavonth of Mem!* Those rasts have sunk her!"

He glared about, distraught, one hand in his hair, tugging, his eyes wild.

"You've your life, Captain."

"My life! My life! And my goods! The profit on the voyage! Oh, why has Opaz forsaken me now?"

Well, it was understandable. He'd be stranded in the inner sea, too.

The boat from the swifter hooked on and men came over

the side, hard, tough men, overlords of Magdag. I nudged Duhrra.

These newcomers took in the scene: The deck cumbered with dead men, running with blood; the few survivors frantically hauling out their dunnage; the captain raving and moaning about his beautiful ship and his lost fortune; and two hard-faced fellows, smothered in blood, who stood where the fighting had been the thickest.

I realized we must stand out, must be noticeable.

"Get some of our dunnage up, Duhrra. Act like the others."

The Hikdar with the green robes and the gleaming helmet and the mesh mail picked his way delicately between the corpses and sidestepped the worst patches of blood. He saluted the captain.

"Your ship is sinking, Captain. You will accept the hospitality of our swifter."

He looked at me.

Again he saluted, his arm raised in that particular Grodnim way. I replied.

"You wear the green, dom. You are of Magdag?"

"No," I said. I had to say something. "I am of Goforeng." It was one Grodnim city of which I knew a little, having raided there and made myself a nuisance—many and many a year ago—and it was a damned long way away to the east.

"They breed fighters in Goforeng it seems."

I knew the correct answer to that.

"You are too kind. But it is we who must thank you for saving us. We were nearly finished."

"So I see." He did not look about him to underline his remark. He was probably the swifter's first lieutenant, a Hikdar being a nice middle-of-the-hierarchy rank. "You had best come aboard at once. This vessel has not much longer to live."

"My beautiful *Chavonth!*"

"Yes, Captain. Now, if you will go . . ."

So he chivied us over the side and into the waiting boat.

Duhrra brought our effects. I hoped if by any chance a scrap of our breechclouts showed the Magdaggians would think them only drenched in blood. Duhrra had his right arm wedged into the front of his robe. I helped him with the dunnage. The Hikdar's black eyebrows rose. He was a most supercilious young man.

The boat pulled across to the swifter. Captain Andapon could not take his eyes off his ship. The argenter, *Chavonth of Mem*, went down in a last froth of bubbles as we climbed up onto the swifter's quarterdeck.

Oh, yes, the memories gushed up for me, who had been a slave in a Magdaggian swifter, and then a captain of a Zairian swifter, the foremost corsair upon the inner sea.

We were escorted below and to the captain's cabin. The men would be quartered on the upper deck, well away from the oar-slaves. Captain Andapon and I stepped into the ornate elegance of the aft cabin, and entered a world of luxury and wealth, of power and the naked display of arrogance and riches.

Aides and orderlies sprang instantly to do the bidding of this swifter captain of Green Magdag. We were waved to comfortable upholstered chairs, wine was pressed into our hands. What the blood was doing to the upholstery seemed to give no one any cause for second thoughts. No doubt another raid would amply repay the cost. The captain walked in.

"Lahal, gernus. You have wine? Good. Now tell me the essentials."

Captain Andapon was not only a tough hard seadog, he was also a man who had had dealings with the overlords of Magdag. He did not beat about the bush.

"Lahal, gernu. We were caught in a calm. We fought. They would have had us but for your timely arrival, for which I thank you from the bottom of—"

"Very good." This captain waved Andapon down. He looked at me. "My ship-Hikdar tells me you fought well. He says you are from Goforeng. I warn you I can smell untruths many dwaburs off. I want the truth."

How typical this was of overlords of Magdag. And, too, how refreshing! I'd been getting soft of late.

I still sat as I spoke.

"Lahal, Captain. If you do not choose to believe I am from Goforeng, that is your concern."

I heard the horrified gasps from his aides. Andapon drew little away on his chair, as though to disassociate himself from this ungrateful and suicidal madman.

Before anyone could say any more, I said, in what I considered a reasonable tone of voice, "You have not told us your name."

Again the gasps from the aides. The ship-Hikdar, who had come in with some importance, half drew his sword. I glanced up at him. "Why do you draw your sword, dom? Do you wish to die?"

The Hikdar's face flushed with painful blood. He blazed out at his captain, "Gernu! Is this to be tolerated? May I have the pleasure of chopping this—"

"Softly, Nath, softly. There is more here than we supposed." He bent a frowning glance on me. I recognized it as a practiced expression designed to overawe. His black curly hair was bunched on his head, oiled and scented. His long green robe was belted in at the waist, and he wore a short-sword there, on his right side. His face was hawklike, bold, arrogant, two blue bolts for eyes, the chin of a swifter's ram —yes, these were the externals. But in that face there was not only the consciousness of power, there was real power also.

"I think," he said, "that you should tell me your name before I tell mine. That would appear equitable."

It was so, on the face of it, according to ship custom.

"Dak." I paused for only a hairbreadth of time. I had to think of some convincing name, and fast. "Dak ti Foreng." I stared up, my ugly old face hard and uncompromising. "And you?"

The Hikdar bustled forward, outraged by my conduct and yet unwilling to allow the pappattu to be incorrectly made.

"You have the honor to be in the presence of Gernu Gafard, Rog of Guamelga, the King's Striker, Prince of the Central Sea, the Reducer of Zair, Sea-Zhantil, Ghittawrer of Genod. . . ."

All the time this Hikdar Nath rattled off the titles, and there were many more in the wearisome way of Magdag, this Gafard sat watching me with a small ironical smile playing upon his lips. In this, if nothing else, he recognized the follies of panoply and pomp. But I fastened on one fact, one single vital item in all that long imposing list. He did not bear a surname. No man with the power and rank he had, starting from that rog—which equaled the roz of the zairians; the kov or duke of the Outer Oceans—would willingly stride the world's stage without a surname. I knew him for what he was then.

The anger and bitterness in me ought not to be present, save as a general principle. I had made up my mind to quit the inner sea. Why, then, worry my head over its intrigues, its deceptions, its treacheries?

When the ship-Hikdar finished and stepped smartly back to his place, this Gafard bent his eye on me and said, "Now you know."

"Aye," I said.

"You have the honor to be in the presence of Gernu Gafard,
Sea-Zhantil . . ."

This man was no true overlord of Magdag. Had I spoken to an overlord as I had to him I'd have been run outside and something diabolical would be happening to me, had I not done as I intended and broken free among the slaves chained below. This Gafard had prevented me from doing that, whereat I cursed within me, impotent to do what I wanted. No novel situation, I know, by Zim-Zair!

Gafard said, "I wish to speak to this wild leem alone. Clear the cabin. Nath, stand close beyond the door with a guard. Come running at my hail."

"Your orders, my commands, gernu!" bellowed the Hikdar, saluting, turning, bellowing the others out. We were alone.

He sat for some time at the long shining table before the stern windows, his hands limp on the balass wood, his gaze unwavering, direct, on me. Then—

"You take terrible chances, dom."

"It is necessary."

"Do you not think you might raise a gernu?"

I had made up my mind as to my tack. It was a chance, but I fancied this Gafard would be in need of what I offered —or would seem to offer, to my shame.

"What do titles mean to such a one as you?"

"Ah!" He rose and walked about the cabin on the soft rugs, his hands at his back, his head jutting forward so that his arrogant beaked nose looked even more ferocious.

"And suppose I give the orders and you are stripped and thrown below, chained to slave at the oar benches."

I did not shrug. "You might try."

He sucked in his breath at this.

"I need men like you," he began.

I felt a premonition that the banal words might cloak a real meaning, that I was on the way to winning. He could see I read the meaninglessness of his words, for he went on, "You say you know who I am. Very well. I own it proudly! The name of Gafard, the Sea-Zhantil, is known upon the Eye of the World. I am rich, wealthy beyond your dreams. I fight for King Genod. I am a Ghittawrer in his very own Brotherhood. All these things I am, but in Zairia I was nothing! Nothing! There was no Z in my name. I fought for the Red—aye! Fought well, and nothing was my reward. I was prevented from joining the Krozairs, from joining any Red Brotherhood."

"So you turned renegade."

"Aye! And proud of it! Now I take what is rightfully mine upon the Eye of the World!"

He stood before me, alert, his right hand resting on the hilt of the shortsword. He turned, ready to draw. It would be a fifty-fifty chance whether or not he could draw and present the point at my throat before I could get out the longsword. I would not attempt to draw. . . .

"You do appear to be doing well. And I compliment you upon your swifter handling."

He saw the arrogance in my words. Yet he smiled.

"You know I am not an overlord of Magdag by birth. But I am an overlord now, by right! Any other Grodnim gernu would have had you chained to a rowing bench by now."

"Yes," I said.

"You wear the green. You carry a Ghittawrer longsword with the device removed. You fight well—or so I am told. Do you not think to ask yourself, you who call yourself Dak ti Foreng, why you were not thrown below, chained, whipped at the looms?"

I looked up at him. "Why?"

His smile mocked me.

"I am a renegade, yes, once of Zair and now of Grodno. And you—you were of Zair, also!"

Chapter Four

Gafard, the King's Striker, the Sea-Zhantil

The secluded courtyard of the Jade Palace echoed with the clash of combat, the quick breaths of fighting-men, the spurting gasps of effort. The streaming lights of Antares flooded down to illuminate the yellow stone wall and the vines rioting in gorgeous colors on their trellises, sparkling in the upflung jets of water from the stone lips of stone fishes surrounding the lily-pool.

I switched up the shortsword and felt the shock of Gafard's point hitting just below my breastbone. We were both stripped to the waist. Gafard's muscular body glistened with sweat. He bellowed to me.

"Again, you fambly! You do not have a great long bar of steel in your hand! You have a shortsword—a Genodder, the great slayer—fashioned by the genius of King Genod himself!" He stamped his right foot and lunged at me again with every intention of spitting me once more. I clashed the wooden sword across and this time I deflected his lunge. I had to force my muscles to lock. I had to stop myself—with some violence—from doing what was natural and looping the sword and riposting and so dinting Gafard in the guts, as he so delighted in dinting me.

He slashed at my head and I ducked, he sidestepped and I let him drive his wooden sword into my ribs. It was damned painful. I thought I had done with this kind of tomfoolery after those days I had acted the ninny among bladesmen in far Ruathytu.

Gafard leaped back and saluted me, ironically.

Slaves advanced to take his sword, to sponge him down with scented rose water, to press a glass of parclear into his hand, to fan him, to fuss about him as dutiful slaves should fuss about a kind master.

"I am a longsword man," he said, sipping his sherbert drink, and then with a single swallow downing the lot. Slaves handed me a glass of parclear, for which I was grateful. I do not usually sweat a great deal. I had had to leap about in the sunshine to work up a glow. Gafard threw the glass casually over his shoulder. A nimble numim girl caught it before it hit the flags. I wondered what the slave-master would do to her had she missed. Now this Gafard, this Rog of Guamelga, this Prince of the Central Sea, this man of many ranks and titles, this man of enormous power and wealth in Magdag—this renegade—looked at me and repeated: "I am a longsword man. But I recognize the power of the shortsword. The Genodder is a formidable weapon."

"Aye, gernu," I said. I wiped my gleaming body with a soft towel. Gafard had narrowed his eyes when I'd stripped off. "It is a knack, surely."

"A knack you must master if you are to be of use to me."

Only a few days had passed since Gafard and his swifter *Volgodont's Fang* had rescued us from the renders. Much had happened in that time, but all the hurry and bustle amounted only to the one important thing. Duhrra and I, as one-time adherents of the Red, were now followers of the Green.

Duhrra of the Days, and I, Dak, had turned renegades.

The scene in which I had tried to convince Duhrra of the wisdom of this course still had power to make me bristle. Of course I was right, and of course Duhrra was right. We'd been standing, facing each other, in the center of the bed-chamber allotted to us in Gafard's Jade Palace. The room was wide and tall and sumptuously furnished and we'd almost hit each other.

"Turn traitor! Bow and scrape to Grodno! You are mad!"

"Not so, and for the sweet sake of Zair do not shout so!"

"I am prepared to go out and cut down these evil rasts of overlords until I am cut down in my turn."

"You may be. I am not."

Duhrra eyed me. He was more worked up than when he'd lost his hand.

"I do not believe you lack spirit, Dak. But you talk like a mewling woman, heavy with child, with another at her breast, whining for mercy."

I compressed my lips. Then, unable to restrain myself, I burst out, "Sink me! Of course I'm after mercy, you great fambly! I'm long past the day when I will fight for the pleasure of fighting, or resist when resistance is hopeless! Have you learned nothing? To turn renegade now and pretend to follow the Green will not only save us from the galleys, or save our lives, it will give us the chance to escape —you great onker!"

"Now who's shouting?"

Before Duhrra had finished his sentence I'd crossed the soft carpet in long vicious leem-strides and wrenched the sturmwood door open. The corridor beyond lay pale and empty, with a tall table bearing a jar of Pandahem ware, the cold sconces upon the tapestried walls, bars of mingled sunlight streaming in past barred windows at the end. I turned back and slammed the door.

"By the Black Chunkrah! I won't shout if you will not shout."

"Duh—who's shouting?"

I breathed hard, through my nose.

"You know where I want to go. We've won through so far. If we are to escape this little lot with our lives we have no choice but to do as Gafard wishes. He's made a good thing out of it, by Krun!"

And, as I said that, I saw a ruse I had overlooked. Well, you who have listened to these tapes will know what the ruse was and how I might have employed it in the argenter. As it was, it was too late now.

So, here I was, a guest in Gafard's Jade Palace, awaiting ratification of my application. King Genod welcomed with open arms all defectors from Zair. He took a dark delight in that. I didn't have to be told that.

We went inside and Gafard insisted I play Jikaida. I like the game. We played jikshiv Jikaida, which is a middling size, for Gafard had an appointment later and could not spare the time for a larger and longer game. As usual we ranked our Deldars and set to. The game proved fascinating, for this Gafard had a cunning way with him that, if I was honest, was not so much cunning as straightforward ruthlessness applied cunningly.*

Rising, Gafard motioned for a slave to clear the board. He looked not so much pleased by his win as puzzled. He nodded.

"Come into my chambers while I dress. I would talk with you."

I followed him.

---

*Here Prescot goes into some detail of the Game. A.B.A.

The rooms were furnished with a sumptuousness and display of luxury that clearly indicated cost had formed no part of the designer's plans. Everything was of the finest. I did not go through into the bedchamber, and sat in a gilded upholstered chair as Gafard dressed. Silks and satins, gold lace, swathing artful folds of green and gold—gradually his clothes were built up. I noticed that he wore a fine mail shirt under his tunic of green and gold. That mail had never been made in the inner sea. That must have come from one of the old, old countries clustered around the Shrouded Sea, in southern Havilfar. He saw my interest, and smiled that slight, down-drooping smile that betrayed so much.

"Yes, Dak of Zullia. Only the best."

My short-lived pretense of being a Grodnim from Goforeng, naming myself as Dak ti Foreng, had given place to my naming myself from another well-known location. This time it was the small ponsho-farmers' village south of Sanurkazz from which hailed my oar-comrade Nath. We had taken a trip there, Nath, Zolta, and I, riding lazily through the warm weather, drinking and singing. Nath had felt the urge to visit the haunts of his youth. One oldster —a man two hundred years old, with a white beard— recognizing Nath, had called him "You young rip Nathnik."

Zolta had near bust a gut laughing. "Nathnik!" he crowed, slapping himself on the thigh, rolling about.

I can tell you, Nath and Zolta lost no opportunity to score off each other in the most outrageous ways, for all that each would gladly lay down his life for the other. They were far-off days now, long, long ago. . . .

So it was that I felt some confidence in naming Zullia. If Gafard had ever by chance been through the place and if by an even greater chance he remembered it, I could answer up.

A long white robe was lifted and set so that the shoulders projected on small wings. Gold chains blazing with gems were draped over his chest. Slaves belted on a broad emerald and gold creation, glittering and gorgeous, and from it hung the jeweled scabbard of a brightly shining Genodder. The baldric for the longsword swung over his right shoulder; the scabbard, brilliant with gems, depending on the left. Finally, two things: the iron helmet swathed in green velvet and silk, with flaunting green and white feathers, and a last sprinkling of scented water.

Gafard, the King's Striker, was ready for audience.

He would be carried there in a preysany palankeen, with

link-slaves, and body slaves, and a strong guard party of his
men clad in his personal livery. He affected the golden
zhantil as his emblem. I sighed.

"The Sea-Zhantil," I said.

"Aye. It is a proud title. It is one I cherish. A certain
man once carried that title upon the Eye of the World. A
great corsair of the inner sea. A Krozair—a Krozair of Zy.
He was the Lord of Strombor."

"I have heard of him," I said. But my heart thumped.

Gafard, in the usual way of Kregans, showed no real
indication of age, and could have been anything from thirty
to a hundred and fifty or so. I fancied he was much less than
a hundred. I, for all that my physical appearance had remained much as it had been when I was thirty and had taken
the dip in the Sacred Pool of Baptism, could subtly alter
the planes and lines of my face, as I have said. I could make
myself look different enough to fool a lackluster eye. But
beside the bulky magnificence of Gafard I looked the younger
of us two—which I was, of course, as entropy if not chro-
nology goes.

"Yes," he said, following my thought. "He disappeared
from the inner sea before you were born, I imagine. A
great man. The greatest Krozair of his time, this Dray
Prescot, Lord of Strombor."

"So I have been told."

I did not say that I practically never used the title of
"Sea-Zhantil" conferred on me by King Zo of Sanurkazz. I
believe I have not even bothered to mention it in these
tapes. It was of no consequence. No title could mean anything in the inner sea beside the simple, dignified, immortal
Krozair of Zy.

Instead, I said, "So you, a follower of Grodno relish using
the title of a Krozair of Zy."

He flashed me a look. I wondered just what I would do if
he considered I had gone too far. But he boomed a laugh
and gripped his longsword hilt where the gems blazed gloriously, and strode for the door.

"A title lost by the Zairians! A title won by the Grodnims! I glory in it! And, for another reason, another reason
far too precious—I am behind my time. Practice your Genodder work with Galti. He is quick and strong and will
test you well."

"Your orders, my commands, gernu!" I bellowed as they
did in the Magdaggian service. I learned quickly when I
wished.

He went out to his appointment with King Genod and I took myself off with Galti to bash around some more with the rudis.

Galti was quick and agile, clever with the shortsword. His chunky body was made for sharp in-fighting. His broken-nosed face with the scar over the left eye danced before me as I parried and shifted and swung and withdrew. I found myself realizing that in my comtemptuous dismissal of that boastful title, Sea-Zhantil, I had allowed something of the old feelings about the Krozairs of Zy to come to the surface. The Krozairs of Zy had thrown me out and de-clared me Apushniad. It seemed that Gafard did not yet know this. So why should I condemn him for taking the title, when it meant nothing, when the Krozairs of Zy no longer meant anything?

Thus thinking as I fought Galti with the rudis I was aware of a blade flashing for my stomach. I found myself doing what I normally do when that happening happens. The wooden blades clashed once, my wrist turned over, my arm straightened, and Galti went backward with a thunk and a yell as the blunt wooden point punched into his belly.

"By Iangle, master! That was a shrewd blow!"

I did not reach out a hand to help him up, as I would ordinarily have done. I must think and act as a damned overlord of Magdag if I were to join their detested ranks.

"I must have slipped, Galti. That will be enough for now."

"Yes, gernu. Grodno have you in his keeping."

"And the All-Merciful, you."

He went out, casting back a look at me and rubbing his stomach. It had been a fair old thwack.

The best thing I could do now was to have the bath I had promised myself, when Gafard had been bathed before dress-ing, and find Duhrra and make sure he did not drink so that his brave Zairian tongue wagged too much.

My mind had been made up, my course set. I wanted nothing further to do with the Eye of the World and the tangled politics of Red and Green. I was for Valka and Delia. Some way must be found. Already I had thought up a dozen impractical schemes. A ship of the inner sea would never successfully survive the long sea-journey back home. There were no fliers. But—this maniacal King Genod would probably bring in fresh fliers from Hamal. When that hap-pened I would steal one. This time I would let my head rule my heart. Zair, Red, Krozairs—all meant nothing to me now.

So why did I feel a continuing repugnance for this Gafard, despite his friendliness, his help of Duhrra and myself, his obvious strength and power and tenacity of purpose, the clearly evident geniality of his personality behind the grim facade of authority he must maintain in his position?

He was a renegade.

He had destroyed all credence. Once a man of the Red, he was now a cringing cur of the Green.

But—Red and Green meant nothing to me now. . . .

All this talk of the great Krozair, Dray Prescot, Lord of Strombor, had unsettled me. That was a long time ago. Now I was a Vallian and wanted to go home.

Finding Duhrra in our room with an opened bottle of Chremson I slumped into a chair and reached out my hand. Duhrra slapped the bottle in. This Chremson was not Grodnim wine; it had been looted from a sinking prize. For all his protestations, Gafard still preferred good Zairian wine.

"Good stuff, Dak."

"Go drink with moderation, Duhrra." I glared at him. "I am still concerned about you and your hook. If word comes back from the Akhram that they fitted a man with hooks and cripple-blades, and that information is joined with the novice Todalphemes' account of what transpired on the Dam of Days, we could—"

"We could find ourselves with a coil of chains about us and our tripes being drawn out! Aye! And we might also find ourselves with brands in our fists smiting down these cramphs of Magdag."

"Your black-fanged wine-spout gapes too much."

"Aye, master, you are right. I will be a good Grodnim."

I did not laugh. But the invitation was there as I said, lifting the bottle, "Then you'd be a dead Grodnim." The expression, crude and cruel, is known on Kregen as on Earth.

Later a slave summoned me over to Gafard's chambers. He was in jovial mood as his slaves disrobed him. He had been drinking and the flush in his hard face and the sparkle in his eyes told me that the drink was only a preliminary for the night's activities.

"I spend the night in the Tower of True Contentment," he said, flinging his green tunic off himself so the slaves might unlatch the mesh shirt. "But, before I go, I have great news. The king accepts you! You have an audience on the morrow. You will be gladly enrolled."

I nodded, not wishing to speak. He took that as a favorable sign, an indication I was moved with joy.

"You will do as I have done. Once I was Fard of Nowhere. Now I am Gafard, a great Ghittawrer, a rog, Prince of the Central Sea. You will take the name Gadak. It is as Gadak that you join the ranks of the Green, serving Grodno, a true Grodnim!"

Chapter Five

Zena Iztar advises me in King Genod's palace

I had been a seaman in the late eighteenth-century navy of England, Nelson's navy, and an education does not come much harder than that. I had been a slave, whipped and beaten and slaving all the hours of the day. I had been a prince, living in luxury, a king, even, leading my ferocious warriors to victory.

Also, I had been a spy, acting a part to steal away secrets from a hostile nation.

As Gafard critically appraised the preparations made for my dress and appearance, and counseled me, sagely, on how to conduct myself during the audience, I reflected that I had had enough experience to pass off this coming ordeal without trouble.

But for all my protestations to myself, for all my newly won wisdom, for all my concern lest I had lost that old cutting edge, I did feel the dangers ahead. I might break out with a furious roar of "Zair! Zair!" and go on bashing skulls until they hacked me down and dragged me out by the heels.

I might.

There was too much at stake for me to allow myself that luxury.

My island stromnate of Valka, a part of the empire of Vallia, would soon be locked, I felt sure, in another bloody struggle with the evil empire of Hamal. My duty lay to Vallia. My Delia, the glorious Delia of Delphond, Delia of the Blue Mountains, awaited my homecoming. I could not jeopardize all that for the sake of the heady satisfaction of swinging my sword against the hated Green. And—I was no longer a Krozair of Zy. Why then did I fear so much what I might do?

My kingdom of Djanduin had not seen their king for many a long day. Strombor, my noble house of the enclave city of Zenicce, no less than my Clansmen of Felschraung and Longuelm, must feel deserted by me.

No.

No, I must mumble and scrape and humble myself to this maniac, this Genod Gannius.

He would never know that it was only because I had obeyed the dictates of the Star Lords on that long-ago day by the Grand Canal and saved the lives of his parents that he had been born at all. But for me he would never have been. I had brought woe to all Zairia with that action, all unknowingly, moved only by selfish aims, for I had dearly needed to continue upon Kregen. . . .

Immense and awe-inspiring is the city of Magdag. Enormous walls defend the many harbors. Tier upon tier rise the costly houses above the waterfront. Many glittering temples rise to Grodno, and the place is forever a babblement of people about the business of a great city.

The single stupendous fact about Magdag, which marks it off from most other cities, is the incredible area devoted to the megaliths. For dwabur after dwabur they stretch along the plain, colossal, blocks of architecture, striding with the insensate hunger of continual growth. Thousands of slaves and workers toil ceaselessly, forever creating new halls and courts and pavilions, raising fresh towers and cupolas to the glory of Grodno the Green. Always, in Magdag, there is building as the overlords indulge their obsessive craze. As a slave, as a stylor, I had worked there, and, too, I had been caught up in the dark mysteries revealing the reasons for this fraught building mania.

As Gafard in his preysany litter and I, astride a sectrix and riding abaft him, made our way through the crowded streets, those enormous blocks, the megaliths of Magdag, fractured the far skyline. Dominant, impressive, brooding, they lowered down over the city of Magdag.

The reception at King Genod's palace proceeded much as I had expected. There were all the usual panoply and pomp and circumstance, the frills and the rituals, the protocols. We were escorted through court after court, up marble stairways, and through immense arches in the tall pointed fashion of Grodnim. Everywhere stood guards, ramrod stiff, on duty, only their eyes moving as they watched every arrival and departure. They wore a variety of fancy uniforms, and I stored away details of armor and weaponry against future need.

The chamberlains in their green tabards and golden wands went before us. Trumpeters pealed a blast as we passed that was designed, I felt damned sure, to make the suppliants to the throne jump out of their skins with fright. On we went and, at last, came to the anteroom to the reception chamber. Like many of the palaces of Kregen of which I had knowledge, this Palace of Grodno the All-Wise contained a maze of rooms and chambers and secret ways. I held myself erect and I looked about openly, as would be expected; but I had loosened my longsword in the scabbard and my right hand remained limp and flexed, ready for instant action.

Trumpets pealed again, the anteroom doors were flung back, and preceded by the chamberlains, Gafard and I marched into the gleaming brilliance of the reception chamber.

Light, color, glitter. The sight of waving fans, bare shoulders, silk and furs, armor of iron and steel, and everywhere the green, that green, shining and refulgent, here in the reception chamber of King Genod Gannius of Magdag.

Designed to impress, the chamber weighed down on my spirits. What was I, who had once been of Zair, doing here, even if the Krozairs of Zy had rejected me?

The device of the lairgodont appeared in many places. Guards with spears and swords, in glittering mail swathed in green robes, stood dumbly along the walls. I marked their helmets. Atop each burnished helm rose the sculpted form of a lairgodnot, in the round, fashioned of silver, shining and winking in the light streaming through the clerestory above. The artist who had created the master image had caught all the violent, vicious character of the lairgodont, portraying him with a half-turned head so the wicked fangs in that gap-jawed mouth showed prominently. The body scales were delineated to perfection, the spiked tail curled high and menacingly, the skull-crushing talons gripped like vises of death.

We marched down the marble length of floor to the throne at the far end. There were three thrones and in the center, higher throne, sat King Genod.

Our studded sandals rang on the marble.

Gafard presented a formidable picture of a fighting-man, loaded with honor and wealth, harsh and cruel, superb in his strength.

I, this same Gadak, marched a half-pace to his left rear. Over the mail shirt he had given me I wore a white robe well splashed with the green decorations, with a green sleeveless jacket embroidered in silver over that, the Genodder scabbarded high on my right side, the longsword swinging from a baldric at my left.

Past the watching lines of guards we marched, past the crowds of courtiers and officials and high officers, past the clustering women who arranged, every one, to wear their flaunting green feathers in ways individual to each. The light streamed in above, the mass of gems and feathers and precious metals formed a chiaroscuro of brilliance, and over all the hated green prevailed.

We halted where a golden line in the marble pavement indicated the distance by which we must be separated from the king and his magnificence. I halted, still that half-pace to Gafard's rear, and the chamberlains wheeled to the side and stood, their heads bent, facing the throne. Deliberately, I looked at the smaller thrones.

The right-hand chair of gold held the small, shrunken body of a man I judged to be well past two hundred, well past the age he should have gone to the Ice Floes of Sicce or, in his case, up to sit in glory on the right hand of Grodno in the green radiance of Genodras. His role, I judged, would be that of court wise man, perhaps wizard, and his lined, pouched face and those dark darting eyes, like lizard eyes, confirmed the shrewd intelligence of the fellow. His frail body was so smothered in green and gold no indication of his figure was possible; I fancied he had little longer to spend on Kregen.

In the left-hand chair sat—My breath sucked in and I forced my ugly old face to remain a carved chunk of mahogany.

Oh, yes, I knew her.

She had changed since I had last seen her. Plumpness had softened the lines of beauty in her face, making her appear more petulant than ever. But she remained superbly beautiful, still lithe and lovely. Her dark hair had been dyed the fashionable green. Her kohled eyes regarded me and I kept my face blank. The last words we had exchanged— so long ago here in Magdag as my old vosk-skulls surged forward to the victory that was surely theirs, that victory so cruelly denied—had been words of anger and unfulfilled yearning. She had said I looked ridiculous, standing there with an old vosk skull upon my head. She had slashed at my

face with her riding crop, and I had ducked and the blow
had glanced harmlessly from the vosk-skull helmet.

The princess Susheeng.

Oh, yes, I knew her.

Would she know me?

How she had recoiled when she had learned I was a
Krozair of Zy, the Lord of Strombor!

I stood dumbly and looked away, daring in the parlance of
the overlords of Magdag to lift my eyes to the radiance of
the king.

He was a man, this king Genod. I saw at a glance the
fire in him, the fierce energy, the deep-banked fires of genius
that could flame and flash as he led his men, driving them,
leading them, inspiring them with all the magnetism of his
powerful personality. And yet in those deep dark eyes I saw
the callous cruelty of a leem. I saw in the bladelike nose, the
arrogant jut of jaw, and the thinness of the lips signs that,
brush them aside as you will, denote the man who puts himself and his own purposes always foremost in all he does.

He sat brooding upon us, and all the gaudy glitter of his
clothes and jewels and arms paled beside the sullen power of
that face.

"Lahal, Gafard."

"Lahal, majister."

That was all, between these two. Yet I swear I understood a little more of the bond between them. Master and
servant, brain and tool, they complemented each other.
Between them they could take the inner sea and wring
it dry.

The princess Susheeng, who had once knelt weeping, be-
seeching, supplicating before me, naked but for the gray
slave breechclout, did not move. I flicked her a quick
glance and saw no outward change in her demeanor. It had
been a long time, and that notorious Krozair Brother, the
Lord of Strombor, was long dead and gone to his grave. And,
perhaps I, too, had changed over all those years.

Also, Gafard's shadow from the clerestory windows fell
across me, and my green silken turban wound around the
plain iron helmet draped half across my face. I breathed
more easily.

Impossible to imagine she would recognize in this new
renegade seeking admission to the king's armies a man she
had once known so long ago and who was now dead.

Gafard had warned me that this audience would form the
public initiation. From this time on I was Grodnim. Later

the king would see me privately, and there I might form a better opinion of what was required of me.

I recognized that Princess Susheeng had achieved much of her heart's desire. She and her brother, that devil prince Glycas, had planned and plotted to raise themselves even higher in Magdag. Now this storming genius Genod Gannius had appeared on the scene and had led his armies in triumph over Magdag and ruled here in the city of megaliths. And he had chosen Susheeng as his consort. She, at least, had achieved much.

The thought that Glycas must be here, if he was not dead, made me realize the latter alternative to be far more preferable.

The short ceremony of admission was about to begin.

The chamberlains unhitched the Genodder from the high belt and carried it toward a Chuktar, a Chulik, who stood enormous and impressive in armor and green. He took the sword.

After some mumbo-jumbo, the Genodder would be blessed by the priests, waiting in their green robes at the side, the king would kiss it, and I would receive it back, to kiss it and so hang it once more upon my person. The admission would have been completed.

So I stood there, waiting for the next move in this charade.

No one moved.

No one stirred.

I looked hard at the king. His right hand was half lifted in the sign to begin. That hand did not move, did not waver, did not tremble. The old wise man's mouth was half open. That mouth neither opened nor closed. Susheeng's hand turned at the wrist and fondled a golden brooch upon her breast. Nothing moved.

So I knew.

Not a sound rose from the mass of courtiers in the bright reception chamber, not a person moved.

I shuffled my feet and turned around, nastily, to face the tall double doors. Now, I said to myself, now what does she want?

Zena Iztar walked in through the opened double doors and past the lines of petrified people. She looked, as always, supremely imposing. She wore her crimson and scarlet and golden robes, with a narrow green sash, and the jewels flamed from her to drown in magnificence the suddenly tawdry splendor of King Genod's glittering reception chamber.

She halted a little way off from me. She shook her head. "Dray Prescot!"

"What do you want, Zena Iztar?"

"I seek to know what you do here."

"It is obvious."

"Not to me, not to the Star Lords, not to the Savanti."

"Then are they—and you—of little wit."

That calm face, imperious, proud, beautiful yes, all those things, but also maternal and wise and sorrowing did not smile. Again she shook her head and the jewels of her head-dress flashed and sparkled. "If we used our wits, as you suggest, we might believe you did an evil thing here."

"Of course it's evil!"

A tiny line dinted between her eyebrows.

I said, "We have met three times, Madam Ivanovna, Zena Iztar. Do you not yet understand I am an evil man?"

"Yet were you chosen by the Savanti and after they cast you off, by the Everoinye, the Star Lords."

"That was not of my seeking."

"Yet were you chosen."

I wasn't fool enough to ask why I had been chosen. The Savanti, those superhuman men of Aprasöe, the Swinging City, selected many men from Earth and subjected them to a test and so, accepting them, trained them to become Savapim and go forth upon Kregen to uphold the dignity of apims, of Homo sapiens. I had been found wanting and so had been kicked out of paradise. I had fought and worked and created my own paradise upon Kregen. All I held dear lay with my Delia. The Star Lords used me when they willed for their own ends. The reasons behind the selection of myself were obvious; the ramifications of the conflicting desires of others were the causes of the way my life had gone upon Kregen. I had no stupid delusions that I was in any way special, destined for a great and glittering fate in this world four hundred light-years from Earth.

"I warned you, Pur Dray," said Zena Iztar, "that you would not be allowed to leave the Eye of the World."

"I am no longer Pur Dray."

"That is sooth. But I would like you to become Pur Dray again, once more to take up your rightful place as a member of the Krozairs of Zy."

"I'm finished with all that!"

"You will never leave the inner sea until you do."

All along, all during the time of my boasting and planning, when I had ridden to Magdag, when I had taken the

argenter, all the time, I must have known—had known—
that I could not leave the Eye of the World. Those vast
and implacable forces operating outside of the time and
space I knew held me fast caught. Until what they desired
occurred I must remain here, a free man within the confines
of the inner sea, but imprisoned here as I had been imprisoned on my own Earth.

"The Krozairs of Zy mean nothing to me now. I am
Apushniad. Had you forgotten?"

"I do not forget important things so lightly."

"It's not important! Not any longer!" I was shouting.
"I have put the Krozairs behind me, cast them off, shed
them as a snake sheds a skin. There are other places of
Kregen I hold more dear."

She bent her gaze upon me. "As a snake, you said . . ."

"Well, then? I am evil, so a snake will serve. Although I
detest the things, even though they live according to
their natures."

"The man of your Earth called Shakespeare had a word
for your conduct now, Pur Dray."

"He had a word for everything."

"And I have a word for you. You are held here. When you
are once more a Krozair of Zy, then perchance you may
return to your Valka—"

"And Delia?"

She put one long white finger to her lips. Those lips, red
and soft, parted and I caught the gleam of white teeth.
She cared for herself, this Zena Iztar. "You know your wife.
You know her mettle. She is safe, as happy as she will ever
be without you—poor soul!—yet will she risk all to find you
again."

"And you condemn her to that!"

She was very brisk about that. "I condemn no one to anything. Men and women have suffered since the beginning and,
assuredly, will suffer until the end."

"You told me I would face a choice, a hard choice—"

"Not this petty business, serious though it may be." She
brushed my words aside. "The choice will come later. Also, I
said that even Grodno might play a part, that stranger
things have happened."

"I remember. That was the first time, in my chambers in
London, before the séance—"

"And when I saw you for the second time, by the banks
of the Grand Canal, I warned you afresh. You have a part to
play. I would you would play it with all your heart."

"When I am parted from Delia, that I cannot do."

"I see that, and I believe it. Then I say this to you: you must pursue the path with every part of you that you can. Put as much of yourself into your struggle as you can possibly spend. I know whereof I speak. I salute you as Pur Dray."

I nodded my head at the thrones. "And if Susheeng recognizes me?"

"I do not think the—the princess Susheeng will know you. For her the Eye of the World revolves about the king. And she will not wish the king to know she once abased herself to you and that you spurned her."

"Aye. She didn't relish that, by Vox!"

"But you did?"

I flicked up my evil old eyes to glare at her. "Sharp, Madam Zena Iztar! No, I do not think I relished seeing a silly hulu make a fool of herself. I do not think I took pleasure from that. But had I done so, I could have understood myself passing well."

"I have no more to say to you now."

I knew that in a moment she would walk off and the silent, motionless people all about would wake to life and the ceremony would proceed. Already the Chulik Chuktar, he who held my shortsword, had the piece of red cloth extended, still and unmoving. There were very many things I wished to ask this woman, and every time she sidestepped them and we got into an argument. I said, "Not the Star Lords, not the Savanti, then who, Zena Iztar?"

She saw my eyes and looked where I looked and saw the scrap of red cloth in the fingers of the Chuktar.

"They will make you—"

"Yes, I know."

"And it will mean nothing?"

"Nothing."

"Remember what I have said. Your only way out. Remember."

"But—tell me who you are and why—"

But she was walking away with that lithe swinging gait, going out the doors. She had passed along all that long expanse of marble with supernatural speed; yet she appeared to be only walking naturally. The double doors closed of their own volition—or so it seemed.

She was gone.

The piece of red cloth in the Chulik Chuktar's fingers

jerked as he finished ripping it from his pocket. He held it up, ready for the king's signal.

Silver trumpets pealed. The high room filled with the sigh and murmur of hundreds of people gathered together to witness the repudiation of the Red and the acceptance of the Green. The king finished making his signal.

So the sorry charade was gone through, when I spat on the red cloth—it was an old swifter flag—and trampled on it. I made various promises which, as they were made in the name of Grodno, meant nothing—and all the time I heard those ominous words clanging about in my vosk skull of a head.

"To leave the inner sea—you must become a Krozair of Zyl"

Chapter Six

Gadak the Renegade rides north

"Such plans the king has!" said Gafard, guiding his sectrix past a broken tree stump in the forest trail. "Such plans, Gadak, as gods must surely dream!"

I wasn't fool enough to point out that the king was no god.

"You may rest assured, gernu, that I will do all I can to help the king." I looked at him as he rode, a tall, strong robust man with that iron profile eager and aimed always for the heights. I decided to take a chance. "I think, gernu, all I can for the king—after you."

He turned his head to regard me. His Zairian face glowered. Then the sheer infectious bubbling of his good spirits broke down that overlaid Grodnim severity. "Aye, Gadak—I know what you mean, and I joy in it, for that is why I chose you. But, for all our good and health, never say it again."

"Your orders, my commands, gernu."

"Remember it!"

We rode for the northern mountains. We rode for battle. The leemsheads—outlaws—had allied themselves with the barbarians of the north and King Genod had arisen in his wrath and dispatched his favorite general to put down the disorders and to drive the barbarians back away from Magdaggian land and to hang all the leemsheads he could lay his iron hands on.

At the least, I had not, for my first task, been called upon to fight against Zairians.

A sizable little force we were, a full ten thousand warriors, led by the overlords of Magdag. And, leading them, a renegade, this Gafard, the King's Striker.

I wondered just when the moment would come when I would have to strike him down.

That, it seemed to me then, was the only course left open to me.

The reasons why he had taken to me, helped me, secured my admission as a Grodnim to the service of the king through him, were perfectly plain. He had many enemies. Many and many a proud overlord of Magdag hated and despised this upstart renegade. That would be inevitable. So he looked for friends, men he could trust, allies in whom he could repose confidence. And of all his friends, bought by bribes and high office and the ear of the king, none would be more faithful than men like himself, once of Zair and now of Grodnim, traitors, turncoats, renegades.

One very simple and effective way of ensuring their loyalty had been spelled out to me by Gafard himself.

"My name is anathema to all Zairians. They know of me only too well. Rest assured, Gadak; your name also has been passed to the king and his nobles in Sanurkazz, to the Krozairs, to the Red Brethren. There is no return for us. Now we are of the Green. I do not believe you plan treachery against me, for I am your good friend and master; but think what will be your fate should you return to Zairia."

Well, that was the rub. That kind of fate did not bear contemplation, and yet according to Zena Iztar it must be dared. How arrogant her display of power, there in the sumptuous reception chamber of King Genod! She had chosen her moment well. How clearly she had shown me my own puniness, the driveling paucity of all men, of Red and Green, here in the inner sea!

There was the other side of this coin of forwarding names of renegades. The Grodnims kept long lists of the names of Zairians who had wounded them. These rolls had been diligently searched and no record of one Dak of Zullia had been found thereon. Gafard had shown his relief.

"Had they found your name on the rolls, Gadak, you would have had to answer for your crimes against Grodno, after you had renounced Zair and taken the Green. The secular and the divine laws catch you between them, like Tyr Nath and his hammer!"

He also took the opportunity to tell me, in a strange tone of voice, that not one of the names on the Grodnim Rolls of Infamy bore a longer list of crimes than the name of Pur Dray, Krozair of Zy, the Lord of Strombor.

His attitude puzzled me. It seemed that he admired this Pur Dray and tried to emulate him from the Green side of the inner sea. More than once he used expressions that I could only construe as envy of the renown and prowess of that foremost corsair of the Eye of the World. "Yet he is dead and gone these many years," he said, as though ramming home a debating point.

We rode together near the head of the army, with a scouting force well ahead and covering parties of sectrix-men to the flanks. The flaunting green banners flew over us and the silver trumpets pealed ever and anon to give orders. In a long toiling column the infantry marched, men of many races, with the varter artillery spaced out, and at the rear trundled the strings of calsanys packed so heavily it was a marvel they could walk. Carts rumbled, harnessed to dour and shaggy krahniks, that special kind of tiny chunkrah, and following all that came the camp followers.

There appeared to be no quoffas, that large and patient draft animal of the Outer Oceans lands. The cavalry right out ahead in the scouting party rode the four-legged hebra, a saddle animal recently adopted from those very barbarians we marched out to chastise. Although not as heavy and stubborn as a sectrix, and that beast, as I have indicated, is barely up to the work imposed on it of carrying a mailed man, the hebras were quicker and more spirited. The whole *trix* family of six-legged saddle animals is not much to my liking: the sectrix of the inner sea; the nactrix of the Hostile Territories and elsewhere; the totrix of Vallia and Pandahem and Havilfar. I prefer the zorca, the superb four-legged, close-coupled nimble-footed animals combining marvelous fire and spirit with an endurance topped only by the legendary vove.

But all the same the hebramen cavorted about in fine style and could whoop up a rousing gallop to go haring away to investigate every plume of smoke or wisp of dust, every knoll and defile on the line of route.

We had left the inner sea far to the rear, marching north northeast. We had crossed the River Dag twice as it curved in one of its huge lazy arcs in its long journey from the distant mountains of The Stratemsk. The enormous river effectively contained the immediate hinterland north of the inner sea. There were many other rivers and mountains; none reached the size of the River Dag and The Stratemsk.

Our march would take us for the best part of a hundred and forty dwaburs. We would cross the River Daphig, which flows southwest from the Mountains of Ophig and joins the River Dag almost due north of Magdag, a hundred dwaburs away. At the junction stands the important trading city of Phangursh. We would cross the River Daphig close under the Mountains of Ophig, some hundred dwaburs east northeast of Phangursh.

Depending on the difficulty of the way and the feet of the swods, the journey might take as much as a month of the Maiden with the Many Smiles.

The camp followers were not allowed to impede our progress. If they could not keep up that was their business.

Among the leaders of the camp followers a huge and ornate palankeen, a veritable house slung between thirty-two preysanys, swayed along. The drapings were of gold and green silk; the curtains were kept always tightly drawn. Beautiful apim and Fristle slave girls served the occupant of the palankeen. No lewd soldier eyes would ever behold the glories of the fair occupant. Every night a gorgeous, sumptuously large tent was set up in a reserved space, marked out and guarded by Gafard's personal bodyguard. Every night he would bathe and change into crisp clean clothes, smothered with jewels, adorn himself with scents, and so, perfumed and handsome under the moons, would go into this magnificent tent and the flaps would be let down and no one would see him until reveille.

As we rode in the long journey he took more and more to calling me up to ride at his side. I was uneasy. This sign of favor marked me among his retinue. Duhrra accompanied me and we slept lightly in our little two-man tent at night when we were not on guard duty.

Gafard summed it all up in a phrase. "I need men like myself, men I can trust, about me. I see in you, Gadak, a man who can go far. Your loyalty is what I ask."

I assented with the usual words. But I knew well enough that he had other men in his retinue who would dispatch me without a qualm if I angered him. Autocratic, absolute power—well, I knew all about those baubles and the paths they led a man's feet into.

For my own good, perhaps, my periods of absolute power on Kregen had been heavily broken up by periods when I was the recipient of harsh authority. Although, as you know, I react with vicious hostility to most forms of authority when they are manifestly unjust.

We crossed the River Daphig at last, a brownish swirling flood running through eroded banks, and pressed on into the disputed territory. We had long left the cultivated areas behind, the enormous factory farms of Magdag, the immense pasture lands, the vast expanses of head-high grasses. Now we ventured into a sparser land, broken, where water became precious. Our goal was an outpost from which we would seek out the leemsheads and the barbarians after we had rested and recouped.

That night Gafard said to me, "I hunt on the morrow, Gadak. You will ride with me."

"Your orders, my commands, gernu."

"Aye."

Of his immediate retinue there were a number of men, not all apim, with whom I rubbed along, quelling my distaste for the Green, consoling myself with the reflection that I planned for the future when the Red might once more rise.

On that morning Gafard rode out hunting. With him went five of his favorite officers, two women, and me, Gadak.

The beaters, simple swods earning a few obs, ran ahead crying up the game, and we rode slowly along after. We all carried the short simple bow of the inner sea. There were, I had noticed, no Bowmen of Loh among the mercenaries of the army. And another thing I took note of—this little army was composed of overlords to command, of mailed men-at-arms to obey and act as cavalry, and of mercenary swods, cavalry and infantry, some mailed, some not, some apim, some not. There was not a single sign of the superb fighting army created by Genod Gannius on the model set him by the slave phalanx of Magdag.

We rode along, bright and glittering under the lights of the Suns of Scorpio. I rode easily, looking about for quarry. We hunted what there was to find, for some would offer good eating and the others would offer the challenge of predators disturbed in their own hunting grounds.

Presently I found I had trended to the left, going through a rocky defile where the sand puffed beneath my sectrix's hooves. A shout from the rear brought back my attention.

Gafard rode up with one of the women, sitting her sectrix in the fashion that told me she was a rider, for all she wore a long green robe concealing her and—most unusual in Turismond—a heavy green veil.

Loh is the continent of secret walled gardens and veiled women.

I guessed this woman to be Gafard's paramour, the woman of the sumptuous palankeen and luxurious tent. He

made no offer to introduce me, and, with a bow, I went to
fall in at the tail.

"Ride with me, Gadak."

So I reined in to his left. The veiled woman rode on his
right, which is a privilege given to very few. I disliked anyone walking or riding on my right.

Even out hunting he could not desist from talking.

"The king's plans, Gadak! I tell you, with our army we
can sweep the southern shore of all the Red! We can turn
the whole inner sea Green."

"If that is Grodno's wish it will surely come to pass."

"You have not seen the army of the king. This is a mere
rabble, a mercenary host hired to put down the leemsheads
and barbarians. Down on the southern shore—that is
where the battles are."

I risked a question.

"And Shazmoz?"

Shazmoz, one of the last frontier seaport fortresses of
Zair, had been heavily besieged. Pur Zenkiren, a Krozair
Brother, now broken because of ill health and disappoint-
ment, held it against impossible odds.

He made a gesture of irritation. "It holds, still." The
woman remained silent, but I knew she listened. "That old
devil Pur Zenkiren holds the city. His days are numbered.
Prince Glycas leads the army on toward the east, on to
the fortress of Zy, and on to Holy Sanurkazz itself."

So that was where the evil rast Glycas had got to. . . .

I did not venture to ask why, if Gafard was the king's
favorite, he was not down there, leading this formidable
army. Perhaps the king preferred him closer to hand.

We walked the sectrixes slowly, hearing the calls and shrill
hunting horns of the beaters ahead and to our right. We
were for the moment alone. Gafard went on talking.

"The kind has fashioned an army like no other upon the
inner sea—save for a contemptible slave army fashioned by
this Pur Dray." Perhaps this would explain his obsession
with the Lord of Strombor. I had learned that Genod
Gannius, fruit of that Gahan Gannius and the lady Valima
whom I had saved at the Grand Canal, hailed from Malig, a
powerful but small fortress city of the northern coast some
twenty dwaburs along from the Akhram. That explained the
presence of his parents there on that fateful day so long
ago. All that area lay under the sway of Magdag, the city
of the megaliths. Even the important conurbation of
Laggig-Laggu, near twenty dwaburs up the Laggu River

and twenty dwaburs from Malig, owed allegiance to the
king in Magdag. It also explained how I, knocked on the
head and captured by overlords, had been shipped to Magdag. They took tribute of everyone for dwaburs about their
city.

Gahan, it seemed, had been in Magdag when I had led my
old slave phalanx of vosk-skulls against the overlords. He had
seen and he had remembered. The old king had been only too
thankful that this dangerous insurrection had been crushed.
He, like the Magdaggians, put his trust in mailed men
riding sextrixes, armed with the longsword.

So Gahan had experimented and fashioned an implement.
But it had been his son, Genod, who with all the ardent fire
of youthful genius had seized on the implement and turned
it into the most formidable fighting machine yet seen, who
had used it to take Laggig-Laggu, to overturn the
mercenary hosts of Magdag, to humble the overlords, and,
eventually, to make himself king, the All-Powerful, the
Revered, the Holder of Men's Hearts.

I knew that fighting machine. The solid ranks of armored
pikemen, the halberdiers and swordsmen in the front ranks,
the wedges of crossbowmen shooting in their sixes. And, because the fighting-men of Segesthes and Turismond commonly derided the shield, the shield-protected phalanx could
simply march forward and topple all the mailed chivalry sent
against it.

"It was this same Pur Dray, the Lord of Strombor,
who created the first phalanx. He was defeated and slain.
And Genod Gannius now rules in Green Magdag."

"But suppose," I said, feeling the emotions in me boiling
up in a rage comical and ludicrous, "this same Dray Prescot
was not slain?"

He reined in his sectrix with a lunging thump of hooves.
"What mean you?"

"Only, gernu, is it certain sure he was slain?"

He eyed me. He licked his lips above the black beard.

"No," he said, at last, reluctantly. "No, it is not certain."

"And has there been no news of him since?"

He smiled, that ironic half-smile. "I can say what is
common knowledge, that men tell stories of two Krozairs
of Zy who claim this Dray Prescot as their father."

How my heart leaped!

"And do they speak false?"

He flicked the reins and kicked in his heels. "Who is to say what is false and what is real? I would that it was true, though, by the Holy Bones of Genodras!"

"Aye," I said. "So that we might go up against this great Krozair and measure swords with him."

"Not so, Gadak!" He spoke too sharply. He saw my expression and kicked in, harder, and sent his sectrix bounding off. The woman spurred up, also, and raced after him. I was left looking at their flying animals, and their tensed bodies, their capes flying, and wondering.

Well, there are none so blind as will not see. But, by the Great and Glorious Djan-kadjiryon, how could I be expected to see then?

I shook up the reins and cantered after them, the sectrix's six legs going in that damned ungainly lumber.

The hunting horns had shrilled and died; the cries of the beaters dwindled and faded to silence. The sectrix lumbered along. I heard a scream. I rammed in my heels and we picked up speed and came galloping out onto a scene that in all its ugly drama made me furious and, had I known it then, would have made me go cold with horror.

Gafard had shot cleanly and had dismounted to dispatch his kill, a small tawny-colored plains ordel. The hunting lairgodont had caught him totally unprepared. The sectrix had wrenched free of its reins and bolted. The woman's sectrix, equally terrified, bolted also and bore her off. After that first scream, which I suspected had been ripped from her when Gafard and she had first seen the lairgodont, she remained silent, wrestling to keep her beast under control.

Gafard stood there, his longsword out, his feet spread apart. Dust puffed as the lairgodont drew itself up ready to charge.

Not so much large in their strength, the lairgodonts, as vicious and quick and damnably difficult to kill. Scaled and clawed, sinuous as to neck and back, with those skull-crushing talons and those serrated, steely fangs in the gap-jawed mouth, the lairgodont presents a terrifying spectacle of feral horror.

Scarlet gaped the fanged mouth of the lairgodont. Pricked ears lay back on its scaled head. Hissing, it advanced, one taloned claw after another. That long forked tail rippled high. When that tail straightened and became a rigid bar . . .

I was minded to let Gafard, the renegade, go to his fate unmourned.

I knew I could not make the sextrix advance any farther.

It pawed the ground, trembling, arching its neck and shrilling in fear. Hastily, I dismounted and hitched the reins to a projecting rock. If I was slain the sectrix would provide a fine second course.

Yes, Gafard, arch-traitor, a man who had betrayed the Red of Zair, yes, why not? Why not let him be pitched to the Ice Floes of Sicce under the fangs and talons of this vicious monster?

The bow in my hands spat four times as fast as I could draw string and let fly. The four arrows struck. Two bounced away, broken. The third penetrated one staring eye. The fourth took the lairgodont in the belly, for it leaped with the shock, not charging. I lugged out my long-sword and ran in, yelling.

"Hai! Lairgodont! Your dinner is this way!"

It whipped about so that Gafard went into its blind side. Then its forked tail lashed sideways and knocked Gafard head over heels. There would be no support from him, then. . . .

What an onker I was! Charging into this mess when I should have wheeled my mount away and let nature take its course.

"The ordel is not yours this day, my friend," I said, and I leaped.

Chapter Seven

The Lady of the Stars

I leaped.

The longsword is a cruel weapon.

Even this longsword, this Ghittawrer blade Gafard had allowed me to keep without comment, could do its work with cunning and smashing power in the hands of a Krozair Brother.

And, as I leaped, I even shouted: "Hai! Hai!"

The sword licked across the beast's near foreleg and almost severed it, crunching into bone. I leaped nimbly away. The tail hissed above my head. Again I leaped and as the vicious head struck at me so I came down and went on, rolling, to come up with the sword blurring for the other eye. The eye vanished in a gout of blood and slime. A blow like—well, a blow like a ripping slash from lairgodont's talon—raked down my side. I thanked Opaz I wore mail this day, even for hunting.

I was knocked over and flying, landing in a spout of dust. I heard Gafard's yell, feeble and coming from a long way off.

Somehow I jerked the sword up and thrust and the lairgodont screeched and hissed and drew back. Blood flecked its snout above the fanged mouth. I got to my feet, drew in a breath, cocked the blade. Then, again, I leaped.

A clawed leg lashed blindly at the sound. The beast's other leg, half severed, collapsed. It toppled forward. I was able to brace myself, feel the ground under my feet, my legs hard, and swing the blade with full force. Full force from all that length of steel. . . .

The lairgodont hissed once. Its head hung askew. Blood spouted from the hideous gash in its sinuous neck. It tried. Yes, it tried. Incredibly vicious and tough, the lairgodont.

It tried to scrabble up to get at me and so, once again, I slashed. It fell. It rolled over and blood pooled away. Its body fell flaccidly. For the space of a few heartbeats I saw its belly heaving; then it slowed and stopped.

Gafard was there. He looked ghastly.

"Hai, Jikai!" he said, and then: "My heart! My love!" He glared distraught after the bolting sectrix bearing the girl away. He staggered and gripped his side. "The pearl of my days! She is doomed!"

I looked. I saw. This lairgodont had a mate. The mate, hissing and screeching, pursued the girl in swift, agile bounds.

There was time for no words, no comment, nothing besides leaping astride my sectrix, freeing the reins, a violent dig with the heels, and a jolting, bouncing, breakneck race to save the girl from certain death.

As I went hurtling past, spouting dust, I heard Gafard yelling, but his words were lost. He called the woman of the palankeen, the woman of the tent, by the tenderest names. But not her name. The endearments might mean anything. But I knew he felt all he could ever feel for a woman and so, too, knew that if I failed I had best never return to the patronage of Gafard, the Sea-Zhantil, the King's Striker.

Head down I galloped, the neck of the sectrix outstretched. It would run for me, lairgodont or no damned lairgodont. I used the flat of my sword, all bloody as it was, on the back of the animal and it responded gallantly. We flew over the ground trailing a long plume of dust. Hard rattled the hooves of the sectrix, a drumming staccato that echoed the hoofbeats of the girl's mount. The lairgodont kept up a hissing shrill that would have unnerved, as it was designed to do, the prey on which it lived.

This Zair-forsaken risslaca was the emblem of the Ghittawrer Brotherhood founded by Genod. I cursed him, too, as I cursed everything else as I thundered along.

The thing would have to be done nip and tuck.

I gained on the risslaca as it gained on the girl. Again and again I hit the poor sectrix—and I felt sorry for the beast then—and we roared on. A sharp cry from the girl, the only one she had uttered since the first, heralded the plunging collapse of the sectrix. It went over in a sprawl of six legs and a wild confusion, dust spouting, the girl flying off to land with a crunch against rocks. I cursed for the last time, stood up in the stirrups, and swung the longsword high over my head.

We galloped madly up to the running risslaca, who was a

mere half-dozen strides from the crumpled form of the girl.
The long bloodily gleaming blade high above my head
blazed as the head of the crazed sectrix reached the tail of
the lairgodont, reached past its flank, panted and gasped
alongside the very fanged head of the monster itself.

Side by side we raced those last few strides, and then the
longsword fell with all the weight I could put into it.

It struck shrewdly, just abaft the head on that sinuous
neck.

The shrill the lairgodont let loose rattled the stones of
the hills.

I swung back with a wrench, prepared to strike again, and
saw there would be no need.

The monster swerved in its dead run, collapsing, toppling,
its head flopping, and skidded in a long swathe of dust on its
belly before it swiveled about, its legs spread, to come to a
stop, tail limp, stone dead.

I hauled up the sectrix and jumped down, keeping the
reins in my left hand. I rammed the bloodied longsword into
the ground and knelt by the girl.

The risslaca had sprayed blood as it skidded past. She
was drenched. Her green veil was torn away. So I looked
down on her as she lay there.

I saw the full firm beauty of her form in the green riding
gown, splashed with blood. I saw the beauty of her face,
superb beauty, a perfection of features such as is seldom
seen—but I must not maunder. She opened her eyes as I
gazed. Her face in all its blood-splashed purity tried to smile.

She licked her lips, those soft, sweet perfect lips.

"The monster—?"

"The lairgodont is dead, my Lady. There is nothing to
fear."

"Then you—" And she raised herself, turning that imperious head to look. She saw the lairgodont. She saw me
holding the reins of the sectrix, and she smiled.

"Yes," she said. "Yes, it is all right now. Hai, Jikai!"

"Perhaps, my Lady," I said. "It was a small jikai."

Her hair was a deep glossy black, curled in the fashion of
the inner sea. A shadow crossed her face and her brown eyes
widened on me. She reached a small firm white hand and
gripped my arm.

"My lord Gafard! He is—he is—?"

"He is safe, my Lady." I felt the enormous attraction of
this girl, a sensation I could not understand or explain. I

thought she would respond to a small jest. "Judging by his shouts he is very sound of wind and limb—my Lady."

She stared at me, a long, level look. "Yes. Yes—I have seen you about the camp. I think I can trust you. You are this Gadak of whom my beloved speaks?"

"I am Gadak."

"And you are—as is he—"

I interrupted, always a rash thing for a mere soldier to do when speaking with a highborn lady. "Yes, my Lady. We are both. But it does not matter—you are safe."

She was a highborn lady. I felt that. I picked her up and felt her firm and warm in my arms and so carried her to the sectrix, who stayed calm now that it could smell dead lairgodont instead of ravening lairgodont. I did not wish to put the longsword all bloody back into the scabbard, even though this scabbard had not been made up for me by my beloved Delia. . . . I noticed the way she spoke so unaffectedly of Gafard. Perhaps, after all, there was a real affection, a deep love, between them?

How painful it must be for her, then! I knew nothing of her history, but if she was Grodnim by birth, then a love for a renegade would reduce her in the eyes of her family. If she was Zairian and had been captured, perhaps made slave, then how much more painful it must be to receive wealth and privilege and love from a man who had turned his back on Zair.

I looped the bloodied longsword through a rear strap and let it dangle. If it thwacked the beast a little it would help it along. It had done well. I would revise my opinion of sextrixes in its favor. Its name was Blue Cloud, and it was expensive, a gift from Gafard.

I took the girl in my arms again and mounted up, a trick I knew well from the days when I rode with my incomparable Delia. I held the girl close to my breast, supporting her, feeling her warm, firm body against mine, and she placed her slender arms about my neck. So we rode back to Gafard.

We spoke but little, silly inconsequential stuff, for she was a great lady and the shock of her experience had not all worn off, although she affected to regard it as a mere incident. A fold of the veil tangled about her waist and the hunting gown were all of green, yet the lairgodont's blood had splattered them with red. I felt the enormous attraction of this girl, for I judged she was still very young, and the perfection of her beauty would set any man mad and inflamed with passion. Yet I felt a strange otherly feeling for her in which my own profound and abiding love for Delia formed an inseparable part. As we rode back over the dust and left the dead monster behind, I thought about the many beautiful women I have known upon Kregen and of them all—even Mayfwy and certain others—none would have moved me had I never known Delia. But this girl might have. . . . Had I never met my Delia, then this girl, I thought, might have come in her time to take my Delia's place. And this, I thought, as I reined up, was blasphemy.

Gafard had limped out after us, raving. He had seen most of what had gone on. Like a warrior he had brought his sword with him. He was shaking. His face showed dirty gray beneath the bronze suntan.

"My heart! My heart!" He limped forward, desperate.

I set the girl upon the ground and she tottered.

"My beloved!" she cried.

Gafard dropped his longsword. The gleaming blade and the ornate hilt encrusted with jewels, all the symbolic power of the weapon, went into the dust. He took the girl in his arms. They held each other close. I walked away.

Yes, I thought, yes, there is genuine love here.

I, a grim old fighting-man, can understand love.

After a space, when I looked back, I saw that Gafard had adjusted what was left of the green veil, drawing it up to hide the glory of the girl's face. He called her his pearl, his heart, the beloved of his days. He did not use her name.

That, too, I understood.

When, after a time, others of his retinue found us, he became all harsh authority, damning and blasting, calling down the wrath of Grotal the Reducer upon the beaters. He shouted passionately for his guards to take the head beaters and flog them and if they would not die to draw out their bowels until they did. Old-snake, torture, hideous death, would be their portion for allowing for a single instant any danger to his divine beloved. He desisted in his anger against them only when the girl pleaded for their lives.

"Jikaider them!" shouted Gafard, incensed, holding the girl as she held him. "Punish them so that all may know their crimes!"

Flogging them jikaider, with a right-handed and a left-handed man to wield the lash, was horrific punishment. But Gafard was at pain to point out why he was merciful. "You deserve to be shipped out to the Ice Floes of Sicce! But my

"Jikaider them!" shouted Gafard.

Lady of the Stars has interceded for you, and I deny her nothing within my power! Thank her, you cramphs! Her orders are my commands! Go down on your bellies, you rasts, grovel to show your gratitude to the divine—to my beloved."

The beaters flopped down, howling, crying, wailing out their gratitude that they were to be flogged jikaider.

They were flogged most thoroughly, jikaider, and that night their howls sounded uncannily over the camp, stopping the cowardly and the guilty from much rest. That vicious crisscross flogging opens up a man's back to the bone. Mere raw lumps of meat, the beaters, by morning. But they would have unguents applied and they'd be carried in litters and, after they'd recovered, would go back to the ranks. Tough, the swod of Kregen, the ordinary common warrior soldier. I wondered if they'd be paid the few obs they would have earned beating for the hunt. The beating had been of a very different kind, poor devils.

And yet, thinking that, next morning as we prepared to get under way again, I realized I'd have done exactly as Gafard had done—more, probably—if harm had come to this girl he called the Lady of the Stars.

In only a few more days we would reach the area in which our operations could start. Then it would be man's work once more. The hebramen scouting ahead kept more particularly alert, for these wild barbarians were notorious for their cunning and skill in ambush in this hard and sere region. Farther north the land of the tall forests led on and on until, at last, the land of everlasting whiteness was reached. I had no desire at all to journey there. What I did now was a part of the plan I had formed. Duhrra followed me still because I had promised him I knew what I was doing and he had had evidence of that in the past.

"We will for a time act the part of Grodnims, Duhrra of the Days. We do not fight Zairians—"

"No! Mother Zinzu the Blessed forfend!"

"Yet when we reach the Eye of the World again we will have proved ourselves of the Green. Then we may escape."

"Duh—let us crack a few skulls before that, Dak, my master."

"I am Gadak now."

"Aye! And they call me Guhrra, may Zair rot their—"

"Easy, easy. The camp has ears."

Duhrra had been about the camp, ears cocked, picking up all the scuttlebutt that forever circulates where fighting-men congregate. I wanted to know about this girl, this Lady of the Stars. There was precious little to know. The men speculated on the mysterious occupant of the palankeen and the great tent, of course, in the scabrous way of warriors. The story that had gained the most currency said that she was a Zairian, from Sanurkazz, and had been taken in a swifter by a squadron commanded by Gafard. He had found her in the aft state cabin and from that moment on no other man had seen her face.

"In a swifter?" I said. "Passing strange, for a woman to be in a swifter in action."

"It is known."

"Aye. It is known. And is that all?"

"None know her name, none know her face. Four men—trusted men—have been flayed alive by Gafard's orders for trying."

The majority of the personal bodyguard maintained by Gafard about the tent were not apims. That would greatly reduce the dangers, of course, although no sane man trusted a woman to the protection of some races of diffs. Gafard chose wisely.

The moment came to which I had been looking forward with an interest that had led me to keep Blue Cloud always in perfect condition, a bag of provisions knotted to his harness, to sleep lightly and to have the edges and points of all my weapons honed razor-sharp.

The summons reached me carried by one of Gafard's aides. I went with him to the campaign tent in which Gafard dictated his orders and kept his official being. Only when he had discharged his duties would he dress and anoint himself and go to the great tent where the Lady of the Stars awaited him.

Among his retinue I had, as I have said, made no real enemies apart from his second in command. This was a certain man called Grogor. He was a renegade, also. The situation was obvious. Grogor feared lest I, the new friend of Gafard's, might oust him from his position. I had been at pains to tell the fellow that I had no intentions of doing any such thing. He had not believed me.

Now Grogor, a bulky, sweaty man, but a good fighter, motioned me into the campaign tent. Gafard sat at a folding table affixing his seal to orders and messages. He looked up and waved me to sit at the side and wait.

His stylor, a slave with privileges as a man who could read and write, was, as was common, a Relt. The Relt gathered up all the papers and their canvas envelopes in his thin arms and, bowing, backed out. The flap of the tent dropped. Gafard lifted his head and looked at me. I had not been called to ride with him since the episode of the lairgodonts and the hunt.

"You have been wondering why I have been cold to you in the last few days, Gadak?"

It needed no quick intelligence to understand why. I said, "Yes, gernu."

He put his hands together and studied them, not looking at me as he spoke.

"I owe you my gratitude. I do not think I would care to live if my beloved no longer lived and walked at my side."

"I can understand that."

He looked up, his head lifting like the vicious head of a striking lairgodont itself.

"Ah! So you are like all the rest—"

There was no way out of this save by boldness.

"I saw the face of the Lady of the Stars. Yes, it is true. You have had men flayed for less. But when a lairgodont rips at one, and the green veil is already torn away, there is not much choice."

He still stared at me. He measured his words. "Have you ever seen a more beautiful woman in all the world?"

I have been asked that question—and most often by silly women seeking to gain power over me—many times, as you know.

Every time, every single time, the answer was automatic, instant, not needing thought. No woman in two worlds is as perfect as my Delia, my Delia of Delphond. Yet . . .

I hesitated.

He thought I feared, perhaps, to speak the truth, hesitated for the reason directly opposite to the truth.

Often, although my own feelings needed no thought to arrive at the truth, that none could compare with me Delia, I had temporized—most particularly on the roof of the Opal Palace in Zenicce. Now my hesitation held none of calculation.

I said, "The lady is more beautiful than all women—save, perhaps, for one."

He seized on that.

"Perhaps?"

"Aye. But beauty is not all. I know nothing of the lady's perfections—and I do know a lady whose perfections are unmatched, in her beauty, her spirit, her love of life, her courage, her wisdom, her comradeship, her love—"

He sat back. That small ironic half-smile flitted on his lips and vanished.

"I do not think you lie. You speak too warmly for lies."

Here there was no need for me to go on. He would decide what to do with me. If he decided against, then I would decide if he must be killed at once or if I dare leave him merely gagged and bound.

Perhaps something of those wild leem thoughts showed in my face, although I own I would have been extremely wroth had I thought that possible: perhaps he realized more than I gave him credit for at the time.

"You know little of my history, Gadak."

"I know little, gernu. Men say you were a Jikaidast. If that is so it is no wonder you always win."

His smile broadened, became genuine, warm. "Were I not so busy—with this and that—I would call for the board at once, the grand board. Yes, I was a Jikaidast, in Sanur-kazz."

These Jikaidasts are a strange lot, strange in the eyes of ordinary men who love the game of Jikaida and play when they can. A Jikaidast lives only for the game. As a professional he plays to earn a living, and these men are found all over Kregen earning their living from the highest to the lowest levels. The greatest of them even aspire to the title of *San*, which is given to great savants, wise men, and wizards.

There is much to be said about Jikaida and Jikaidasts, as you will hear. The odds would be against the manner of the master's winning, not if he would win. Handicaps would be set, a simple matter of removing a powerful piece, say a Paktun or a Chuktar, or of giving the privilege of extra moves.

Gafard, the King's Striker, said, "I was known as a Jikaidast who could win after having surrendered my Pallan from the call of 'Rank your Deldars'."

I resisted the temptation to fall into the deadly trap of talking Jikaida. That way lies the engulfment of many burs of a man's life.

"You were a hyr-San, gernu. But of aught else, I know nothing."

He showed his pleasure. This was the first time I saw him as a human being apart from those traumatic moments when he had clasped his lady to him after the hunt of the lairgodonts.

"There is little to tell, as a Zairian. My home was too small, the people too small, my opportunities too small. When I fought for Zair men smiled. I was taken by the Grodnims. I did as you have done. I think the decision hardened me, made of me different flesh. I am a man among men now, the keeper of the king's confidence, his Striker."

"And Sea-Zhantil," I said.

I couldn't resist that little dig. He nodded. "Aye. I value that. You know it. It was borne by a man who—" He glanced up sharply at me, and I saw he felt his own surprise.

"You were brought here to listen to me, Gadak. I tell you this because I have taken a liking to you. But treachery is rewarded by a knife in the back, just under the ribs."

"Aye. Perhaps that is all it deserves."

Again that probing look. If I was to take him seriously, for he was a mortal powerful man in his own surroundings, I would have said, then, that he was puzzled by my attitude, realizing he dealt with a man who might be of more use to him than he could have imagined.

"That is sooth." He picked up a dagger that threw scattered shards of light from the gems packing the hilt, and he twirled it as he spoke. If there was a meaning here, he was underlining it too obviously. "I am a king's man. King Genod is a wonderful man, a genius at war, commanding, powerful—he has the yrium. I do not forget that. But—" Here he again broke off and flicked the dagger into the ground. The sharp blade struck and stuck, the hilt vibrating just enough to fill the tent with leaping colors. "But he demands women. He takes women and uses them and discards them. It is his only weakness; and, for a man such as he, it is not a weakness."

"I can see that. But the princess Susheeng?"

"She carried much weight when King Genod defeated the overlords of Magdag and took the throne. She supported him and in return is his official queen—although, well, it is all in the loving eye of Grodno. I tell you this, Gadak—" He interrupted himself yet again, rising and prowling about the tent, his fierce face thrust forward. "It is all probably common knowledge. Susheeng has her powers. She must tolerate Genod's caprices. Do not whisper this in your cups, for you may wake up minus your head."

"I believe I understand, gernu. The veil, the concealment so that no man may see her face—yes, I understand."

"Be sure that if you do understand you tell no one."

I felt it was about time he eased up from this fraught excitement. And, anyway, confidences like this were damned dangerous secrets. So, to goad him, I bellowed.

"Your orders, my commands, Gernu!"

He turned on me, saw me standing bolt upright, my ugly old face blank, and he caught himself and lowered his hand.

"Yes, yes you are right, Gadak. That is the way it must be. Regulations. Just remember. I let you live even though you have seen the face of the Lady of the Stars."

"I shall not fail you."

"I do not think you will. I would have you slain out of hand, you know that. And yet I would feel sorrow were that to be so."

As I went out I said to myself, rather obviously for all it was the perfect truth, "Not half as sorry as I would be, dom!"

Chapter Eight

Concerning the mystery of the escaped prisoners

There followed a short campaign that, although viciously and bloodily fought, contained nothing of interest apart from a demonstration of the overlords' methods of maintaining order in their own lands and of dealing with incursions over their borders.

The people who lived beyond the river were mainly nomads, although cities existed as well, built by settlers in favored positions. No one knew very much of this whole vast area of Northern Turismond, and we were much less than two hundred dwaburs into a space of land stretching, it was estimated by the Todalpheme, for six hundred dwaburs to the pole.

These nomads did not remind me of my own Clansmen.

Oh, they possessed vast herds of chunkrah, and they lived in magnificent tents, and when they moved they shook the earth. I do not think the land was as rich here as it is in the Clansmen's areas of Segesthes. These folk had their ways and their customs, traditions and folklore, and pretty and fascinating it all was to me at the time, to be sure. These people called themselves the Ugas, in their various tribes, and many races of diffs formed the tribes and nations. They had no zorcas. They had no rarks. Their weapons were inferior longswords and small bows. They did have the hebra, which I have mentioned, and a form of dog I believed they called *ugafaril*—the derivation is obvious—but which the Grodnims called rasts and cramphs and all manner of obscene things, for the dogs kept watch and alerted the camps and it was damned difficult to carry out a neat smart raid.

84

In all this I acted my part with as good a grace as I could muster. Duhrra, rumbling like a vessel of San Evold's boiling with the cayferm, followed.

I will not weary you with the details of the campaign. We caught leemsheads who were very dreadful men with atrocities upon their heads, so that I had no compunction about dealing with them. The Ugas were another matter. But they were worthy foemen and after they caught a strong party of Grodnims and slaughtered them to a man the atmosphere eased. And, anyway, I did not see much fighting, being used by Gafard as an aide, a messenger, a trustworthy conveyer of orders and instructions.

One day we surprised a war party of Ugas, and Duhrra and I had a taste of the reckless charge, swinging our swords, going up and down on the sectrixes, lumbering into a bone-crunching collision with the Ugas. Hebras went down. Swords whirled. The dust rose in driven clouds. When it was all over we inspected what we had captured.

This had been a slave caravan. The Ugas required slaves, as was common over Kregen except where Delia and I had stamped out the practice, and we were happy to release a number of Grodnims who fell on their noses and upended their bottoms and gave long howls of thanks to Grodno for their rescue.

Among the slaves I saw a group of men and women with stark white hair.

I thought, as was natural, that they were Gons, that race who habitually shave their white hair religiously until they are bald, out of shame.

"Not so, Gadak," said young Nalgre, the son of an overlord of Magdag on Gafard's staff, and therefore one day to be an overlord himself and so a candidate for the edge of my sword. He would have been a smart young man had he worn the red. As it was, he had no chance to learn what humanity meant. "They are the Sea-Werstings. Best we slay them all, here and now, and so save trouble."

"Are they so dangerous?"

"Little you know, renegade." They liked to rub our noses in it, these puppies, when Gafard was not around. "They are a sea-people and they should be sent sailing to the Ice Floes of Sicce, by Goyt!" He half drew his Genodder, scowling at the huddled group of naked white-haired slaves, and thrust the shortsword back into the scabbard with a meaningful snap.

Later there was a chance to talk to these Sea-

Werstings, for Gafard had issued orders they were not to be slain but were to be kept awaiting his pleasure.

Their language was but little different from the universal Kregish, an imposed tongue, and it would have been easy to talk with them even had I not been blessed by Maspero's coded genetic language pill given to me in Aphrasöe, the city of the Savanti.

I selected a strong man in the prime of life, who sat with bound hands and feet in a protective fashion by the side of a woman who, although not beautiful in the accepted sense, was firm of body and pleasantly faced, with a fineness about her forehead where the white hair had been cut away.

"You have fallen on hard times, dom," I said, sitting at his side and offering him a piece of bread soaked in soup. He opened his mouth sufficiently to speak, and shut it at once.

"Thank you, master. Give it to my woman."

I did so and then gave him a second piece from the earthenware bowl. I kept my weapons well away from his bound hands, just in case he had been working on his bonds.

"You are Sea-Werstings?"

He scowled. "That is the foolish name given to us by these barbarians, and by you ignorant Grodnims."

"Then what is your name, and where is your home?"

As we talked so I fed them soup-soaked bread, and gave also to the others nearby.

"We are the Kalveng. We are a seafaring folk, with havens all along the western coast of Turismond. When our long-ships breast the foam and our weapons glitter across the dark sea, then all men tremble."

"I have never been there. Is it very cold?"

He looked at me as though I were an idiot. "No more than a warrior may bear, wearing mail and wielding a sword."

"And a woman?"

"They, too, are handmaidens of Veng."

We talked more. It seemed to me the spirit of these people would not be broken by fetters and chains. Had I been a king ruling a country menaced by their depredations, I fancy I might have heeded well the advice of that young puppy Nalgre, the Magdaggian overlord's son.

This Kalveng, Tyvold ti Vruerdensmot, clearly a proud and stubborn character, told me much of the unknown lands of northwestern Turismond. In the map I roughly sketched out I indicated that coast with a mere scrawl, a line of no meaning, for the coast there had no part to play in my story then.* The inner lands are riddled with vast lakes and inlets of the sea; there are fjords and rapids and marshes, a whole vast area aswarm with life and people on the move and people in their keeps and towns. As the folk of the inner sea face inward, to the Eye of the World, so the nations of the northwest hold themselves aloof from others.

"What is your name? said this Tyvold ti Vruerdensmot.

"I am called Gadak."

He looked astonished.

"And is that all?"

"Aye."

"You do not trifle with me, for sport?"

"No. You are bound and I am free. There is no sport in that."

"I have seen it, though, when the slaves ran and the torches flew and the brands bit. You are a man with a secret."

I stood up, easily enough, and stretched my shoulders under the mail and the white tunic and the green sleeveless jacket. I looked down on Tyvold.

"And if you escaped this night . . . would you return home direct?"

The hunger in his face moved me.

"Aye!"

"Direct?"

He took my meaning. "Aye, master. Direct."

I said no more and turned away, leaving the empty bowl.

That night a thief broke into a stores tent and a quantity of food and clothing was taken. Also, in the morning, a Rapa guard was discovered unconscious but otherwide unharmed where the Sea-Werstings had been chained to stakes driven into the ground. The Sea-Werstings had vanished, every one, and a search failed to discover any trace of them. Gafard entrusted the leadership of the search party into the hands of his fellow-renegade, Gadak; and Gadak, although he searched diligently to the north, failed to find a single trace of the escaped slaves. With that, amid a smother of curses, the affair was forgotten.

As Nalgre said, lifting his manicured fingernails to the

---

*This refers to the map Prescot drew that is appended to Volume 5 of his saga, *Prince of Scorpio*. It is quite clear that this map was a mere sketch to indicate the main landmasses and seas. No doubt more detailed maps will eventually appear. Prescot has provided a map of the inner sea and this will be appended to Volume 3 of the Krozair Cycle.　　　A.B.A.

gold lace at his throat, "They do not make good slaves. We would have had to slay them, in the end." He couldn't leave it alone, for he added with selfish venom, "A fine opportunity for sport, lost!"

I did not answer, but walked away. I wondered what that cold northland of the Kalvengs was like.

When the Grodnims said the Sea-Werstings would not make good slaves I knew what they meant. Some races seem destined to be enslaved and one must fight for them and put iron in their backbones, for no man is born slave in the eyes of Zair or Opaz.

Of the diffs of Kregen, the Xaffers are a case in point.

Other races breed men and women who will not tolerate slavery, and these simply will themselves to death, or seek release at the hands of their masters in the final death. I will not speak of these races now.

And there are races of people with a stiff-necked pride that bends ill beneath the yoke. There are many of these. My fearsome four-armed Djangs will accept slavery if forced upon them; but they make their masters damned uncomfortable all the time these masters are foolish enough to enslave a Dwadjang.

I had been slave many and many a time, as you know. So had my Delia, to my shame. I wondered how my children would tolerate slavery. I had last seen my eldest twins, Drak and Lela, when they had been fourteen, just at the time when they were burgeoning into manhood and womanhood. Now they were all of thirty-six. Prince Drak ran my island stromnate of Valka and was a Krozair of Zy, and was a powerful man. Lela had refused the offers of marriage five times—at the last count. My other twins, Segnik and Velia, would now be twenty-five years old, and I had last seen them when they'd been three, running and laughing upon the high terrace of Esser Rarioch, forever plaguing Aunt Katri, joyous, gorgeous, wonderful children; and now Segnik would have himself called Zeg and was a Krozair of Zy, and Velia had received the same education as Lela with the Sisters of the Rose and was no doubt in her turn refusing offers of marriage. I wondered what they were like now, and if I would ever see them again, and so that made all the dark powerful forces of obstinacy rise up in me.

I would play out this hand and act like a Grodnim and so use that as a springboard to escape with Duhrra and once more become a Krozair of Zy. Oh, yes, I'd set my hands to that task. I'd become a Krozair of Zy again, for only by doing that would I escape the Eye of the World and once more clasp my Delia in my arms, see my twins Drak and Lela, and my twins Zeg and Velia.

As to the Red Brotherhood of Zy—the Krozairs—I swung a Ghittawrer longsword at my waist now and wore the green and swore luridly by Grodno. Nothing mattered besides escaping and going home to Valka and my family.

When the last barbarian chief in this area had been captured and had his head removed Gafard said we would return to Magdag. A strong force would be left against future disorders. None of these Grodnims seemed to realize that the Ugas were not barbarians. There were savages in the north, we all knew that, but they lived farther off, and they cut up the Ugas cruelly. One day, no doubt, the barbarians of the northern hills would foray down south, past the tribesmen and the citizens, past the Ugas, and come rolling down to find out what pickings the Eye of the World might offer.

History and destiny follow their own paths, on Kregen as they do on Earth.

On the march south a messenger rode up on a foundering hebra and was instantly escorted to Gafard, where he rode at the head. He had remained cold to me, reserved, but not hostile. Shortly thereafter Nalge summoned me. Gafard looked at me stonily. He had given orders that closed up a bodyguard, ready to ride.

"Orders, Gadak, from the king. We ride for Magdag and must reach there faster than the wind." He bent closer from his mount. "There is serious trouble in the inner sea. I want you at my side, for I smell treachery." He lifted himself in the stirrups, a powerful, compelling figure. He waved his sword. "We ride! On for Magdag!"

Chapter Nine

Museum pieces

The red sun of Antares, Zim, preceded the green sun of Antares, Genodras, across the heavens. A small but powerful body of men rode hard across the plain kicking dust in a straight line for the northern gate of sinister Magdag. All about on the plain stretched the megaliths, monstrous edifices, cutting enormous blocks of darkness against the radiance of the suns.

When the red and green suns passed in eclipse awful rites took place in those megalithic chambers, which only the highest of the land might see. The ordinary folk must huddle in their hovels and shudder at the wrath of Zair upon the land.

Always, Genodras would emerge from the pierced flank of Zim, and thus proclaim that Grodno still ruled.

We rode hard. The suns were drawing apart again in their cycle and were about a quarter of the way through that outward and inward movement. Our cloaks flared in the wind of our passage and our sectrixes labored with snorting nostrils, for they sensed the stables ahead and knew the journey was almost over. There was no time to reflect on the mysteries of Grodno and Zair within the spider-webbed shadowy chambers of the megaliths.

The sky held a high, drawn look, streaked with ocher clouds, and a few magbirds fluttered and cawed, whirling spots of blackness against the light. Heads low, trailing dust, we raced for the northern gate of evil Magdag.

Among our company, surrounded by Pachaks, rode a figure in armor and green robes glittering with precious gems. She was clad and accoutered like a warrior, but I could not mistake the erect, graceful carriage of the Lady of the Stars.

I was grateful that her protection had been entrusted to Pachaks. They are intensely loyal, honoring through their own system of nikobi the obligations of their hire; mercenaries whose code places them above the common herd. Two left arms has a Pachak, so that with a shield he is a formidable fighter. A long, sinuous tail equipped with a strong hand has a Pachak, so that he may slice you down from aloft or spit you clean as the blade leaps between his legs. Oh, yes, I employed Pachaks whenever I could.

There were no Rapas among our company.

The hooves of the sectrixes rang loud on the stones beneath the gate. Passing archways with that pointed Grodnim shape, we saw the alert forms of guards and watchmen, the slanting rays of the suns bright on their weapons. The echoes bounced from the yellow stone walls and the dark granite walls as we clip-clopped along. People scattered from our path. A basket of gregarians overturned and the ripe fresh fruit rolled, squishing.

Straight to the Jade Palace we rode, and Gafard, lost in thought, led us, his head sunk upon his breast and his powerful body lumbering along in time to the ungainly gait of his mount.

As in any well-run palace everything was prepared against the master's homecoming.

In the hullabaloo and uproar as slaves ran and men bellowed Duhrra and I took ourselves off to the small chamber we had been allotted for our personal use. This lay under the roof to the rear, overlooking a courtyard where daily vast amounts of sweat were spilled by swods drilling. When Gafard needed us he would call. In the interim we spent the time arguing, as was inevitable, here in Green Magdag, about the best ways of getting back to the Reds.

I felt sure that Duhrra had either completely forgotten or had never really understood just who I was. After all, there had been only the scraps of quick conversation between Pur Zenkiren and myself, there in besieged Shazmoz, to afford any inkling that I was not the Dak I claimed to be. For Duhrra the task was simply that of escaping from Magdag and returning to the Zairian side of the inner sea.

For me, of course, there awaited slavery at a galley oar in Zairia, for I was an unfrocked Krozair, Apushniad.

After we had bathed and eaten a huge meal and were thinking about emptying a few pots, the call came.

I took care to dress in my mail and to bear my arms as I followed the Relt messenger along the corridors and so down to Gafard's private suite, secluded in a separate wing of his palace with the windows cunningly angled so that the occupants might not be overlooked. The suns had long set and She of the Veils rose over the steep roofs and the flat roofs, set alternately in pleasing patterns. The long shadow of the Tower of True Contentment lay across the last corridor. The shimmer of golden light at each end burned unfocused. The Relt hurried on, silent on his foofray satin slippers, and I in my mail clumped on after in my studded sandals.

This was not a private audience. A number of Gafard's chief officers crowded the anteroom to his study. Grogor, of course, was there, to favor me with a scowl as I entered. The others looked up without speaking and then went back, as I considered, to biting their nails. They knew far more than I of the intrigues festering in Magdag; whatever news Gafard had brought back from the king was not good. The close, oppressive atmosphere as we sat in silence and waited told me that.

We were called in at last and trooped through the green velvet-draped doorway and so came into Gafard's study. There were books here, papers and charts, maps and the paraphernalia of the fighting-man by both sea and land. Also on separate tables lay spread out six separate games of Jikaida, all in different stages of progress. Gafard waved us to seats.

We sat, expectantly, waiting for him to speak.

"Gernus," he began, and so we knew this was a serious business, for he used the usual euphemism, calling us lords. They do not go in for *koters* and *horters* in Green Magdag. They fancy *kyrs* and *tyrs* are below their gernus—as, indeed, they are—their overlords of Magdag.

"There is serious work afoot. I have to tell you the king is highly displeased with some of the recent actions over against the rasts of Zairians. Shazmoz is not taken. Shazmoz is relieved."

There was a stir at this, a buzz, a murmur of speculation.

"Yes, well may you be astonished. For was not Shazmoz closely ringed, besieged, due to fall like a ripe apple? And now the king, may his name be revered, tells me that not only is Shazmoz undefeated, it is relieved, and the cramphs of the Red press on to the west."

I own I felt perky at this news. Mind you, I had given

up any concern over the outcome of the internecine strife
between the Red and the Green; but I own I felt a lift of
the heart at this news.

"What, gernu, of Prince Glycas?" Grogor, Gafard's second
in command, spoke up.

"Aye, well may you ask, Grogor! The king has heard ill
words of Prince Glycas, who commands our armies there
against Zair. But the disaster cannot be put down to him.
He was to the last, pushing ahead, when two things
happened that deprived us of Shazmoz."

If Pur Zenkiren, who commanded in Shazmoz, was still
the powerful force I had known, for all he had sadly fallen
away after he had been passed over in the elections for
Grand Archbold of the Krozairs of Zy, then I was not at
all surprised at what miracles he might achieve.

Gafard went on speaking, and he ticked off two points
on his fingers,

"One, a new, fresh strong force came up out of the
hinterland and caught the besiegers of Shazmoz unprepared.
They were led by a damned Zairian noble, a Roz Nazlifurn.
He coordinated his thrust with the commander of their
eastern army, Roz Nath Lorft."

Now I understood what Pur Zenkiren had stopped himself from saying, and I rejoiced. How the Krozairs must be
laughing!

Gafard went on, "And, two, a freak tide swept away the
shipping. We lost a great deal of supplies. Explanations are
being sought from the Todalpheme, whose task it is to
prevent such catastrophes in the Grand Canal."

I kept my hard old face straight. So the tide had reached
Shazmoz and had swept away the damned Grodnim shipping! Well, that was good news. No doubt, also, the tide
had created havoc on its way, and many a good man had
lost a boat, a shed, a house. I felt sorrow, I felt the guilt
I carried, but most of all I felt some deep pleasure that
the tide I had created had not only swept away the Menaham argenters carrying King Genod's damned vollers, but
had also contributed to the Zairian victory at Shazmoz.

"So we are for the southern shore, gernu?"

"Aye. We take a swifter squadron, and broad ships with
mercenaries and men-at-arms. We make a landing and we
strike at the rear of the combined Zairian army. The king,
whose name be revered, is confident we can restore all
that has been lost."

Here, then, was a task set to the hand of the king's favorite general and admiral.

Preparations were already well under way under the aegis of the king's hyr gernu admiral—his lord high admiral. He was a man past a hundred and seventy who would be only too grateful not to have to command the expedition, for he was a hedonist much given to the daily inspection of the bottoms of many glasses. He held the titular rank, to keep up the face and the pretense for the overlords of Magdag; it was Gafard, the King's Striker, the Sea-Zhantil, who held the real power.

In all the bustle, as the final details were attended to, I had to take serious stock of my position.

For Duhrra, the future was clear. The moment he reached the southern shore he would break free and rejoin his comrades. With contempt he would hurl the name Guhrra back in the teeth of the Grodnims, and as Duhrra would joyfully embrace Zair.

I said, in the privacy of our room, "The Grodnims have sent your name to Zo, the king in Sanurkazz. You are renegade."

He swelled his enormous plated chest. "Maybe so, Dak—Gadak—but I shall explain. As you have explained to me. The king will understand, for he is wise and just."

I hadn't seen King Zo in fifty years; I did not smile.

"As to his wisdom, it would be impolitic to doubt that. But his justice—you will run a mortal danger."

"I know. We both will. But I have faith in the justice of Zair."

You couldn't say fairer than that.

What I did say, and at that merely giving expression to a thought that had been building for some time, was, "And if when we were thrown down before King Zo, crying piteously for mercy, we could bring with us, in chains, this same Gafard, the renegade?"

Duhrra turned slowly to stare at me. His idiot-seeming face bloomed with blood, a flush seeping from forehead to neck. He half lifted his good left hand, and let it fall slowly to his side. His hook trembled.

"That would be a deed, by Zair!"

"Think on, Duhrra of the Days."

He surprised me.

"I hate the Green as any man of the Red must hate the Green. I do not forget my brother. All my friends who are dead and gone. But, yet—for all his villainy, I would not joy in delivering up my lord Gafard to his enemies."

I looked at him. He was sincere. He shared my thoughts.

In so many ways the early life of this Gafard—who had then been fard—paralleled my own. From a humble birth he had faced a life completely without prospects. He had striven to improve his lot and had become a Jikaidast, and a good one. Then he had fought for the Red, and fallen foul of Zairian justice—from what I gathered he had knocked the teeth out of a Red Brother—and had for a space served in the galleys and then had been taken by the Grodnims. As he had said from the moment he had changed his allegiance, aiming for the main chance, his fortunes had dramatically improved. Would I, having served a similar apprenticeship, not have embraced the Green? Was I not a newly converted enthusiast to Zair? All my early convictions remained unimpaired, merely overlaid with newer convictions of Kregen.

"No, Duhrra," I said. "He is a man, for all he is a renegade. He is very likable, for all his villainy. And, do not forget, the Lady of the Stars loves him dear."

"There must be good in him." Duhrra rubbed his hook flat over his bald head, a trick that, at first, had quite turned my stomach. Now I was used to it. He put his thoughts awkwardly into words, reverting to his old ways. "Duh—I wonder if his good outweighs his bad. A rogue, yes, but I believe his heart still belongs to Zair."

He could have said "his heart is still in the right place," but that would not have conveyed the flavor of his thoughts.

"Then," I said, "he has sent a damned lot of good Zairians up to Zim to spy out his welcome."

"That, of course, he will pay for."

For my own plans to prosper I needed something like the enormous prize that Gafard would represent. If I could haul him in at the end of a chain and dump him down in the Krozair Isle of Zy, display him a captive to Pur Kazz, the Grand Archbold, might not that win me back my place as a Brother of the Krozairs of Zy?

I believe the sight of my Lady of the Stars affected my decision, even then. I had seen her face, and talked with her, and I felt this spiritual attraction, and I felt absolutely confident she loved Gafard as he loved her. And there was the man himself, confident, hard, but likable, generous, friendly. The two halves of his personality were not any the stranger than the two halves of my own.

The thought of betraying him so basely, after his extended hand of friendship, despite all the hidden threats, sickened me.

I'd do it, of course, like a shot, for my Delia.

Nothing could remain undone for Delia.

Even this Lady of the Stars could not stand against Delia, could she . . . ?

My unforeseen, too familiar brush with the Lady of the Stars led Gafard to appoint me to a task of some honor on Kregen. I have indicated how the banners and standards of armies and ships are regarded with deep veneration—not the tawdry bit of cloth, but the meanings the bright colors and symbols contain—and men have had their arms hacked off rather than give up the standard. This is known on our Earth, also. In certain armies men vied to carry the standard into action and when honored prepared everything for their own deaths. The honor of bearing the banner into action was so great they were prepared to give their lives, for they knew as everyone knew that the standard-bearer was the target for the most violent attack. So they would dress themselves in their full-dress uniforms, clean and smart, would go through their necessary religious observances, make their farewells of their friends, and then take up the standard and march into battle, expecting to die. Usually they were not disappointed.

Summoned to the presence of Gafard, I found him lounging in a long white silk robe, his concerns for the moment thrust aside. He had chosen one of the luxurious saloons of his palace, with padded walls and soft furnishings, mellow lamps and many potted flowers, the scents heavy in the close air. There was a great quantity of different wines from which to choose. He waved the majordomo away and beckoned me in. I wore mail and my weapons, a custom I had faithfully followed since I had turned Grodnim.

"Sit down, Gadak—wine? There is a matter I wish to tell you, and, after that, another matter."

"I await your commands, gernu."

A Fristle slave girl dressed in bangles and pearls poured wine. Gafard waited until she had finished and then waved her away. We were alone. He handed me the wine goblet; it was all of gold with great rubies set about the bowl and stem. I sipped, making the sign to him of salutation and thanks. It was Zond.

"When we used to drink this, gernu," I said, wishing to

get him started on this interview, "we would say: 'Mother Zinzu the Blessed! I needed that.' "

"Those days are best forgotten." He drank quickly. He looked not so much agitated as keyed up. "You, Gadak, will carry the standard of my Lady of the Stars."

I gaped at him.

"Close your mouth, you fambly, and listen."

I shut my mouth with a snap.

"My Lady will accompany me on this expedition. She will dress and travel as a man, a great gernu. This for reasons that need not concern you. Arrangements have been made for her cabin in *Volgodont's Fang.* She will not be seen. But, as an overlord, she must needs have her deviced banner. This will be your charge."

I knew what was required of me. I bowed my head, and then looked up. "The honor is undeserved, but I will serve till death."

To a Green Grodnim, such a promise meant nothing; it was rote.

"Good." He stood up. "I have taken a liking to you, friend Gadak. After this expedition, who knows, you may well be Gadak of some honorable title. Come—there is that I would show you."

He led me toward a tall single door, which he unlocked with the bronze key on his belt, and we went through into a tall narrow room lit by lancet windows. The room flamed with color.

Red!

Banners and standards of all kinds hung from the walls. There were stands of arms of Krozair manufacture— although there were no Krozair longswords I could see—and I looked.

"Aye, Gadak. This is my trophy room. These are the trophies of my battles and actions."

I swallowed down hard. I recognized some of the devices.

There was much there I was dismayed to see. This man, this King's Striker, had roamed the inner sea like a leem. I walked slowly along, looking up. At the far end in a small alcove stood a balass-framed glass case. The light struck across it and lit its contents. I looked.

A scrap of red cloth, not eighteen inches square, with faded gold embroidery, and, along one edge, a strip of yellow cloth. Also in the case lay what was clearly a fragment of mesh mail. Also a main-gauche. . . . A main-gauche? The left-hand dagger was not a familiar weapon in the inner sea, for they were not rapier-and-dagger men.

I looked back at Gafard. He stood there, one hand to his beard, staring at the case with an expression I found hard to read.

"You wonder at these pitiful relics, Gadak?"

"Trophies of your first action?" I suggested, doubtful.

He smiled. "No, Gadak. My first victim sank in a bubble and all was lost." He came closer and stood looking down at the red cloth, brooding. "No. These are precious to me. Most precious. You will not understand, and yet, I sense in you a spirit, a spark that can ignite if fanned with skill."

"Swifter actions are violent and bloody—"

"Aye! And the man who owned this red flag, and this mail shirt, and this dagger, was violent and bloody above all."

So I knew.

I looked closer.

Well . . . the bit of red cloth with the yellow edging could be a quarter ripped from my flag, that yellow cross on a scarlet field fighting-men call Old Superb. The colors were faded and, like museum pieces, gave a fusty, dusty faded look. The mesh mail, a scrap from a left shoulder and breast, might also have been mine. As for the main-gauche—my mind went back fifty years. . . .

Yes, I was almost sure it was one given to me by Vomanus, the young man who had so recklessly come seeking me in the inner sea because he had been told to do so by Delia. He was Delia's half-brother. He was now Vomanus of Vindelka. I thought he was a good friend. Yes, it could be his. A spot of dirt about the ornate hilt where the metal had corroded bore that out, for he was always careless of his weapons.

And damned funny it was, to be sure, to stand and look down at bits of one's own belongings all solemnly laid out in a glass case in a museum, relics to be sighed over with awe.

I tapped the case lightly. "How can you be sure these belonged to Pur Dray?"

He smiled, and the smile was neither ironic nor wolfish; it was the smile of the collector who has paid a price for a dearly desired object of his affections.

"I know them to be. I have been given proofs."

I decided I had best display some of the chauvinistic ignorance of the warriors of the Eye of the World.

"This dagger. It is of strange design." I put my hand on the glass and twisted it about—my right hand. "You would hold it, but with difficulty."

He laughed. This, the first genuine laugh I had heard from him, for he could contort his face to a polite grimace when the occasion warranted, sounded light and happy and carefree.

"Your left hand, Gadak."

So I went through the pantomime of putting my left hand on the glass and holding the main-gauche. I was suitably amazed.

"You have heard of Vallia? The king no longer desires to trade with them, for now we are allied to the empire of Hamal, wherever that may be, and the ships of Menaham ply here. But there are many things of Vallian make in Magdag. This dagger is one, and it was owned and used by the Lord of Strombor."

He did not offer to take the precious objects out of the glass case. I hadn't the heart to ask him. I could feel the weight of all those years rolling down on me, like the peaks of The Stratemsk toppling upon me, and I felt my spirit reducing, as though Grotal had me in his grip.

Truthfully, I, an Earthman, had not yet adjusted to the normal and accepted life-span of two hundred years usual to the people of Kregen, let alone the thousand years that stretched ahead. To Gafard as well as other Kregans, the past fifty years was like twenty to an Earthman.

And I knew what twenty years trapped on Earth was like, Krun rot the Star Lords!

Gafard was speaking again, and I roused myself to listen. ". . . honor of the most high. She will be waiting in my saloon now. Show no surprise, Gadak, I caution you, for she has chosen this from the Vallian goods I have told you of. It is a bauble, but it augurs well for your future with me."

Not quite sure what he was talking about I cast a last look at the scraps and relics of what once were mine, and went with him back to the saloon.

My Lady of the Stars waited for us.

I bowed deeply, very deeply, going almost into the full incline, and this I did without conceit or embarrassment.

"Rise, Gadak, for I think you would be a friend to my lord Gafard and to me."

Her voice, musical, filled with light, entranced me.

"I will serve you, my Lady. Your standard shall never be dishonored."

She wore no veil. She was dressed, as was Gafard, all in white. Her black hair was piled in ringlets upon her head, and she held that head erect and yet, although she held herself with pride, there was nothing of arrogance in her. I looked at her, drinking in her beauty, and then looked away, for I felt the desolation within me.

"I wish you to wear this, Gadak. It is a trinket, a foreign bauble from some unknown place far over the Outer Oceans. Yet it has value. I would wish you to wear it in remembrance of me, and as a thanks for your jikai with the lairgodonts." She held out a golden chain. "And, for what is far more important, you saved the life of my beloved."

I took the bauble. From the golden chain swung a miniature made from bright enamel and precious gems. Red and white. The semblance of a tiny bird in red and white, with spread wings and beak agape. A valkavol. This bird, this tiny harmless bird, could become frighteningly ferocious when attacked or if its young are threatened. I knew the valkavol passing well. Native to my island stromnate of Valka, in far Vallia, the valkavol had been adopted as the emblem set atop my warriors' standard poles.

I looked at it, there in my hand, a tiny scrap of gold and red and white. I was to be her standard-bearer and she, all unknowingly, had given me the very symbol that decked my Valka's standards.

"I thank you, my Lady. . . ." I could say no more.

Gafard boomed his laugh again. "I can spare you two burs. Then my Lady and I return to the Tower of True Contentment."

I have absolutely no idea of what passed during those two burs. I regret that now, regret it bitterly, as you shall hear.

Chapter Ten

Of red sails and green banners

The crushing power of Magdag reached out a mailed arm across the Eye of the World.

Ten topclass swifters, the smallest a hundred-and-twenty swifter, escorted a hundred and fifty broad ships carrying twenty-five thousand troops, infantry, cavalry, artillery. The force was sizable, well-balanced, the varters brand-new, and their equipment did credit to the slave armories of Magdag.

I would as lief have seen the lot at the bottom of the sea, save for the swifter *Volgodont's Fang,* which carried my Lady of the Stars.

That flagship carried me, also, but I am an old hand at shipwreck, and so did not count myself among the blessed.

We sailed on southerly with a fair wind and a calm sea and the oar-slaves were relieved from their intolerable burdens of pulling, eternally pulling, and the breeze blew their stinks away from the functional quarterdecks and high ornate poops.

To me, who had once been a Krozair of Zy and devoted to the Red of Zair, the sight of all those miserable naked slaves came as an affront, but a subdued one. I could never have sat still and done nothing previously. Now I accepted what fate had to mete out—or nearly always—and reflected that I, too, had slaved at an oar not only for the overlords of Magdag but for the Krozairs of Zy as well.

One day, Zair willing, I would return to my true allegiance. Now, I was Grodnim and intended to play that role until the bitter end. Poor Duhrra scarcely ever showed himself on deck. We had a little cubby under the forward part of the quarterdeck—the half-deck of a seventy-four—and I, too, stayed there for long periods.

The standard for which I was responsible hung racked with the others of the overlords in the great cabin aft, blazes of green and gold and white about the cabin. My Lady of the Stars had chosen—or someone had chosen for her—a plain white and green banner with a gold device of a zhantil, a rose, and three stars.

I harbored no thoughts that she might be from Earth, thus explaining the familiar name given to her, that was not her real name. She was a Zairian, as the tightly clustered, shining jet-black curls showed.

She kept to the suite of cabins allotted to her. The king had appointed an agent—a kind of crebent—to sail in the flagship, and we all knew his eyes were everywhere and full reports would go back to the king. We were all on our best behavior during the voyage.

This galley, *Volgodont's Fang*, proved to be an exceptionally fine craft. She was an eight-six-three hundred-and-eighty swifter. That is, she had three banks of oars, thirty to a bank, each side. On the lowest tier there were three men to an oar. The middle bank rowed six to an oar, and the upper bank eight to an oar. These men were stripped stark naked and, as we had recently cleared the ship sheds of Magdag, every man's head was shaved as smoothly as a loloo's egg. They had no need to wear the conical straw hats, dyed green, that rowers in an open-decked swifter were issued with, for this swifter was cataphract, decked in to give protection and space for the fighting-men to operate.

Although Gafard had shown signs of haste during the fitting out in Magdag and the final clearances of the mole, now that we were on course he gave orders for the slow cruise speed to be maintained. Only one bank of oars was manned and the slaves took turns to pull, thus conserving their strength.

The swifter still carried only one mast, I noticed, and I wondered yet again why the overlords did not do as the Zairians did and give their galleys two masts. Both types carried the forward boat-sail, a kind of sloping bowsprit not unlike the artemon of merchant vessels. The sail was square and reefed from the deck and was dyed a brilliant emerald green. At its center the golden device of the zhantil, rampant, glowed and glittered in glory for the Sea-Zhantil, Gafard, the King's Striker.

The breeze remained fair and we reached the various tiny islands that lay on our course in good time each day before the suns sank. Because war vessels must be as light as possible commensurate with the strength they require, their bottoms are not sheathed in lead or copper. So they must be hauled out of the water as often as possible, otherwise the old devil teredo will go to his devastating work. I knew that the teredo worm was nowhere as active or vicious on Kregen as on Earth and warships for all their cunningly light construction lasted longer than the flimsy vessels of the Ancients of Earth. The Ancient Greek penteconters and triremes and the Phoenician biremes were manned with one man to one oar; but there is room to conjecture that the quadriremes and quinquiremes of later times had four or five men disposed pulling one or two oars. Certainly, this makes more sense than to suppose there were four or five banks vertically separated. As for the later giants of Classical times, these must have been crewed with more than one man to an oar—and, indeed, as we know, there were giants in the Mediterranean in those days.

The Roman dekares probably crewed five men to an oar with two banks barely separated vertically, the distancing being done laterally and fore-and-aft. This is a neat system, for it reduces the height needed to contain the oarsmen and also gives the chance of a decent freeboard. This is, as I have said, always a problem with galleys. Before I'd left the inner sea all those years ago a squadron of these dekares was being built up in Sanurkazz and trials were planned in competition with swifters of comparable power in oarsmen.

The major disadvantage of the dekares is the necessity for adjusting the beam. Kregan galleys are notoriously long and slender craft, for all the controversy over the short-keel and long-keel theories, and there were shipwrights who swore that five men above five men, giving that desirable narrow beam, were better than five men side by side with five men. As you know, I'd left the inner sea before any of this could be worked out.

So when I say that Gafard's swifter *Volgodont's Fang* was a fine craft, you must understand me to mean it was a fine craft of its class.

The two projecting platforms in the bows were armed with large and impressive varters. They were not, of course, as powerful as the gros-varter of Vallia, but they would hurl a rock with power enough to smash into light scantlings. I walked forward and studied the weapons, thinking back to wild times with Nath and Zolta, my two oar-comrades, my favorite rascals.

Gafard found me there, leaning on the rail, watching the break and spume and the white water curling below.

He came straight to the point.

"I spoke to you of treachery, Gadak."

"Aye, gernu."

He leaned back against the rail and swept his gaze across the decks. People moved about their business. We could not be overheard. His bronzed face scowled and his right fist gripped onto the hilt of his Genodder.

"I tell you, Gadak. For all I do for Magdag, and the king, the overlords would gloat to see me torn down and brought low.

"Yes, I can believe that."

"After we left the army it was surprised in the night by raiders wearing black clothes. My belongings were rifled, the great tent belonging to my Lady of the Stars destroyed."

"But why?"

"Why do I bring my Lady always with me, on campaign, where there is no fit work for a lady's hands?"

He was making an opening for me. I took it, taking a chance as usual. It would be a damned long swim from here to the next island on our course to the southern shore. . . .

"The king sends you on errands and when you take my Lady with you he sends men to surprise you and steal her away."

What reaction I had expected, and been ready for, mattered nothing. For this man, this bronze-faced, black-haired, fiery-eyed renegade boomed a huge laugh. He spluttered.

"By Genodras, Gadak! You take the chunkrah by the horns!"

I said nothing.

He wiped his eyes and then said, sharply, "You are right. It would be your head to repeat it."

"Aye."

"I like you. There is something—I cannot put a name to it—that appeals to me in you. You would have been strung up by your entrails by any other overlord long before this. I do not understand why I listen to you—"

"If the certain person we know of wishes to take my Lady from you, I do not think there is a place in all Grodnim you may hide."

He scowled blackly and swore. But it was true.

"Then must the guard be at all times ready. If they slay men skulking by night, clad in black, no man can point the finger at me. I am a loyal king's man. Aye, by Goyt! Despite all, I admire that man, for he is a true genius in war and statecraft, in all things, save this. And in this he has the yrium to do as he wishes and make it the right thing."*

I wondered, privately, however much yrium Genod possessed, if he took the Lady of the Stars from Gafard how that violent man would console his conscience for his master. Or would he take sword and seek to redress his wrong, authority and power or no damned authority and power?

Next day we all knew we faced a long haul ahead. The warships were run down into the water, the slaves in their chains whipped on into putting their backs to it. They merely labored to float the ships that were their floating prisons. The suns shone. The sky lifted high and blue, with a few lazy clouds. There would be little wind today, although I fancied a breeze would get up toward evening and if we were unlucky would be dead foul for our southerly course.

There are many small islands dotted all over the inner sea, which is often a very shallow sea; but this day we faced a haul that would take us through the night and well into the morning of the day following before we sighted Benarej Island. Here we expected to be joined by a squadron of swifters for the final passage to the southern shore.

Well, the day limped along. The rowers pulled. The suns shone brassily, mingled jade and ruby, streaming down on the decks and casting strange-colored splotches of light through the awnings. Everyone sweated. The thought of the slaves below and the agonies they were enduring as they took their tricks at the looms made me fidgety and irritable.

Had I been still a Krozair of Zy I would have found an excuse to go below, would have slain the whip-Deldars and would have freed the slaves and so taken the ship back for Zair. But that, by itself, would not be enough to reinstate me. That would be the simple, ordinary, and obvious thing for any Krozair to do. And I was no longer a Krozair. So I sweated and was unpleasant to Duhrra and took my-

---

*Yrium: a word of profound and complex meaning, more than charisma—force, power conveyed by office or strength of character, or given to a person in a way that curses or blesses him with undisputed power over his fellows. A.B.A.

self off to stand in the bows and watch the bar-line of the horizon, burning against the sky.

That sky changed subtly in color. I watched. This might be a normal rashoon, one of those suddenly explosive storms of the inner sea, or it might be the far more sinister manifestation of the Star Lords once more taking a hand in my destiny.

"It would have to strike us now, when there is no lee to run under."

I turned.

The ship-Hikdar, Nath ti Hagon, had walked forward to stare with great animosity at the growing storm. He did not like me still, and who could blame him after that scene in the aft cabin when I had first come aboard *Volgodont's Fang?* But the annoyance of the moment made him speak.

"We are in for a blow," I said, feeling that the calmest and most obvious thing to say. I turned away ready to go aft. He stopped me by speaking in a low, hurried voice.

"You know I do not like you, Gadak. But hear me in this. If you prove false to our lord in anything I shall surely slay you."

Shock, pleasure, annoyance? The emotions clashed in me.

I said, "I do not need you to teach me my duty, Nath ti Hagon. But, for your peaceful heart, I am charged to protect my lord. You see that you do not fail him." And I stalked off.

He said no more and I guessed he was staring at me with baleful eyes and wishing to tear me to pieces as I walked aft. Hagon, his home town, lay in one of the huge looping bends of the River Dag, some sixty dwaburs north of Magdag as the fluttrell flies, although more than twice that far if you followed the curves of the river itself. Guamelga, of which province Gafard was rog, lay some eighty dwaburs to the west of Hagon, still on the same river, which looped sharply north and east, going upstream. Phangursh lay fifty dwaburs farther upstream, to the northeast. In all our operations across the River Daphig, to the east, Gafard had never troubled himself to ride across to the west and visit in his rognate of Guamelga.

That made me think of all my own fair lands in Valka and her nearby islands, in Strombor and in Djanduin, and I cursed and hurled off below to make sure everything in our cabin was tightly lashed down against the force of the coming blow.

The swifter herself was snugged down. Gafard, who had

been a swifter captain for a long time, knew how to handle ships on the inner sea. His first lieutenant, this Nath ti Hagon, had already proved to be a tough nut, able to run a trim swifter. I had no real fears we could not ride out the rashoon.

This displayed another facet of Gafard, for a man in his position as king's favorite, Sea-Zhantil, would act as an admiral and have a captain under him to run the ship. Not so Gafard, the King's Striker. He ran his ship like a captain, and joyed in the doing of it. Not for him the sterile and removed glories of admiralty.

The rashoon swooped down on us and the suns vanished in gloom as the dark cloak of Notor Zan enveloped us. The wind screeched and whitecaps ran and were blown away across the tumbling sea. A galley is no ship to ride in during a blow. Men were frantically baling, and I took a hand, with Duhrra, cursing and swearing. The boat-sail was torn to shreds. In the gloom and the heaving movement, the wild shriek of the wind, the roil of the sea, I took a savage and bestial delight in battling those natural native elements, for the Everoinye had no part of this.

When, at last, the rashoon blew itself past, its violence intense and short-lived, we saw the scattered mess in which the convoy had been left. Mind you, Duhrra had a hard time not to crow aloud in his glee.

"Keep your black-fanged wine-spout shut, Guhrra! And that stupid grin off your chart-top!" I was harsh with him, for his own good, as he knew.

We had in sight across the still tumbling sea some fifty or so of the broad ships. They were scattered, but already sails were breaking out aboard and they began to straggle back into formation. I scanned the horizons; past the sails of the convoy, around over that islandless sea, and could make out not a single other swifter. Well, I knew *Volgodont's Fang* had been handled superbly. She had kept up to the wind, being as weatherly as any lubberly galley ever can be, and the other swifters had all been blown down to leeward.

They'd row back when the breeze finally died. We set about sorting the convoy and heading on for our destination on Benarej Island.

"Sail ho!" bellowed down from the lookout perched on the high prow beside the beakhead swivels. Then: "Red!"

Swifters of the Eye of the World commonly carry three sets of sails, white for normal duties, black for night work,

and red or green for business, depending on which side of
the sea they harbor. I felt a thump of the old heart, at
that call of "Red!" I can tell you.

Many of the Zairians ship blue sails as well as red, for
red is a color not conducive to slipping up unseen, and their
hulls, too, are often blue instead of red. It is a matter of
common sense. When the strange sail showed, gleaming a
bright ruby-crimson in the opaline light, I saw moments later
the long, lean hull show up with the same brave color.

This fellow was a fighter, then. . . .

A tremendous bustle and scurry thundered along the
three rowing decks of the swifter as the slaves were
rousted out and the spare slaves brought up for extra
power. They were whipped and rope's ended along to their
benches and shackled down. Every oar would be in use and
every loom would be fully manned. The green sail came in,
in a booming rustle, and was fought into a long sausage-
roll shape and stowed. Soldiers poured up onto the upper-
works from their quarters on the open upper deck. The
varters were cast loose and the men bent to the wind-
lasses.

Gafard, the Sea-Zhantil, appeared on his quarterdeck
gorgeous in white and green, with an enormous mass of
feathers in his helmet to mark him. I stood nearby, ready
to hand, with my green feathers in my helmet.

The drum-Deldar, in obedience to the orders of the oar-
master in his tabernacle, raised the beat. The double note
sounded, treble and bass, thumping out the rhythm. Now
the whistles all stilled. The sound of water hissing past the
sides reached everyone. The creak of the woodwork and
the rush of water, the long groaning sigh of the slaves as
they pushed and pulled, the sounds of the oars grinding,
made a pattern of sound very familiar. Also familiar,
dreadfully so, were the sharp, vicious cracks as the long
whips snapped over the backs of the slaves. A snapping
crack and a jerked shriek, and then the usual sounds until
another lashing blow produced another agonized screech.

The whip-Deldars of the swifters of Magdag are skilled
with old-snake.

And, too, there sounded the shouted word I hate, the
vicious, sadistic bawling of: "Grak! Grak, you cramphs!
Grak!"

Grak means work and slave and jump to it until you
can work no longer and are dead. Grak! Oh, yes, I have
heard that foul word many and many a time on Kregen, and

many and many a time in evil Magdag and on her hellish swifters.

"Wenda!" bellowed the ship-Deldar, bashing his fist against the quarterdeck rail. "Wenda!"*

Gafard stood still, his head lifted, grand in his armor and blazonry. He looked across the starboard bow. Over there the square red sail still bore on with the wind. But even as we looked so it shriveled, shrank in size, became distorted and so disappeared to be rolled and stowed out of the way, as we had stowed our green sail.

Very quietly Gafard said to his ship-Hikdar, Nath ti Hagon, "Break 'em out, Nath."

"Your orders, my commands, gernu!"

Nath bellowed his orders and the hands ran. I watched, fascinated, for it had been a long time.

From the masts raised along the sides of the swifter's apostis broke the green flags of Grodnim. Two parallel rows, those flags enclosed the ship in a box of green power. With an apostis some one hundred thirty feet in length and the flag-masts set at ten-foot intervals, there was room for some twenty-eight flags. This coruscating mass of green and gold and white fluttered in the dying breeze, magnificent, really, bold, daring—and damned well green.

I saw that the standard of the Lady of the Stars had been placed right forward on the larboard side. The standard of Gafard matched it on the starboard. I looked at Gafard and caught his eye as he turned to survey his quarterdeck, and I nodded my head, hitched up my sword, and started off forward.

I was used to fighting an Earthly ship from the quarterdeck. In swifters and swordships it was often preferable to fight them from the beakhead itself.

The Norsemen of Earth, those hard, tough warriors their enemies called Vikings, held to the tradition of the fighting-man being right forward. They called the warrior selected to fight in the prow *stafnbui,* stem-fighter; the Kregans call him *prijiker,* which is much the same thing.

As a stem-fighter I could wish to have Nath and Zolta with me. But what they would say of me now, as I went forward with every prospect of coming to hand-strokes with men of Zair, I did not care to contemplate.

As for Duhrra, I had spoken to him most severely. If he could get across to the Zairian without being killed he

*Wenda: Let's go.

would do so, win or lose. Otherwise he would stay close in his cabin and hope to escape detection, and failing that—and it was a remote chance—must plead illness, an old wound, his stump giving him trouble. I knew he would never strike against a Zairian. He would hope to escape among his comrades. I just did not know, as I strode past all that panoply of the Green, just what I would do.

I thought of the Lady of the Stars. She had entrusted her standard to my care, and had given me a little valkavol symbol as a sign. If a tough, carefree Zairian sailor tried to slash that standard down and carry it back to Sanurkazz or any other Zairian town in triumph—what would I do? Could I cut him down? Could I let the standard go? For the sake of my Lady, who trusted me, I really believe I might have cut a Zairian to pieces. I thought of Delia, and I knew my decision would not be affected.

Across the narrowing stretch of water the Red oar blades all lifted and fell as one. The swifter came on as though on tracks, every oar parallel, rising and falling like the red wings of a great raptor of the air.

The bronze rostrum cut through the water with a swirl of blue and white, curling into a white line tumbling and flowing past her sides. That cruel ram would rip the guts out of a ship. Above it the center wales curved to join at the proembolion, which would force the rammed ship off and thus prevent her in her sinking from dragging down her victorious enemy with her. The beakhead was lifted and men in the brave red worked there ready to drop it with stunning force onto our deck, or to run it out ready to form a boarding gangway. The two forward varter platforms showed busy activity, as did ours.

The first darts flew, massive, long bolts of wood tipped with iron. Soon bolts entirely of iron would be used as the range, closing minute by minute, dropped. And then the chunks of rock, which would smash and rend their way through wood and flesh alike. A dart hissed in to pierce a varterist near me clean through. Blood burst from his back, spraying everywhere as he gave a last screech and spun and toppled overboard. He went under the thrashing lines of oars. Another man of the Green stepped up to take his place at the windlass. The varter clanged and a wicked bolt flew off in reply. The air filled with missiles as more and more varters and bows could be brought to bear.

The two swifters bore down on each other, their whip-Deldars frantic with lashing, their drum-Deldars bang-

He gave a last screech and toppled overboard.

ing out the stroke, the oar-masters bellowing the time, and the two opposing captains watching and waiting for the first glimpse of intention in their enemy. One or the other must sheer. The diekplus might be used, the ram-to-ram, the straight shear. The time for decision was running out with gathering speed. And then I, an unfrocked Krozair of Zy, deciphered the devices of those red flags. I stood ready to engage in bloody combat with a swifter of the Krozairs of Zy themselves.

Could I, even Apushniad as I was, fight and slay my Red Brothers in Zair?

Chapter Eleven

The *Golden Chavonth* leads us a dance

The two swifters leaped across the last gap of water at each other like sea-leems.

The answer to the question that formed in my mind was: Of course I damned well could! I was an old mercenary, an old reiver. When men sought to slay me no matter who they were—by the Black Chunkrah!—I'd slay them first! And there was the green standard of my Lady of the Stars to consider. Was a man's life, the life of a Brother Krozair of Zy, worth more or less than a scrap of green silk given into my care by a girl? How could such idiotic and callous thoughts even occur to me? Had this girl, this beloved of Gafard, this Lady of the Stars, addled my wits?

There had to be a way—a way of honor.

The arrows rained down about me now and I cursed the stupidity of the men of the inner sea, no less than of Vallia and Segesthes, that they despised the shield as the coward's artifice. Turko the Shield should be with me now, his great shield upraised, deflecting the arrow storm.

I flicked away two arrows that would have pierced me.

An officer at my side, a Chulik mercenary and a man with long experience in artillery, in command of the bow varters, coughed gently to himself. He pulled an arrow from his arm where the keen steel head had bitten clean through his mail. He threw the two halves to the deck, with a Chulik curse.

The gap of blue sea between those two closing rams narrowed with dreadful rapidity.

I stared wolfishly at the Red swifter. She was two-banked and the two tiers were set closely together. Her beam appeared broader than I would have thought neces-

sary. I could see the heads of the men clustered abaft her
forward breastwork, across the forecastle. The beak remained aloft, ready to drop down if her captain chose to
board. Our beak likewise remained lifted. Both captains
considered this to be ram work.

How quick would Gafard be?

He was a fine swifter captain—he must of necessity be
so to have earned his reputation. He was called the Sea-
Zhantil, a name taken from the Zairians, a name taken from
the renowned Krozair, the Lord of Strombor. He measured
himself against that long-dead Krozair, did Gafard. Whatever Pur Dray had done, Gafard, the King's Striker, would
do better—or die in the attempt.

The hail from aft reached me attenuated and thin. The
breeze had almost died after the rashoon. The order of
command from the Red swifter reached me as clearly.

Both swifters hauled out, spinning. I had thought the
Zairian would try the diekplus, the maneuver in which the
attacking swifter abruptly swivels and turns so as to smash
her ram hard against the leading oars and the apostis forward frame, what the Ancient Greeks called the epotis. As
I have said, in the swifters of the inner sea this framework
remained a supporting member and, forward, a true cathead
of substantial construction, designed not only to secure the anchor but also to smash on down the line of oars,
was fitted with that intention. The diekplus was thus
rendered less of a formidable weapon than of yore. In a
ram-to-ram the stronger cathead would win the day, provided the attacker's oars could be hoicked up out of the
way, and this presented difficulties.

I had thought that a two-banker would not try the
ram-to-ram against a three-banker.

I was right in that. And I was wrong about the diekplus.
Gafard had thought the same and had sought to take his
vessel into the accepted method of attacking defense: a
rapid wheel and a reversal so he had the enemy's tail in front
of his ram.

But the Zairian went on spinning. She turned past the
ninety-degree point, turned more, and then all her oars
went down as one and she shot off, away from us. Gafard's
vessel, still turning, the water a welter of white along its
sides, was left facing at an oblique angle. I could hear
Gafard raving as he bellowed his orders to bring the swifter
back on line.

As the Zairian thus impudently fooled us I saw the bows

flash past, turning. I had seen the men there, close. And I had recognized the Krozair Brother in command, the prijiker in command of his party of prijikers. Their hard bronzed faces in the glittering helmets turned as they flew past. Arrows crisscrossed, but no man flinched.

That was Pur Kardazh over there, one of the five Krozair Brothers who had been accepted into the Krozairs of Zy at the same time as I was. I would have thought he would have reached higher in the hierarchy than a prijiker commander, no matter the glory and honor of such a position. Perhaps he had taken the world-stance, as had I, and the call had brought him back to the service. As the swifters bore on I pondered. Could I slay an old friend, Pur Kardazh, for the sake of a scrap of green silk?

The ship-Hikdar, Nath, came running forward again, bellowing. He was not satisfied with our bow varters' performance. That the Chulik in command had an arrow wound in his arm meant nothing. In that, of course, he was right.

"The cramph! You see what he is after!"

Indeed, I did see, and I felt most pleased.

For the Zairian was not after a fight with the Magdaggian. He was after the plump chickens of the convoy. As the breeze dropped so conditions became impossible for the sailing broad ships and ideal for swifter work. The Red swifter made no attempt to take prizes. With *Volgodont's Fang* on her tail there was no time for that luxury.

Sharp cries of anger rose from the men. They were filled with rage that they were standing idly by. For long, graceful streamers of smoke rose from the Red swifter, arching over, curving to land with precision on the decks and in the rigging of the broad ships. First one and then another burned. We were flying along at full speed, every slave hurling every ounce of his being onto the looms. But the Red swifter kept ahead, and the fire-pots blossomed from her, and she left a blazing wake of ruin as she went.

"By Grodno! I'd like to drop our beakhead on her quarterdeck now!"

"That would prove interesting," I said.

Nath shook a fist at the Krozair swifter.

"Krozairs! The bane of Grodno! They are damned and doomed to all eternity! May the Green strike them."

I didn't bother to reply. I now realized what had puzzled me at first about that double-banked galley as she had pulled toward us. I'd lost a great deal of the sharpness of a swifter captain. The two banks of oars had been lifting and falling at a speed much below that of *Volgodont's Fang*. I had assumed that to be because not only was Gafard's swifter in perfect fighting trim with a trained crew, but more probably because the Krozair swifter had been newly commissioned with an inexperienced crew. More than ship quality, crew quality can win an action.

Now the Red swifter's wings beat in furious tempo.

In a bur or so the slaves being lashed by Gafard's whip-Deldars would be unable to keep up the stroke. His spare oarsmen would be insufficient to make up the numbers required to propel the swifter at her top speed, and the time taken to change rowers would disrupt her smooth effort. But the Red swifter's oarsmen were fresher. She could outrun *Volgodont's Fang*, that was certain.

And, too, I had noticed that the Zairian, with the figurehead of a chavonth, had possessed no less than thirty-six oars in each of her banks. I had counted them quite automatically as she flashed past, as I had recognized Pur Kardazh, as I had stood under the arrow hail. She was of the long-keel construction, then. Slow to turn, perhaps, although her spin when she broke and fooled Gafard had been executed smartly enough. She would be very fast. It was clear that Gafard had come to the same conclusion.

The oar-master shouted, and the drum-Deldar subtly smoothed his frenzied banging and the bass and treble rang out with a slower rhythm. The Green swifter plowed more slowly through the calm blue sea.

Now Gafard showed his seamanship.

The contest presented itself to me as a problem. The Krozair swifter had cut through the convoy in a straight line. Now she was beginning to turn. Gafard followed, more slowly, and pulled out free of the convoy flank. Orders rattled and the whistles blew and the oars came up, level and still.

Like a faithful rark guarding a flock of chunkrah, the Green swifter hovered, ready to dart larboard or starboard to catch the Red swifter in the flank as she bore in again.

The oars in the Krozair swifter leveled.

Both vessels drifted.

If this was a waiting game, then every advantage lay with Gafard. As though to confirm that a hail reached us and the news flashed like wildfire about the swifter.

"Swifters! Coming up fast!" And, then, "Green!"

The Krozair captain made out the fresh vessels at about the same time. Immediately he put up his helm.

"He's running! May Grotal the Reducer grind his bones!"

By the time the Green swifters, four of them from the scattered squadron, hove up, the Red swifter was a brilliant dot on the horizon. I gazed after that speck of color, and I sighed. I wondered who her captain might be. He had struck a shrewd blow for Zair. He had struck like a leem and destroyed, and had vanished the moment the odds altered. He had acted as a proper ship captain and not as so often the Krozairs did as a crusader willing to die for no good purpose.

I would remember that golden chavonth figurehead. Maybe I might live to shake that Krozair captain's hand.

Gafard was livid with rage.

He looked dangerous.

"The rast! Twenty good broad ships—burned! And I'll wager he has no more than twenty casualties, if that."

We had thirty dead and wounded.

Later, when Gafard's anger had cooled—and this was after he had spent a bur with the Lady of the Stars—I said to him, when it was safe, for I had no wish to puncture the boil of his anger again and drown in the suppuration: "An interesting vessel, that Krozair swifter."

"You must have seen them, as have I. They play about with their ship specifications, the shipwrights of Sanurkazz. I'd say she was a seven-seven hundred-and-forty-four. Double banked, shallow draft, broadish in the beam, but quick and deadly."

"I saw the oars, gernu. Seven-seven, you say?"

"Not tiered—raked. A diabolical design. But, given a fairer margin, I'd say *Volgodont's Fang* could catch her."

Yes, I said to myself. Yes, I'd risk that. The speed of turning had been found in a greater beam for length ratio; maybe there was more than just the one controversy in Sanurkazz these days. Maybe the short-keel people had gone over to the long-keel argument and then given their ships a broader beam and so regained their original position.

She'd been low in the water, long and deadly, and I knew she was a highly tuned precision fighting instrument.

As she'd cut through the sea a deal of spray had flown over the prijikers, wetting my old comrade, Pur Kardazh.

Where I had stood the spray had flown clear.

Maybe the swifters of the inner sea were developing faster than I had given them credit for, for with a man's life-span extending to two hundred years, change was bound to be slower on Kregen than on Earth.

"The *Golden Chavonth?*" said Gafard, pulling his black beard. "Aye. Aye, I'll remember her."

For the rest of that day we went on our way, slowly gathering up the convoy, for the breeze I had expected got up. I wondered how the captain of *Golden Chavonth* would have dealt with a hundred and fifty of the broad ships instead of the fifty he had met, and of which he had destroyed twenty.

The swifters closed up, the sails were set, and we passed the rest of the night on course for Benarej Island. We were late for the rendezvous; but we met the other squadron, fifteen swifters of various sizes, and, after a day spent recovering, we all weighed or were slipped for the southern shore.

By Zair, though! Hadn't that Krozair swifter presented a grand sight with all her flags red and glorious under the Suns of Scorpio! And hadn't her captain led Gafard, the King's Striker, the Sea-Zhantil, a right merry dance!

Chapter Twelve

Of Duhrra, dopa, and friends

I, Gadak, a Green Grodnim of very dubious reliability, watched moodily as the army disembarked. There seemed to be no end to the lines of marching men, the strings of sectrixes, the rolling thunder of the varters on their wheeled carriages. There were hebramen, also, and the Grodnims considered these would give them a decided advantage in scouting against the Zairians.

So I stood on the quarterdeck of *Volgodont's Fang*, where she had been pulled up onto the shelving beach, and I brooded.

Duhrra stood with me and he breathed harshly through his opened mouth, his hook hidden within his green robe.

"You are sure he did not recognize you, Dak—Gadak?"

"No. Anyway, I had a fold of white cloth about my face. I fancy it is a precaution we could both do well to adopt all the time. The sand in the wind here gives ample excuse."

I had not told Duhrra that it was a Krozair Brother I had recognized and he no doubt took it that I referred to one of the seamen, one of the prijiker party, or the varterists. I fancy he wanted to know nothing about Krozairs. They are regarded as men apart, dedicated, austere, giving their whole being to fighting the Green for the glory of Zair. Those Brothers who choose to take the world-scene, as had I, achieve this sense of awed mystery when they adopt the Krozair symbol no less than the Bolds, who are men dedicated for every single mur of their lives to the Krozair Brethren.

That symbol had been displayed in *Golden Chavonth*: the hubless spoked wheel within the scarlet circle. That device had stirred me. I felt uneasy. I had been ejected and I must regain my place in order to leave the inner sea and I was doing precious little about it. That there was precious little I could do at the moment had no importance in the sense of nagging frustration.

My plans depended on a great stroke, a High Jikai.

I was kept running about on errands for Gafard.

He provided me with a hebra, a spirited little animal, for all it was no match for a zorca, and I grew to like it. Its name was Grodnofaril, and I thought it inexpedient to change that, so I called it "Boy" and left well alone.

We had landed on the main southern shore in a deeply indented arm of the sea some twenty dwaburs to the east of Shazmoz. The east. About twenty dwaburs across country to the east of us rose the Zairian fortress town of Pynzalo. It goes without saying that any town or city on the Red or Green shore must be strongly fortified if it lies within a day's march of the sea. These frowning battlemented places must be strong. Most towns and cities are inland, well away from raid and foray.

King Genod's idea was simple enough. Reputed a genius at war, he demonstrated some of the necessary qualities of genius by issuing instructions to his subordinates that were easy to comprehend. Their execution would be another matter, of course.

After Shazmoz had been relieved the combined Zairian armies had fought on to the west, rolling up some of the Grodnim defensive positions, for they had been weak, every mind being set upon advance to the east. Now the advance had stalled and both armies lay in stalemate.

Our descent onto the rear like this would seriously disrupt communications, at the least. We had already caught a supply column—and there was nothing I could do about that. Even ships that coasted along the shore could be snapped up. Once the fleet of broad ships had discharged the army and supplies for a period they left us, to return to Magdag. They were expected again very shortly, bearing the main supply buildup. So, here we sat, astride the Red communications, and very ready to strike in any direction.

More fleeting raids by Zairian swifters had bothered us, but since that destructive onslaught by *Golden Chavonth* nothing so damaging had been achieved against us. I fancied that Gafard might not wait for his full supplies. They had been faced, the king and the King's Striker, with the alternatives of dispatching half the army with full supplies, or all the army with limited supplies. In my view, given the caliber of Gafard, the king had chosen correctly. One must always remember the slowness of armies when men march on their feet, and draft and pack animals carry their gear and supplies and there are no mechanical contrivances for transport.

I fancied Gafard would strike east, at Pynzalo.

With that fortress reduced and its supplies captured, and with his swifters dominating this whole stretch of coast through their use of slipways and bays and beaches, Gafard could then form a firm rear on Pyzalo and turn west. With Prince Glycas to the west, they would have the Zairian forces caught like a nut between crackers.

Just how long it would take for Sanurkazz to realize the position and scrape up another army to fling against Pynzalo could, for me, remain only conjecture. I did not know how far the treasury's resources had been depleted. I did know that both sides had expended vast amounts of treasure on this internecine warfare. Red and Green! Well, I was supposed to have grown to a more mature wisdom, but I own I still felt the old surge when Red rose up to challenge Green, still the blood thumped quicker through my veins.

One night after I had been all day chasing hither and yon carrying orders—and, incidentally, coming to know the composition of this army, its strengths and its weaknesses—Duhrra rolled into the tent we shared, not so much drunk as fuddled and annoyed.

"Tonight," he said, slumping down on his cot with a crash. "Tonight, my Gadak of the Green—I escape!"

I took the bottle from his hand and sniffed. Dopa. I threw the thing into the moon-shot darkness and I followed it out to the hanging water bottle and I took that into the tent and sloshed the entire contents over this Duhrra of the Days and his cot. He spluttered and roared and I reached down and put a hand over his mouth.

"Duhrra of the Days," I said, in that kind of penetrating whisper that smacks of drama. "If you wish your entrails to be drawn out, then by all means continue to shout of your intentions."

His eyes glared up at me over my hand.

He put his left hand on my wrist and tried to draw my hand away. I resisted. I did not let him take my hand away.

I said, "If you wish to go over the hill you must plan. There must be food and water, a mount, a plan of escape. Onker! Think on, Duhrra of the Days."

I took my hand away.

He dragged in a harsh breath. His eyes were bloodshot.

"Aye, Gadak of the Green! You argue well and shrewdly. Yet you do nothing to escape. I begin to think you really love these zigging Grodnims. You wish to stay with them forever. I do not think—"

"No, Duhrra, you do not think."

"Duh—I do, so!"

I shook my head. I know I wore that old evil expression on my face in the moons-glow, for he flinched back.

"I do not intend to escape, meekly run away, like a cur with its tail between its legs. When I go, I go in style, in a way all men may see, and say—'That was a Zairian!'"

"Fine words."

"Aye."

He still did not know what to make of me. Of late I had been your true dyed-in-the-wool Grodnim. The religious observances that amused me had been dealt with faithfully. I think that Duhrra did doubt me then. And he had every right so to doubt, for I doubted myself.

All my life I have been a loner. With the exception of my Delia I have never revealed myself. And yet I have good friends, as you know. Seg Segutorio and Inch—great men, fine blade comrades, true friends. And there were others you have heard me speak of—Hap Loder, Gloag, Prince Varden Wanek, Kytun Kholin Dorn, and Ortyg Fellin Coper. And there were my friends who lived in Esser Rarioch: Turko the Shield, Balass the Hawk, Naghan the Gnat. And I included here Tilly and Oby. There were others of whom you know. There was most particularly here in the Eye of the World Mayfwy of Felteraz. How could I face them with the knowledge I bore? I do not make friends easily. When I do make a friend I tremble lest I destroy that friendship through one of my typical, stupid tearaway actions.

Not for me the easy assumption that friends remain friends no matter what atrocities I commit.

How would Rees and Chido regard me? They were of Hamal, the empire ruled by mad Queen Thyllis, and were deadly foemen to Vallia. Yet during my days as a spy in Ruathytu, capital of Hamal, I had found true friendship with Rees, Trylon of the Golden Wind, and with chuckling, chinless, pop-eyed Chido, a courtesy amak. I had been tortured by the decisions forced on me, the honest attempt to rationalize the friendship I felt for Rees and Chido and the numbing knowledge that our countries fought and hated each other.

Duhrra punctured my problems with a new brashness owing much to dopa.

"So, Gadak the Great Planner. When is this to be?"

"As soon as the right opportunity offers." I did not smile at his words. But this was much more like it—much more a cheerful companion, this Duhrra who chided me for my lapses from grace, my omission of good works. That to him these good works could exist only in labor for the Red of Zair meant only his vision was scaled to the Eye of the World. Maybe I had been slack of late. But, despite all, for me, still, it was Red and not Green. The conflict in the Eye of the World might be of tiny dimensions when compared with the dramas of the Outer Oceans. When a fellow was caught up in them they tended to reduce visibility to the immediate horizon.

Duhrra possessed the appearance of that kind of superbly built idiot calculated at first glance to deceive. I have met your true moron from time to time, and usually give him a wide berth. They do not amuse me, as they appear to amuse so many people, these slack-faced giants with muscles of gods and brains of calsanys. Duhrra was basically right in his desires to go and *do* something for Zair.

My problem was that what I did must rank as a High Jikai, a world-shaking feat of arms that men would talk about and nod their heads over sagely and consider to be worthy to stand in the legends of Kregen along with the other high feats of achievement. That it would be damned difficult to do I knew. Maybe I overmatched myself against fate.

"We will strike for honor, Duhrra, but I do not believe I shock you when I say that honor is a poor substitute for life."

"Duh—you threw away my bottle!"

"Aye—now get some sleep. I must think."

But my thoughts coiled around my friends and my shortcomings.

These feelings of dissatisfaction with myself prompted me to the reflection—which I try always to keep somewhere near the forefront of my mind—that a man must work hard at keeping friends. At least, I know this was so for me. I did not feel that no matter what I did my comrades would remain loyal to me forever and ever. I know this is the counsel of perfection, the David and Jonathan summit; and I knew, too, I would never lose my affections for Seg and Inch and the others just because they were foolish at some time or other, or played me false out of a lapse from the counsels of morality we all accepted in our own ways; but I felt always that I was under trial. If this proves me lacking in understanding, as I suppose it does, it also proves that I am a true loner.

I would not have understood had someone at this time pointed out to me that—in my assumptions that no matter what my friends did I would forgive them but if I erred they would not forgive—I did my friends a grave injustice and imputed a higher value to my friendship than I was prepared to extend to theirs. I knew, then, I was not worthy of my Delia, and, also, not worthy of the friendship extended to me by Seg and Inch and the others. This is what I believed.

So, with Duhrra as with Melow the Supple, with Vomanus of Vindelka, with all my comrades, I chose to hew to the line of rectitude—and as always the savage barbarian that is the true me, I often think to my shame, would break out and I'd go raving off doing all the things that should, if my philosphy was correct, have resulted in the cloak of Notor Zan falling on me from a great height.

Kytun Kholin Dorn—that magnificent four-armed warrior Djang, a kov—and Ortyg Fellin Coper—a wise and learned Obdjang statesman, a Pallan—ran my kingdom of Djanduin in the southwest of Havilfar for me when I was away. I had been away on Earth, banished by the Star Lords, for twenty-one Terrestrial years, and since my return and all this imbroglio in the inner sea I had not been back to Djanduin. I had no doubts whatsoever, no doubts at all, that Kytun and Ortyg ran the country with all the efficiency and honesty we had built up between us. I was still the king of Djanduin, and when I returned I would be greeted as such. Provided, of course, they were both still in power and no further revolutions had taken place. Against a warrior of the caliber of K. Kholin Dorn and the statecraft of O. Fellin Coper, I did not fancy the chances of new revolutionaries, for we carried the people with us. I give this example to illuminate my tangled feelings about friends.

Twenty-one years' absence and then a cheerful "Lahal, Ortyg. Lahal, Kytun," and I would resume the throne as though I had not been away. Blind I was in those days, for although I gave thanks to Zair—or, in this case, to Djan— for my friends, I did not fully understand the quality of their friendship, and how blessed I was in the receiving of it.

All of which led to a very subdued Duhrra, with a hand to

his bald head, crawling out of the tent on the following morning and moaning for a handful of palines.

"Dopa," I said.

"Aye, master. Dopa. Duh—a fearsome drink."

"And suitable only for those who wish to become as calsanys."

"There are many bottles in the infantry lines. I was led astray."

Dopa if drunk in sufficient quantity is guaranteed to make a man fighting mad. Did Gafard, then, need dopa to whip his splendid army to fighting pitch? I was surprised.

When I was summoned to the usual morning briefing ready to begin a day astride my hebra, Boy, carrying messages, Gafard appeared to be wrought to a high pitch himself, as though he, that hard, practical, seasoned warrior, had been drinking dopa.

"Gernus," he said to the assembled officers and the aides standing respectfully in the rear. "Great news! We are highly honored. The king himself, the All-Highest, sends news he will pay us a visit—we must expect him today."

Later I saw the arrival of King Genod. He flew in by voller.

The moment I saw the petal-shape of the airboat flitting in over the camp from the shining sea, I knew the instrument had been placed into my hands.

This, then, would be the means of creating a High Jikai.

Chapter Thirteen

King Genod reviews his army

A considerable bulk of the army drew up on parade to greet the arrival of their king, this Genod Gannius, genius at war.

In my capacity as aide to the general in command here I rode my sectrix, Blue Cloud, and clad in mail and green, waited respectfully among the ranks of the aides, well to the rear of Gafard and his high officers.

The trumpets pealed, the flags flew, the twin suns cast down their mingled opaz radiance, sectrixes snorted, and the mailed ranks stood immobile, splendid, imposing, their pikes all slanted as one, the suns-light glittering from their helmets.

There were two vollers.

One was the small two-place flier I had seen over the Grand Canal, before I'd released the tide and so swept away the vessels carrying the consignment of vollers from Hamal.

The other voller was larger, higher, with three decks and varter positions, with room for a crew of eighty men—a pastang. As she flew in I was forcibly reminded of the power an aircraft must possess over the earthbound fighting-man marching on his own feet.

Rumors had floated about sufficiently for me to know that these were the only two vollers Genod possessed. I took no pride that I had deprived him of the squadron supplied by Hamal; the relief I felt was tempered by the knowledge that with these two alone, against totally unprepared Zairians, he could do a great mischief.

The reception went off smoothly enough—I was sorry to see—and with the bands playing and the flags fluttering and the swods marching in perfect alignment, King Genod made his way into the camp of one of his armies upon the southern shore.

There was no doubt as to the polished drill of these swods. There is a great difference between your wild warrior and your disciplined soldier, for all they are both fighting-men. The mercenaries Genod had hired were not on parade. He was being welcomed by the army he had helped create, the killing instrument with which he had won his victories and carried the Green triumphantly to the Red southern shore. This was a family reunion, as the long ranks of pikemen marched past, with the halberdiers and swordsmen leading, and the wedges of crossbowmen, closed up to march, followed, their crossbows held all in strict alignment across their chests. Each man in the ranks with his green plumes and insignia, I felt sure, owed a special and personal allegiance to King Genod. Genod had forged his army and it was his, in his hand, to do with as he willed.

He trusted this army, out of the greater army he had created, to Gafard, the King's Striker.

There was a deal of affectionate greeting, and much bowing and saluting, the pealing of trumpets, the curvetting of sectrixes, the green flags proud against the sky.

A little breeze had ghosted up, and this added a fine free atmosphere to the occasion, a zephyr breeze foretelling the great wind of destruction that would sweep the Green to victory over the Reds all along the coast.

The king and Gafard and a sizable body of their immediate officers and retinues disappeared into the tall pavilion erected against the king's coming. Treasure was being spilled here. Yet for this genius king, this superman with the yrium, such attendances were not only expected and demanded—they were essential to his life-style.

A powerful Pachak guard surrounded the two fliers, and the gaping swods were kept well away. I stood in the crowd with that fold of white silk across the lower half of my face. Many soldiers affected the style, for here the wind carried stinging sand. I stared at the two vollers.

For my money they would both be first-class specimens. Hamal habitually built and sold inferior specimens to foreign countries. That had been one cause of a war that, while it lay in abeyance for the moment, was by no means over. The Hamalese had supplied these two vollers as examples, and on their performance the balance of the order might rest, although I knew well enough that any nation which did not manufacture fliers was only too pleased to buy examples from Hamal even if they were less than perfect.

"Real boats! That fly through the air!" observed a swod, his full-dress uniform now changed for his fatigues. The other pikemen and arbalestiers were likewise changed. Full dress was costly and reserved for occasions like this grand parade and, ironically, for battle.

"I'd never have believed it, if I hadn't seen it with me own eyes!" declared a dwa-Deldar, wiping his nose with his fist.

"Gar!" said a wizened little engineersman, spitting. "They be just ordinary boats, fitted with the power o' Grodno, if you ask me."

"Nobody's asking you, Naghan the Pulley."

They would have wrangled on, in the press, amicable in this off-duty period as swods usually are. I moved away with Duhrra. I would see all I wanted of the positions of the vollers. I did not like the guards being Pachaks. That complicated matters.

In less than a bur I would be on duty again, and just before Duhrra and I went to dress into our mail and greens, a fresh interest cropped up in the army. Two swifters came in bringing with them a captured Zairian swifter.

We all trooped down to the beach to look and jeer and shout mocking obscene threats as the Zairian prisoners were marched ashore in chains.

The two swifters were from Gansk, a powerful Grodnim fortress city of the northern coast opposite Zy itself. The Zairian was from Zandikar, a fortress city up the coast to the northwest from Zamu. So, of course, the Ganskian sailors and marines were cock-a-hoop over their victory and very mouthy about it to the men of Magdag.

Duhrra spat. "Zandikar," he said. "I've been there myself! I fought a bout there and won two zo pieces. I think they fought well before they were beaten."

The sight of those chained men displeased me. Zandikar, the city of Ten Dikars, was nowhere near as powerful or wealthy a city-state as her next-door neighbor, Zamu; but her small fleet was considered smart and effective and she had a reputation for her archers and her gregarian groves. There was no order of Krozairs associated with Zandikar, not even a Red Brotherhood, but she was of the Red and of Zair, and an ally.

The two Gansk swifters were six-five hundred-and-twenty swifters. The Zandikarean was a five-three hundred swifter.

There must have been great slaughter, for far less than a full swifter's crew trudged ashore. As for the oar-slaves, they were sorted out, Green and Red, and sent the one to recuperate and rejoin their fellows, the other to further slavery on the oar-benches of Grodnim swifters.

After this excitement Duhrra and I had to be quick about dressing and reporting in for duty. There were more messages on this afternoon than there had been for the entire previous three days. The king had stirred things up, although I had no feeling that Gafard had been dragging his heels. Strong scouting forces had already probed east and west, and weaker patrols had gone south to check out if the Zairians had yet returned to the villages of Inzidia, which had been evacuated earlier when the Grodnims had advanced. I knew that the scouts going east would have to halt long before they reached Pynzalo, for the base camp at which I had met Duhrra, and where he had lost his hand, lay in their way.

From the nature of the messages I carried it was perfectly clear that the king endorsed Gafard's view that a strike to the east, the quick capture of Pynzalo, a consolidation on that strong line, and then a chavonthlike spring to the west represented the best strategy. They both agreed with my views, then. . . .

As the suns were dipping into the sea to the west with the nearest of the confused mass of islands known as the Seeds of Zantristar—the damned Grodnims called them the Seeds of Ganfowang—black bars against the burning glow of sea and sky, it chanced that Gafard called me into the inner compartment of his campaign tent. I went in and saluted and noticed he looked keyed up. He paced about, as he spoke, over the priceless carpet, well pleased over some matter.

The imposing many-peaked tent provided for his lady had been taken down long before the king arrived, and the tent, the lady, her retinue, and a strong guard of Pachaks had left the camp, no man would say where. I had seen the king's crebent wandering about looking exceedingly bilious. He was one Grodnim among many we could do without.

"Such news, Gadak!" Gafard greeted me. "We are on the move. The king approves—but these are matters not fit for the ears of a mere aide. Look—" He gestured to a side table. "Help yourself to a drink. It is all Grodnim stuff."

I refused politely. He'd had to stock Grodnim wine when the king came here.

"The king also brought me an item of information interesting to him; an item of supreme importance to me!" He was expansive; I had never seen him more febrile, alert, restless, pacing about, a flush beneath his mahogany suntan giving him even more of that voracious carved beakhead look I know so well from the mirror.

"Yes, gernu?"

"You asked me once if it was sure the great Krozair, Pur Dray, the Lord of Strombor, was surely dead. And I answered it was sure. Well, Gadak—" Here, he stopped pacing and turned and glared at me with a look of unholy triumph. "There is news, sure news! The king's spies brought it; it cannot be doubted. Pur Dray has reappeared in the inner sea from—from where no man knows. He is still alive!"

"You honor me with your confidence—" I began. He brushed that aside.

"It is no confidence. The news will soon circulate. The greater the news the faster it travels. But, Gadak, there is more. . . . Pur Dray has been ejected from the Krozairs of Zy! He is Apushniad!" Gafard shook his head in bewilderment. "I cannot understand how they can be such fools, such stupid idiot onkers; but the fact remains."

"Then if he is Apushniad,'" I said, speaking slowly, sizing him up, "you think, perhaps—?"

"Aye, I do! There is a certain matter between us. I must meet him. Now that I know he is alive and not dead I am overjoyed!"

How badly he wanted to overmatch the old reputation of that Krozair of Zy who was dead and was now alive!

I said, "You would seek to come to hand-strokes with him, to slay him, to prove yourself a greater Ghittawrer than he is a Krozair?"

He looked at me as though I were a mewling infant, or a crazy man screaming at the lesser moons to halt in their tracks. He opened his mouth, but the tent drapings ripped up and Grogor, his second in command, appeared, throwing a quick salute, butting in, interrupting: "Gernu! The king! He calls for you—at once, gernu!"

Gafard's mouth snapped shut. He whipped up his green cloak and threw it over his shoulders. His longsword clanked once as he strode past me. He said, "Get about your duties, Gadak. Serve me well and you will be rewarded."

"Your orders, my commands, gernu!" I bellowed blankly.

That small incident had shown me in more revealing drama the situation between these two, between King Genod and

Gafard, the King's Striker. For all the talk of brain and hand, of genius and executive, still when the king whistled Gafard ran. Gafard was tough and strong and ruthless and high-handed and all the things a man needed to be to survive upon Kregen and attain a position of comfort—quite apart from power and wealth—and his authority within the army was unquestioned. Still, King Genod whistled and Gafard ran.

Then I checked. Did I not run when Gafard whistled?

The answer to that question should be satisfactorily answered this very night.

After the suns had gone down and the Maiden with the Many Smiles began to climb the heavens, I found Duhrra thinking about wandering down to the infantry lines after more dopa, and told him what I was going to do.

His broad idiot face broke into one huge grin. "About time, master! Huh—I'm with you, by Zantristar the Merciful!"

I said, "We will take both the flying boats, for that will be easier. The little one will rest on the big one's deck."

We gathered up all our fighting gear we would ordinarily use on duty and left our sleeping silks and spare clothing scattered about as though we had just left casually. I wanted to leave a bolt-hole in case the damned voller was not a first-class example and played up. That is a thing anyone of foresight would do, even though I did not expect to see this place again for a long time.

The Maiden with the Many Smiles, Kregen's largest moon, gave more light than we needed for a desperate enterprise of this nature. But I would not wait. The king might leave on the morrow after his inspection. And my impatience had now boiled over. Rashness and recklessness—they are a mark of my own stupidity, I own.

Acting perfectly normally we walked through the moon-drenched shadows to the edge of the bluffs overlooking the beach. In one of the curved beach hollows fenced on its seaward side the Zairian prisoners had been lodged. They would be chained and the chains stapled to stakes driven deeply into the sand. Here lay one chance; the sand would give more easily than earth. I had brought a length of iron filched from the engineers' stores, just in case. As it turned out we were lucky here. One of the Rapa guards, who toppled over after Duhrra hit him on top of his crested head, carried keys on a large bronze ring. Cautioning silence, we went among the prisoners, releasing them. They gathered about me in the pink and golden shadows, breathing hard, hardly believing.

"You are men from Zandikar. I salute your prowess. Now we strike a blow for Zair and we strike in absolute silence!"

"I am Ornol ti Zab, ley-Hikdar, third officer of *Wersting Zinna*." The man looked squat and hard, a real sailorman, his black curly hair smothered in sand, with the black dried blood crusting about a wound. "We are with you in this escape. But—you and this giant with one hand wear the green."

"Aye," I said. "Aye, Hikdar, we do. And if there is a scrap of red about we will gladly wear that! By Zair, yes!"

There were dead men in the dunes. Red cloth was to hand. I wound the crimson about my loins, over the green, draped an end over the green tunic. There was no time for more. We all stole silently across the sand. The Hikdar halted as I put my hand on his shoulder and whispered in his ear.

"Not that way, Hikdar."

"But," he whispered back, "that way lies our swifter, our fleet *Wersting Zinna*."

"There is a greater jikai tonight. You are a ley-Hikdar.* Success this night will leap you at a bound to Jiktar. I promise you. Your king Zinna will do no other.

He looked doubtful. I did not blame him. I could be a part of a trap, devilish sport of the Grodnims with Zairian captives.

"King Zinna is an old man now, dom. He would sooner see his swifter back in the ship-sheds of Zandikar."

"Yet the way I show you will deliver up a greater prize. Did you not see the flying boats land?"

He gasped. "Aye—aye! This will be a great Jikai!"

So we went on through the moonlight in the way I directed. Of course, King Zinna must be old—I'd last seen him fifty years ago and he'd been middle-aged then. The cities and states of the Red southern shore hang together in a sketchy alliance against the Greens, but they are touchy of their national honor. I didn't care to which Zairian city-state the voller went just so long as I stopped off at Zy first.

Although, come to think of it, my allegiance should go to Mayfwy of Felteraz and through her to King Zo of Sanurkazz. That was, if I had any allegiances left.

The night guard on the two vollers had been changed from Pachaks to Fristles. No doubt apims and Chuliks and any

* Ley: four.

other diffs on the roster might have been used as required. My sea-leems of Zair dealt with the Fristles; the cat-faced diffs swiftly disposed of, the Red swamped over the Green.

The moon glistered on the ornate scrollwork gilding of the sternwalk. The hull bulged with power. Yes, this was a fine handy craft, equipped with varters, decked, a superb fighting machine of the air. We swarmed up like ants, climbing up onto the deck and taking by surprise the remnant of the guard sleeping off watch there.

With brands in their fists, with their blood up, these men of Zandikar showed their mettle.

Their captain and ship-Hikdar had been slain in the battle with the two swifters of Gansk. Many of their comrades had gone up to sit in glory on the right hand of Zair in the radiance of Zim. Now they sent a covey of Grodnims down to the Ice Floes of Sicce without compunction.

Some noise fractured the night in that swift struggle. That was unfortunate but seemingly inevitable. I belted for the control deck shouting to Duhrra to make sure everyone was aboard safely. The controls were perfectly familiar to me. I hit the levers and we went up in a smooth, swooping rise, a rush of power. The smaller voller was not in its mooring place and so King Genod must be sending more messages. I chilled.

Suppose he had taken the voller himself? But no—no, Zair would not play that trick on me. I did as I had planned and brought the voller to earth again in the first spot that appeared suitable from the air. I knew this terrain from carrying messages and had selected a number of deep gullies where the voller might be hidden. I double-checked the best place from the air as we slanted down, and was satisfied she would not be spotted if the two-place flier nosed over.

Hikdar Ornol ti Zab organized his men into throwing the scrubby branches of nik-nik bushes over the deck to shield her. The nik-nik is a nasty plant and the men were scratched. They did not care. My plan appealed to them.

But, Hikdar Ornol and Duhrra both said to me, growling: "We shall come with you, Gadak."

"Not so," I said. "I am able to pass easily where you would have trouble, Duhrra, and you, Hikdar, could not pass at all."

They fumed and argued, but they knew I was right. The voller had to be secured first. Now came the tricky part.

I started to leave them and as I did so Hikdar Ornol said to me, "There is one among our company who claims to have

seen a flying boat before. He even says he can fly one through
the air like a bird."

The urgency in me, I now admit, made me gloss over this
information that would normally have been startling. The
Hikdar went on, speaking in his growly graint voice: "If
you do not return within two burs of dawn we shall decide
—"

I knew what he was going to say. I stopped him.

"You will get this young fellow to fly the boat out. You
will all be trapped if you return. You know this to be
true."

"Aye." He spoke surlily, a warrior deprived of a fight.
"It is sooth. But we are loath to do this thing."

"I shall not say Remberee."

"Hai Jikai!" he said to me, and so I went back toward the
camp and to King Genod and Gafard, the King's Striker,
the Sea-Zhantil.

There was a quantity of confusion going on about the
vanished voller. Guards ran and shouted and torches flared.
This was all to the good. I ran in as though most busy about
my work, and almost forgot to rip off the red cloth. I
bundled it up and stuffed it inside the green tunic over the
mail.

"It must be cramphs of Zair!" men bellowed. "Rasts of
the Red!"

In all this confusion I ought to be able to take Genod and
Gafard. At the least, I ought to be able to do that. So
I planned as I ran and shouted with the rest and worked my
way around to the tent of the king.

How man proposes and Zair disposes! Or Opaz or Djan.
I wouldn't give the time of day to Grodno or Havil or Lem.
I ran through the moon-shot darkness. This was where I let
rip all the frustrations, where I really hit back, where I at
last created a High Jikai that would reinstate me among
the ranks of the Krozairs of Zy.

All the stupid pride flooded me, onker that I was. What
would that oaf Pur Kazz say when I landed with a magnificent flying boat of the air, with rescued Zairians, and with
the enormous prize of not only Gafard, the Sea-Zhantil, the
most renowned Ghittawrer of the Eye of the World, but
his liege lord also, his king, this same king Genod, the genius
king of evil Magdag!

Well, onker I was and onker I remained.

The king's tent was flooded with light. Orderlies and

sectrixmen waited outside, nervous, fidgety. I marched through as bold as Krasny work, up to the tent flaps and the guards.

I thought—well, that would be to reveal too much. Suffice it to say I thought it could be done and I could do it. I think, now, in all sober truth, I could have done it. It was, after all, a thing I had done before and was, as you shall hear, a trick I was to pull off again, more than once.

But could the Star Lords have had a hand in this? The Savanti, perhaps? I did not know. I do know that as I bluffed my way past the guards and entered the first of the canvas-sided anterooms leading into the king's quarters a number of what I then considered impossible events occurred.

There were far too many men here to be accounted for by the loss of the voller, serious though that was. These were men who should be out hunting for the king's airboat.

I heard a man shouting: "I tell you it is sooth! I saw him. I saw him as he climbed up the side of the flying boat and the moon shone on his face. He wore the red. I would know that devil's face anywhere, for did he not give me this scar on my own face, these many years ago!"

I halted in the press, at the back, unable to pass through, cursing to get on and yet halted by these words.

"It was the infamous Krozair himself! Pur Dray. The Lord of Strombor! Come back from the dead!"

Other men shouted that how could Golitas be sure, and this Golitas with the scarred face bellowed that, by Goyt, he knew the most renowned Krozair of the Eye of the World when he saw him!

This made it more tricky. Golitas must have come in with the king, for he had not been about the camp. Had he been he would no doubt have taken longer to recognize me for the circumstances would have been far less dramatic. I had best place my white scarf about my face again, but my groping fingers encountered nothing where the scarf should be. Of course, I'd lost the damned thing somewhere along the way.

This was bad enough. But then—and I swear I was in so ugly a mood I might have done something I would have regretted for all the thousand years of life vouchsafed me—I heard two voices I just could not believe in, could not, for they were of another life and another place many dwaburs removed from the problems of the inner sea.

The first voice boomed out in a great numim bellow.

"What a gang of onkers, by Krun! Can't even guard a voller the empress Thyllis sends out of friendship!"

And the other voice tripped up and down the scale: "This is a wight leem's-nest, Wees! We can't walk all the way home, now can we, dear fellow?"

Chapter Fourteen

I avoid old comrades

Rees and Chido!

Incredible. Impossible. But true.

The crowd swayed as guards opened a path through. In the uproar that roaring numim voice of Rees's blasted out again. He was upset. He didn't mind who knew.

But—Rees and Chido! All the way from Ruathytu in distant Hamal, to the Eye of the World. They must have been with the voller. No other explanation was possible. I stood back, no longer pushing forward.

They had not seen me for over twenty years, but I had no doubts that I would be recognized. They'd know me. They'd be as thunderstruck as I was myself.

They'd know me. They'd know me as Hamun ham Farthytu, the amak of Paline Valley. They did not know their friend Hamun whom they had tried to make into a bladesman was the Prince Majister of Vallia.

What thoughts tumbled pell-mell through my dizzy mind! I had stepped back purely involuntarily. The onker Golitas was still babbling on about it being sure that he had recognized the notorious Krozair, the Lord of Strombor, and over that Rees's lion-roar blattered against my ears.

"By Krun! What a bunch of onkers! Chido, old fellow, this is a right leem's-nest!"

And Chido's light voice, turning all his R's into W's, a mode of speech I seldom attempt to reproduce, saying: "I suppose you can't blame 'em too much, Rees. If this fellow who stole the voller is as good as they say—"

And a rumble from Rees, indicating to me that he had been learning wisdom in the years separating our last meeting. By Krun! But was I glad to know he and Chido were still alive! After the Battle of Jholaix in which Vallia had smashed the Hamalese Army of the North anything could have happened to them. Maybe they were even back in the good books of the empress Thyllis. If they were, they were even more of an enemy to Vallia. . . .

The swirls in the crowd as the closely packed men reformed to let the high dignitaries through pushed me against a wooden post holding a peak of the side wall. I could see past the heads and shoulders of those moving in front. I saw Rees and I saw Chido.

They looked just the same.

Well, of course, twenty-one years made little if any difference to the appearance of a man on Kregen, once he had reached the age of his maturity. They looked great. The flaming golden mane that marked Rees for a numim, a lion-man, glowed in the lamplight. His broad, powerful lion-face scowled and those tawny eyes caught the light and glittered. And Chido, just the same, popping with excitement, spluttering, his chinless face and pop-eyes bringing back the memories. Dear old Chido!

If they saw me they would call out in huge surprise. What explanations had they thought up to explain away to themselves the vanishment of their comrade and fellow bladesman Hamun?

I caught a quick glimpse of a black-browed fellow with a hard, blocky face beyond Rees. Across this fellow's features an old scar showed livid as the blood flushed.

This must be Golitas.

If he saw me the next few murs would be exceedingly tricky and complicated. They might be interesting, too.

Maybe, maybe I might have risked it. For if this Golitas hauled out his sword and ran at me, and Rees and Chido saw that, might they not shout in shock and run to stand with me?

They might.

Somehow, I did not think they would.

My shock had been great at seeing them. They might put two and two together. I had plans for Hamal and I wished to preserve my identity as the amak of Paline Valley.

I turned my head away.

Yes, I, Gadak, turned my head away.

A table lay cluttered with cloaks and capes and scarves dropped by the officers and aides as they had entered. A green scarf, snatched up, covered my face. I do not disguise my own feelings of contempt for myself. But much, much more depended on my actions now; my freedom meant more than the freedom that has so often been denied me —it meant getting out of the Eye of the World and back to Delia. That must come first.

There seemed to me to be more than an inkling in my head why these two, Rees and Chido, had come to the inner sea with the voller for King Genod. I guessed they had fancied the adventure, no doubt feeling at a loss in peacetime Hamal. Had Rees's estates of the Golden Wind all blown away yet? Was he now merely the owner of an empty title? How was Saffi, his daughter, that glorious lion-maiden I had rescued from the Cripples' Jikai, snatched from the Manhounds of Faol?

The interruption in my progress, the check as the crowd surged back making way, the shock of seeing old comrades again, all conspired to thwart my plans.

Chido gesticulating violently, and Rees stalking on arrogantly, they passed through the crowd and on into the moonlight outside. I roused myself. The idiot Golitas would follow soon. After he had gone, would there be a chance to snatch Gafard and the king?

"Ah, Gadak! Just the man!"

I whirled about and my hand fell to my longsword.

Gafard stared at me, and past me at the others in the canvas-walled anteroom.

"All of you! Out searching! The king is most wrathful. The flying boat has been stolen and stolen by no less than Pur Dray, the great Krozair. Stir yourselves!"

He saw the movement of my hand.

"Yes, Gadak. It is a time for swords—but only when we find the flying boat."

"Yes, gernu."

How easily I slipped into the ways of Grodnim that had encompassed me these past months!

My prime responsibility was to Delia. I had to get out of the inner sea and back to her. I had to get back alive, for she had warned me, long and long ago, that she would be cross with me if I got myself killed. Beside her anger at that kind of foolishness on my part the anger of King Genod over the loss of his voller was as the mewling of an infant.

There were many men, both apim and diff, in the anteroom of the king's tent. A guard party of bowmen stood with bows held up and arrows nocked, a part and parcel of the king's security. Word that the Lord of Strombor had been seen was enough to make every man stand to arms and tremble, sweating in anticipation.

The events that had taken place since I had bluffed my way in here to hear Rees's great numim bellow to the moment when Gafard ordered me to join the search had taken practically no time at all. Words and thoughts and actions had tumbled one over the other.

My plan had failed.

There was no chance at all to take Gafard and less chance, even, than that to take the king.

If I put a sword-edge to Gafard's throat and forced my way in to the king the bowmen would feather me, and if Gafard died as well that was the price Grodno exacted. I remembered, here in the very Eye of the World, the callousness with which Prince Glycas, the embodiment of all that was evil in the overlords of Magdag, had told me that I could slay his guard-commander, but that he would surely slay me, anyway. The only life with which to bargain with King Genod was the life of King Genod himself.

"Don't stand about, you calsanys!" bellowed Gafard. No doubt he had had the rough edge of Genod's tongue. His fierce face showed all the venom I might have shown in a similar situation. "Schtump!" He used that coarse and abusive word to these officers, the word that conveys in such a vivid way "Get out! Clear off!"

"Schtump!" roared Gafard, the King's Striker. "Find the flying boat of the king!"

Even then, as the men elbowed out carrying me with them in the press and I saw the tall, scar-faced form of Golitas approaching Gafard, the King's Striker had not made any evil promises as a reward for failure. He was canny enough to see the apparently obvious. If the flying boat could sail through the air faster than a galloping sectrix, then she would be away and gone and no torchlight search in the darkness would find her again.

As we mounted up I had to stop cursing. My hands did not shake, but in all else I felt myself to be the greatest rogue in two worlds. My nerve had not failed me, for I knew it was Delia who had restrained my hand. But I knew what my conduct would appear to my comrades, to my Brother Krozairs—I had failed in my plans and had not taken the opportunity to cut down all in my path until I died still striking out with the cry of Zair on my bloodied lips.

That, of course, was the maniac's way, the battle-lover's way, the berserker way I had renounced with disgust.

But—would that not have been a Jikai?

Possibly, but a damned little one in my view.

I gave up making excuses for my feeble conduct and spurred off into the darkness with the others, the link-slaves astride preysanys lighting our way, and precious little chance we had of finding the voller, I can say.

The torches flared their blazing hair over the shadows and we rode and men shouted and there was much hullabaloo. I took the first opportunity to ride off and lose myself in the darkness.

The Maiden with the Many Smiles made that difficult, for the darkness was a matter of a pink-lit radiance, gloomy only in comparison with the glory of the daytime suns; the torches emphasized the darkness. I slipped away at last and cantered along to where I had left the voller. No one followed.

I had miserably failed in the main elements of my plan. I did not return with the king and Gafard. But the second part of the scheme could still work. I would take the voller and we'd fly out over the inner sea and when the convoy bearing the supplies for the army appeared off the coast we would swoop down and sink and burn the lot.

Yes, that would at least salvage some part of my Jikai.

With a voller of the quality of the airboat we had captured under my command I would be master of the situation.

Grandiloquent ideas burned in my mind. I felt the power of madness and of supernal power flowing through me.

With the airboat I could be master of the coast, and destroy utterly all Genod's plans.

He had no varters that could deal with vollers. The armies of the Hostile Territories and of Havilfar contained high-angle varters, artillery designed to hurl bolts upward and so bring down the flaunting ships of the air. These devices were unknown in the inner sea. I would be unchallenged. I would be unchallengeable.

So it was that with the hateful word "I" ringing in my head I reached the place where the voller had been hidden.

Approaching cautiously, for there had been weapons aplenty in the flier and I did not want an arrow through me, I gave a low-voiced hail.

"Duhrra! Hikdar Ornol!"

The camouflage had been well done. The nik-nik bushes concealed all. My sectrix lumbered on, his hooves near sound-less on the sandy soil. The pink and golden moonlight flooded

down and away from the interference of the torches' glow
I could see well. I called again, louder.

No answer. Nothing.

The sectrix slipped and skidded down the incline. I was
enclosed by the bushy walls. I looked about.

The voller was not there.

I looked again, and shouted, and spurred up and sent the
sectrix crashing down into the bottom of the gulley.

Nothing.

The voller was gone.

Just how long I rode up and down, flailing at bushes with
my sword, yelling, bellowing, I have no idea.

At last the realization reached me that, in truth, the
voller had flown. I could not curse. For the last time I galloped lumpily across the sandy soil, flailing away, and bits
of bush flew into the air, spinning in the moon-drenched
darkness. The smell of night blooms hung strongly in the air.

Nothing.

No voller.

Duhrra and the men from Zandikar had gone.

I was alone.

Now, if ever, was the time to remember that I, Gadak
of the Green, was not and never could be Gadak of the Green.

Chapter Fifteen

My Lady of the Stars wields a dagger

"The onkers rush upon their own destruction," said Gafard with great satisfaction.

We sat our sectrixes upon a slight eminence in the nik-nik covered bluffs. The sea sparkled bluely away to our left. The land to the right trended, flat and interesting, to a far horizon where heat shimmer broke outlines into blue and purple ghosts. Blown by the wind drifts of sand swathed the scene below.

Below us and less than half a dwabur away marched the hosts of Zair, advancing to the west. How marvelous they looked, with their many red banners fluttering, the suns striking back in gleam and glint from armor and weapons. Sectrix cavalry trotted on the flanks. Infantry marched at the center. On they came, proud in their might, a splendid army gathered from the fortress cities of Pynzalo and Zimuzz, from the inland towns of Jikmarz and Rozilloi, and from many of the villages of the fertile inland territories.

In all those brave banners of the Red I saw the proud devices, and recognized many of them. Justice and hope marched there, pride and honor. On the right flank, their sectrixes' hooves sometimes cutting through the surf, trotted a contingent of splendid cavalry on whose red banners the device of the hubless spoked wheel within the circle blazed and coruscated.

Only a small contingent of Krozairs of Zy there were. I guessed that the bulk of the Krzy would be far to the west, fighting with Pur Zenkiren and the two generals of the combined armies there.

My heart lifted when I saw that grand and formidable array advancing toward the massed green banners before me.

Gafard, the King's Striker, sat his sectrix and chuckled and ever and anon he pulled that black hawk-beard of his. He had given no further orders after those that had drawn out the army of Magdag into its allotted positions.

Two sennights had gone by since my disastrous debacle on the night the king's voller had been stolen by the famous Krozair, the Lord of Strombor. Although a strict watch was kept against the flyer's return, no more had been seen of her.

I had hoped she would be flying over the host of Zair when they marched to the attack. The Zairians had worked like demons to collect this army to reinforce the armies of the west. Now we had appeared unexpectedly in their path. They attacked recklessly. This was the way they reacted to the descent upon their coasts of the Green of Grodno.

The king and Gafard had been highly delighted.

All thought of investing Pynzalo had been abandoned. The garrison of the city marched in the host fronting us. Gafard had said, "They save us much labor and casualties." He had slapped his thigh with his riding glove before throwing it to a slave and taking up the metaled war-gauntlets he would wear for the battle. "You ride as aide to me, Gadak. Nalgre and Nath and Insur, with Gontar and Gerigan, will be all I need. Once the battle is joined there will be little need for messages. The army of the king knows what to do!"

"One wonders," said Gontar, who prided himself that his father was an overlord of Magdag who owned estates requiring ten thousand slaves to run, "if that cramph the Lord of Strombor is with the onkers this day."

"One," said Gafard, Sea-Zhantil, "sincerely trusts he is not."

They took that to mean the obvious, but I glanced at Gafard—and away smartly, to be sure—and guessed he meant he hoped Pur Dray would not be there to be slain by a casual pike-thrust. Gafard wanted to cross swords with the great Krozair in person, so I said to myself, pondering imponderables.

I admit, in all fairness, that I was not only coming to share these damned Grodnims' obsession with Pur Dray, Krozair, and regarding him in the third person, but also was still much surprised that his legend persisted so vividly after fifty years. I could scarce credit that no other Krozair had risen to a similar eminence in the Eye of the World.

The truth was that Gafard so hungered after a similar renown his well-known obsession fostered the persistence of the stories and tales of the Lord of Strombor. Now that Pur Dray had returned to life, had been declared Apushniad by the Krzy and had actually been seen back at his old activities, no wonder speculation and rumor buzzed around the camp like flies over the carcass of a chunkrah slain by leems on the plains.

Also in this fascination with a Red Krozair must be the dread knowledge in the minds of the overlords that Pur Dray had witnessed the private, terrible rites that went on in the utmost secrecy within the megaliths at the time of the Great Death, when the red sun eclipsed the green sun.

I suppose, trying to think about it logically and restraining myself from taking the amused and cynical line that was too treacherously easy, there was a terrible and malefic aura about the name and deeds of Pur Dray, the Lord of Strombor, Krozair of Zy.

The hosts of Red marched on, their banners flying. The ranks of Green waited calmly, silent, and their green banners flaunted no less vividly under the suns.

Gafard was eyeing the distances. We could all see the restiveness in the Red cavalry on the wings. They would charge at any moment, a torrent of mailed men bursting down on the ranks of Green footmen. Those footmen were fronted by a glittering, slanting wall of pike-heads.

I knew the heart of that formation down there below us on the sandy soil. I had created it myself. The serried mass of pikes in the strong phalanx to take the shock of the cavalry change. The halberdiers and swordsmen to protect the pikes from swordsmen. The wedges of arbalestiers shooting with controlled rhythm. And the shields—that cowards' artifice—the shields to protect the men and deflect the shafts from the short, straight bows and the crossbows of the enemy. Oh, yes, I had designed that fighting machine to destroy mailed overlords of Magdag. And now those same devilish overlords used my fighting instrument, remade by them with their own swods, to destroy my comrades in Zair. I tell you, my thoughts were bleak and spare.

I hoped that the Zairians would win.

I knew the worth of my work and the genius of Genod Gannius, whose parents I had saved from destruction, and I knew, darkly and with agony and remorse, the inevitable outcome of the battle.

What I would do was already worked out. I knew that despite all I could not stop myself.

The red cloth was stuffed again within the breast of my

tunic. I would don the red, draw my longsword, and so hurl myself into the rear of the pikes as the charges went in. Perhaps there would be a little chance for the Krozairs, for the Red Brethren, for the warriors of Zair.

That chance was slender to the point of nonexistence. But, despite all, I could not stop myself.

Sharply, a shadow fleeted over the ground and we all looked up and there, skimming through the bright air, flew the two-place voller with Genod Gannius gorgeous in green and gold leaning over and encouraging his troops.

If he had fire-pots up there . . .

The army of the Green let out a dull surf-roar of welcome and greeting to their king. Very pretty it was. And in defiant answer rose the shouts from the Reds.

"Grodno! Zair! Green! Red!" The shouts rose and clashed. "Krozair! Ghittawrer!" The yells twined in the brilliant atmosphere. And, a new shout, a shrill screeching: "Genod! Genod! The king!"

The Zairian cavalry charged, a torrential mass of steel and red bearing down on the massed pikes. I reined Blue Cloud a little way back of the other aides. They were all standing in their stirrups, craning to look down from our eminence onto the drama spread out below. Now was the time to don the red and so charge down and make a finish.

It might not be a Jikai, but with those Krozair shouts ringing through the air and the brave scarlet fluttering I could do no other. . . .

A shadow flitted into the corner of my eye and I turned, quickly, the red half drawn from my green tunic.

A Pachak with only one left arm, and a bloody stump where the other should be, rode frantically up to Gafard, his hebra foundering. He yelled at Gafard. I heard his words, caught and blown by the wind; I saw Gafard's hard mahogany face turn abruptly gray within the iron rim of his helmet.

"My Lady—treachery—we were surprised—slain—black —men in black—my lord. . . ."

The Pachak fell even as his hebra collapsed.

Gafard lifted his head and screeched.

I thrust the red away and kicked Blue Cloud over.

"Gadak! You I trust! Find Grogor! Find Nath ti Hagon! Take men—anyone—ride, Gadak, ride! My Lady of the Stars —my pearl, my heart . . . ride, Gadak! Ride as you love me!"

I didn't love the devil. But—my Lady of the Stars!

What do I know, now, of my thoughts, my emotions, and my feelings? I know I knew the Zairian army below me was doomed, for I had wrought the instrument of their destruction. But there would come another time, another field, and another battle. Now all my blood clamored that I save my Lady of the Stars.

I rode. I did not ride wearing the red. I rode not for my lord Gafard, the King's Striker, the Sea-Zhantil—but for my Lady of the Stars.

Even now, after all that happened, I do not regret that decision.

If only some easy power of sorcery had been open to me!

If only by some magic formula I could have prevented what was fated to occur.

But I am a mortal man and the fantasies of wish-fulfillment belong to the myths and legends of Kregen, not to the hard reality of that beautiful and terrible world beneath the Suns of Scorpio.

Yes, there is seeming magic on Kregen, and the wizards practice mighty sorceries, but they are of a piece, following ordained paths. The wonder and mystery of Kregen can never be denied, but it is men and women with hope and courage who flesh out the true fantasies.

I rode.

Grogor, Gafard's second in command, that surly man, did not hesitate a fraction. He screeched a savage order to a squadron of sectrixmen, all picked men-at-arms, apims and diffs, and wheeled his mount and was away with streaming mane and flying feathers. We picked up Nath ti Hagon, Gafard's trusted ship-Hikdar, and then, in a compact body, we rode from the battlefield. Sand blew from our sectrixes' hooves. The wind of our passage blustered in our plumes and scorched into our faces. So we left the action, the battle, that debacle for the Red, which the mad genius king Genod called the Battle of Pynzalo.

Wherever Gafard had hidden his beloved, the rasts of men in black had found her. I had one hope. The voller had been flown by Genod himself and it had flown over the battlefield. We had to deal with men mounted on sectrixes like ourselves.

In one item of my reading of the situation I was wrong.

We went flying through the near-deserted camp, sending the camp followers stumbling out of our way, only the green of our plumes and dress able to convince them they were not attacked by a raiding party of Zairians. We belted past the lines of tents. I had nudged Blue Cloud gently to the head of the pack, for although I wished to conserve him for what I thought would be a long ride, I still felt the mad desire to hurry on like a maniac and be the first there to rescue my Lady of the Stars.

The Pachak of her guard who had escaped to warn Gafard must have been a most intelligent as well as a brave man. He must have fought until he saw there was no hope left and then, instead of going on fighting and throwing his life away, had turned and raced for the King's Striker. Out past the camp we saw the flurry of green cloaks. I looked closer. A party of sectrixmen was picking its way down the sandy slopes toward the beach. A swifter waited there, her stern ladder erected, one end on the quarter and the other on the beach. Beneath the green cloaks I saw—instead of the expected white, or green, or the flash of mail—black.

Grogor saw, also, and shrilled and we all pelted along, hurling ourselves madly over the bluffs and so roaring down the sandy slopes in great clouds and smothers of sand.

Somehow Blue Cloud kept his six legs under him. We were on the beach. I yanked out my longsword, that Ghittawrer blade with the device removed, and whirled along the packed sand.

The black-clad men saw us coming.

There was a struggle in their midst.

Grogor and Nath were neck and neck with me. Our three swords thrust forward, three-pronged retribution.

The black-clad men tried to face us.

There must have been few men who could have stood up to us in that frenzied moment.

In the moments before we hit I saw my Lady of the Stars.

She wielded a long, thin dagger in her white hand, and she toppled one kidnapper from his saddle and whirled on another who tried to spit her through. She parried—it was marvelously done, marvelously!—and riposted and stuck the rast through the eye. He screamed and fell and then we were upon them.

Our rage was terrible and genuine.

The longswords whirled and glittered, split and cleft, and whipped aloft again for the next blow, dripping red.

Blade clanged against blade. My Ghittawrer longsword sang above my head. Aye! It sang as I whirled it up and down. I smashed with full force, seeing a head spin off, seeing a black-masked face abruptly disappear into a ghastly red mask, seeing an arm spin up and away as a back-hander curled beneath a blow. It was all over in scant murs. We panted. I dragged in a great lungful of air and then, dismounting, walked over to my Lady, who lay in the sand. Her green veiling remained in place, for she had one hand to it. But she knew me.

"Gadak! So you rescue me again."

"Aye, my Lady. You are unhurt?"

She stood up. She put a hand on my shoulder. Her left hand. In her right hand, smothered in blood, she still gripped the slender, jeweled dagger.

"I am unharmed. They tried to—at the end—when they saw you coming. But—"

"Yes, my Lady. You yourself created a Jikai. I saw." Then I smiled—I, who am a surly beast and with a face like the ram of a swifter. "I am minded of another lady, my Lady."

"I would not have thought—" she began, and then stopped and threw the dagger to the sand. She took her hand from my shoulder and drew herself up. She put that clean left hand to her hair. Typically, the next words she said were, "And my lord? How goes the battle?"

"The battle will go well enough."

She sighed.

She, like myself, had been Zairian once.

"I returned to the camp, Gadak, and they were waiting for me. Men in black. Stikitches—kidnappers for a space—but real stikitches, nonetheless."

"Aye."

My men were inspecting the corpses. The swifter was gone, pulling madly out to sea.

Grogor turned one body over with his foot and then cocked an eye at me. I looked down.

The brown face with a livid scar all across it showed where Golitas, who had received that scar from the hands of Pur Dray, had died in agony.

"It would be best to heave these carrion into the sea." Grogor took out his knife. "But first—My Lady, would you please retire for a space, for there are things that must be done."

She understood well enough. A warrior maid, for she had fought magnificently, now she was a practical lady with a man to protect. So we disfigured the corpses so that they would never be recognized and heaved them into the sea. When we had finished we escorted my Lady back to camp and had anyone challenged us he would have been a dead man.

We had saved my Lady of the Stars for Gafard, Sea-Zhantil; we had saved her from the clutches of King Genod himself and no one to point the finger of accusation at us. Also, a man who knew my face was dead. Besides the safety of my Lady that was of no importance at all.

Chapter Sixteen

Grogor surprises me

Black magbirds flew overhead. To larboard the lesser Pharos passed at the end of the mole. The stones gleamed in the slanting lines of masonry, and the curve of stone-work opened out into a broad view across the outer harbor. Two swifters rode to their moorings here, their yards crossed, and the last preparations caused a bustle on their long, lean decks as they were readied for sea. *Volgodont's Fang* glided on, the oars pulling with a slow, steady rhythm that drove our stem through the water with a low musical chinkle.

The frowning stone gateway to the cothon, the inner basin, lined up directly with our ram. Nath ti Hagon stood staring directly ahead, lining up the ship, giving quick, di-rect orders to the oar-master in his tabernacle and to the two helm-Deldars at their rudder handles. These two old tarpaulins turned the curved steering oars with cunning, smooth movements that kept the swifter dead on track.

The group standing with me on the quarterdeck included Gafard, but he was in this matter quite content to let his trusted first lieutenant conn the ship. Hardly a breeze ruf-fled the still surface of the water in which reflections stood out in perfect mirror-images.

The entrance to this cothon had been excavated widely enough to accommodate the spread wings of a swifter. Many cothons have narrow entrances, so that a galley must be drawn through by pulling-boat or, more usually, by gangs of men hauling hawsers from the dock side, all heaving to-gether at the crack of a whip and the yell of "Grak!"

We glided on smoothly. I had no doubts that Nath would take the ship fairly through the center of the narrow chan-

nel with not a single oar splintered. Swifters habitually
carry as many as half the number of oars again to replace
broken oars, for breaking oars is a familiar hazard to the
swifter captains of the inner sea.

Once we were fairly through the whistles shrilled and the
drum-Deldar tapped his peculiar terminal notes and every
oar lifted and remained level. Swifters of the size of *Volgodont's Fang* are reasonably stable in the water, unlike the
smaller swifters that rock so much a man must step lightly
and the oars must rest in the water to ensure stability.

How familiar the details of bringing a vessel into port!

I watched, storing away the nostalgic memories and refusing to become maudlin. The sides of the cothon were
lined with the long, slanting ship-sheds, narrow structures,
two slips to a roof, inclined toward the water. Ingenious
capstans and pulleys were arranged so that the swifters
might be drawn up out of the water and gangs of slaves
whipped to the work. The open fronts of the sheds with
their ornate columns and Magdaggian arches could be closed
by wooden doors in inclement weather—of which there is,
thankfully, very little in the Eye of the World—and as they
clustered closely together they presented a compact,
crowded nesting effect. Little over the width of a swifter,
probably not one being more than forty feet wide to accept the apostis, they were long, a hundred and eighty feet
or more. This was not the king's harbor. Over there the
sheds were, of course, larger. The massively impressive building rising to the rear, sculptured almost like a temple, was
the Arsenal of the Jikgernus—the warrior lords—and there
were kept the multifarious stores demanded by the swifters.
The smell of that place could waft me away and away four
hundred light-years in my mind's eye.

Farther to one side and lifting grandly over the ship-sheds
the bulk of a real temple glittered in the suns-light. All
smothered in green tiling, ceramics of the same high quality that decorated the megaliths, the temple of the sea-
god, Shorush-Tish, sparkled and glistered in the light. Set
at the apex of its many-peaked roofs the marble representations of swifters, one third full size, leered down over the
mariners and marines and slaves who crowded the narrow
streets, busy about the sea business of Shorush-Tish.

It is a remarkable fact—at least, at that time it was
remarkable to me—that the blue-maned sea-god, Shorush-
Tish, is shared by Grodnim and Zairian. In all else they
clash in their beliefs, for all that they sprang from the same

original religious convictions. Temples to Shorush-Tish are obligatory on all the seafronts of all the ports of the north and south, the Green and the Red. Even the Proconians erect altars to Shorush-Tish. Even the many races of diffs who live up in the northeastern areas of the Eye of the World—and particularly around the smaller sea known as the Sea of Onyx to the apims because of the many chalcedony mines around its shores—build their temples to their halfling representations of Shorush-Tish. Even the Sorzarts who live and reive from their islands up there respect the power of the universal sea-god of the Eye of the World.

It would be a foolish and reckless captain who did not make an offering to Shorush-Tish before he observed the fantamyrrh boarding his vessel.

For all my own dogged beliefs I complied with the custom, and many were the rings and cups I had given to the blue-robed priests of Shorush-Tish in his great temple on the waterfront of the inner harbor at Sanurkazz.

Over by the near wall as we glided on busy gangs of workmen swarmed over an old swifter of that class rowed in the fashion the savants call *a terzaruolo*. I have mentioned that the extra power gained by using a number of men on one oar rowing over an apostis in the *a scaloccio* system had reached the inner sea; but, like the swordships up along the coasts of the Hoboling Islands, the older system still clung on. This swifter with her five men to a bench, angled to the stern, each man pulling on one oar, could not hope to match the speed of a modern swifter of the type of *Volgodont's Fang*. Yet she had been built well and the teredo had not got her, and her timbers were still sound. She had been a fairly large example, rowing five men to a bench each side and with thirty-two oars in each bank. This gave her a total of three hundred and twenty oarsmen and three hundred and twenty oars.

When I say she would not reach the same speed as the more modern examples, I mean essentially the same sustained speed and the same driving power. To improve her it would be necessary to place the five men of each bench all pulling on the same oar, and to increase the length and strength of that oar out of all recognition of the smaller loom and blade hauled by a single man.

This is exactly what the workmen were doing.

When completed, she would be classed as a five sixty-two swifter. I looked to see if they were building a second bank, but saw no sign that this was proposed in her rebuilding.

We went through all the usual formalities of landing. The slaves were herded off to their bagnios. They would very quickly be pressed into service again, for, as the conversion of the old swifter of the *a terzaruolo* system showed, Magdag was scraping up all her resources to fling into what everyone here must consider as the final stages of a victorious war.

The omens looked propitious for King Genod and the overlords of Magdag as for the whole of the Grodnim alliance. I had more or less recovered from the smart of that series of disasters on the Red southern shore. Now we had come back to Magdag. For all the others here this was a homecoming. For me it was the chance to further my plans —those plans that envisaged the king, Gafard, and a voller.

King Genod had duly won his Battle of Pynzalo. There had been few prisoners, and while I was glad of that, I knew the truth lay buried in the sands or running back to Pynzalo and beyond. That, I tell you, was one battle I was glad with a heartfelt gratitude to have missed.

Gafard did not tell me of what passed between him and Genod.

After all, I was as far as he was concerned merely a fellow renegade he had befriended and given employment and who by chance come into contact with his beloved in ways that, hitherto, he had rewarded with death. I did have a privileged position of a sort, that was clear, but it did not extend past the concerns of his household and domestic matters.

He had thanked the group who had rescued the Lady of the Stars, thanked them profusely and with gold. We were only too well aware of what we had done; but the squadron under Grogor was composed of picked men, every man loyal to Gafard personally. No possible blame could attach to the King's Striker for having his men cut down black-clad assassins and kidnappers.

All the same, at the first opportunity, Genod handed over command of the army to Genal Furneld, the Rog of Giddur, and called Gafard back to Magdag. A gloss was put on this by the announcement to the army that soon Prince Glycas would take over command of the combined armies and Gafard, the King's Striker, was required for further duties.

This Genal Furneld was of the usual cut of unpleasant overlords of Magdag and I avoided him. Giddur was sited on the River Dag in one of the great sweeping bends south

of Hagon. He had arrived on the southern shore breathing
fire and slaughter and having fifty men of a pike regiment
punished for dirty equipment. I thought the army was welcome to him. Gafard had said, lightly, concealing his feelings,
that Genal Furneld could sit down in front of Pynzalo and
freeze for all he cared. No one imagined that he would carry
the city with the same panache as the Sea-Zhantil. That
had cheered me a little.

Little time was given me for moping.

My Lady of the Stars returned to her apartments in the
Tower of True Contentment and Gafard called me in to
tell me that he had decided, if I was to earn my keep now
that he no longer commanded actively, that I was to
stand guard with the others of his loyal squadron. I do not
like guard duty. But I accepted this charge with equanim-
ity.

"The matter is simple. Grogor will give you your orders.
Do not fail me, Gadak. I am a man of exceeding wrath to
those in whom I have reposed trust if they betray me."

So, I bellowed "Your orders, my commands, gernu!" and
bashed off to see what unpleasantness Grogor might dream
up for me.

He surprised me.

He sat in the small guardroom in the wall hard by the
entrance to the tower. It was plain and furnished with a
stand of weapons of various kinds, a table and chairs, no
sleeping arrangements, the toilet being outside, and was a
harsh and unlovely room.

"Now, Gadak, who was once a Zairian, listen to me and
listen well."

I was not prepared to strike him, so I listened. I had
plans. I thought Grogor as a vicious killer was not worth
my destroying what slender chances my plans possessed. But,
as I say, he surprised me.

A bulky, sweaty man, this Grogor. He said, "You told me
you did not aspire to take my place in the affections of our
lord and I did not believe. I was wrong. I do believe you
now." He reached over a leather jack and drank with a
great blustering of bubbles. He started to say "By Mother
—" and stopped, and swore, a rib-creaking oath involving the
anatomy of Gyphimedes, the favorite of the beloved of
Grodno.

I said, "It is hard, sometimes."

"Aye."

"I serve my Lady," I said. "As you know well."

He slapped the jack onto the scarred wooden table. His sweaty, heavy face lit up. "By Grodno! But it was a good quick fight, was it not! We tore them to pieces like leems."

"Yet you missed the battle."

He looked up at me, for he sat while I stood. "Aye. What of it?"

"Nothing. Except that you strike me as a man who enjoys a good fight."

"I do." He nodded to the interior door leading into the tower. "And if anyone save the lord or people bearing his sign attempt to pass that door, it is a fight to the death."

"I understand that."

"Good. It is well we understand each other."

There was no doorway at ground level leading into the tower from the outer four courtyards around the base. The only ingress was through the guardroom in the wall. And we guarded that room and that wall and that door.

A second chamber lay alongside the guardroom in which the guards on duty but off watch might sleep and clean their tack. This room smelled of spit and polish, of sweaty bodies, of greasy food. One day, Gafard said, he would have a fresh chamber constructed and so separate the various guard functions. As it was, our prime duty was to guard my Lady.

I sent in a formal request to see Gafard. When he received me, it was in the armory, where he was inspecting a new consignment of Genodders of a superior make. They would bear the Kregish block initials *G.K.S.M.* in Kregish. This, quite obviously, stood for the sword from the armory of Gafard, King's Striker.

"You want to see me?"

"Aye, gernu. I guard the tower and am happy to do so—honored—"

"Get on with it!"

"We guard the door. But the roof—we have all seen a certain flying boat—"

He slapped a shortsword down so the metal rang.

"By Grodno! No honest man would think of such a thing —which proves you are no honest man and therefore of great use to me. By Goyt! We'll fix any onkers who try to fly down like volgodonts onto my roof! We'll impale the rasts!"

All this meant, of course, was that he had not lived, as had I, in a culture where vollers and flying animals and birds are regularly used. It was a thing he would not have thought of in the nature of his experience. But he sealed the roof as well as any roof was sealed in the Hostile Territories.

Kregen is a harsh and cruel world for all its beauty, and there a man must protect his own, a woman protect her own. I had done precious little of that, lately, but I had supreme confidence in my Delia. She, at the least, would give me firm assurance that I did the right thing in thus helping to protect this unknown Zairian girl, this Lady of the Stars.

I felt sure I was right in this, and yet could give no real reason to myself. I have tried to explain as best I can the effect this maiden had on me, and although I intended to knock Gafard on the head when I could get him and the king together with a voller, I fancied I'd think of her as I hit him.

One night I went on duty earlier than usual, because I was fretful and wanted to get away from some of the diffs of the squadron who were playing dirty-Jikaida (a game I do not care for), and so I wandered along by the wall thinking of Delia and all manner of distant dreams. The guardroom door was open and I went in and almost stumbled over the body of young Genal the Freckles. His neck had been cut open.

The longsword was in my hand, a brand of fire in the torchlight.

The inner door to the off-duty room was shut and logs jammed it.

Three men in black swung about as I stumbled. They lunged at me. I shouted before I bothered to deal with them.

"Guards! Guards! To the tower! Treachery!"

Then the blades met and rang in a glitter of steel. These three were good and they used Genodders. They would have had me, but I whipped out the shortsword and with that in my left hand fended a little, foining as I would with rapier and main-gauche. With a longsword and a shortsword this is not easy; but the second man dropped with the longsword slicing his throat out, and the third man screeched and tried to run as I chopped him as he turned.

The first man was clawing up from the floor, the shortsword still transfixing his throat where I had hurled it. He collapsed in blood and then Grogor burst in from the courtyard.

"Aloft, Grogor!" I bellowed.

We kicked the logs away and the men inside, alerted by

the scuffle and baffled by the jammed door, poured out. In a living tide of fury we went up the stairs. The fight was not long. The kidnappers had posted three of their number to watch the guardroom and sent three aloft. We had no mercy on them. We did not wish to hold them for questioning. We knew who had sent them.

I did not see my Lady then, for she had taken her dagger and gone to her private rooms beneath the roof. We caught the kidnappers, but not before they had slain a beautiful numim maiden, her glorious golden fur foully splattered with her own blood. I cursed. When we trooped downstairs again, assured by an apim girl, a handmaiden to my Lady, that all was well, we took the three bodies and disposed of them along with the first three.

Gafard, livid, twitching, raced up the stairs without a word. He came back furious. I wondered what he would do. I knew there was nothing he could do—save send the girl to the king with a handsome note, a gracious gift.

"This is becoming expensive for the king," he said.

That was all.

I think I admired him then, as much as ever I'd done. We kept the guard even more alert after that.

Three days later I had occasion to go into Magdag on an errand for Gafard. This was all a part of my duties as his aide. He was ordering a pearl necklace of many strands, an enormous pearl choker, for his lady, and I was to deliver gold for the fittings and clasps. He trusted me in this.

The souks of Magdag are strange places, filled with all the clamor one expects of markets where all is bustle, but yet completely lacking the bright, cheerful sounds of markets in sanurkazz. Dour people, the folk of Magdag, resting on a slave foundation for labor, giving orders and whipping and shouting "Grak!" and taking the profits for themselves. They have this marvelous way with dressed leather, as I have said, although the best leather comes from Sanurkazz. I found the jewelers' arcade and the right shop, with its barred windows and narrow door, and transacted my business. Awnings stretched out overhead and the suns' glare was muted into gentle saffron and lime and pink. The sounds of the souks penetrated in a buzz. The walls were yellow and bright, but few vines or flowers grew, where in Sanurkazz in such a place the whole area would have rioted in blossom.

I came outside, bending my head to duck under the low Magdaggian door, and a dagger presented its point to my

I was staring at a crossbow . . .

throat, a hand gripped my arm, and a voice said, "We mean you no harm, dom. Just come quietly with us."

In the normal course of events I would not have abided this. To slide the dagger was not all that easy, for the point pricked just above my Adam's apple; but I did so, anyway, and kicked in the direction of the voice as I gripped the hand and twisted up and back.

Then I was outside the door, dragging one screaming wretch over the stones, seeing another reeling away—most green and bilious and vomiting—and staring at a third who held a crossbow spanned and loaded and pointing at my guts.

"We said we would not harm you, Gadak. We are on the business of a man you would do well to heed. You will come with us."

A fourth man, dressed like the others in the usual green and white robes with tall white turbans, approached and bent to say in my ear: "You are an onker! This is king's business."

The moment he spoke I saw the next few burs in all clarity—and damned awful they would be, too.

If I had been recognized—but this was very much an outside chance. As we went along the crowded streets where it would have been easy for me to slip away, I did not do so. I had already convinced myself that scar-faced Golitas had recognized me only because of the stark illumination as I'd climbed up into the voller. The corner of the eye and the quick, illuminating flash can often reveal far more than the long stare. So, as I went along, I wetted and pulled my moustaches down even more into that ugly soup-straining fungus the Magdaggians think of as proper moustaches. No —I did not think the king wished to see me because I had been recognized as the arch-enemy of Magdag, the notorious Krozair, Pur Dray.

In that—about the king seeing me—I flattered myself. Everything was conducted in the chilling, efficient way of machine governments. The house to which I was conducted was not a villa, not a hovel. It was nowhere near the king's palace. The king would not dirty his hands with the details of his desires. The man who told me what he wanted me to do was puffy and limp-fingered, with a green-swathed paunch, bloated eyes, and moustaches so long and thin and black I felt he could tie green ribbons in each side.

He did not condescend to tell me his name; he told me I might call him *gernu,* and if that was not sufficient, when

I received my pay I might address him as Nodgen the Faithful.

It did not take a genius to understand what these cramphs wanted.

I was to arrange to open the guardroom doors, to arrange to let the kidnappers in, and this time when we jammed the door we would stand guard with more spirit and at a proper time. Of course, this Nodgen the Faithful had no idea of what had happened to his party of kidnappers. I told him, simply, they had all been slain.

"Then this time it is your neck, Gadak. We know you, renegade. You will sell your ib for an ob."

I might sell my soul for a penny—but not on Earth or Kregen.

"And young Genal the Freckles? Will you serve me as you served him after I open the door, as he did?"

"He was an onker. He would have talked."

"And I will not?"

He looked annoyed. I realized I had best not pursue that line too far, otherwise he would release me from the contract prematurely—with a free passage to the Ice Floes of Sicce. So I agreed. They had a lever.

"If you betray us, be very sure you will end up on the oar benches, pulling your guts out in a swifter, flogged . . . you will not relish that, I assure you."

"How would you know?" I began to say. I did not add, as I would have done were I not meditating great, evil joy, "You fat slug!"

We agreed terms. Fifty golden oars. A large sum. I managed to get them to give me ten golden oars on account. No doubt they thought they would take them back from my dead body after I had opened the doors to them. Arrangements were made, the day was set, three days' time, and I was taken away and left in the souk. It would be useless to return to the house. That was a mere convenient place to meet; the owners were probably bound and gagged in the cellars. I returned to Gafard's Jade Palace. As I went in I glanced up at the Tower of True Contentment. I did not smile. But I thought of my Lady.

Any man would do anything for the king to escape the galleys.

What was a mere slip of a girl besides my freedom to pursue my quest in the Eye of the World, to return to Delia?

Would not any sensible girl rejoice in the wealth and

luxury the king would heap on her in return for her favors? The princess Susheeng was out of Magdag, visiting friends in Laggig-Laggu to the west. The king had a free hand. Would not any girl leap at the chance to become the king's favorite, and use her wits to keep her head on her shoulders when he tired of her? Wouldn't any beautiful girl of spirit leap at the chance?

I thought of the very real affection I knew existed between Gafard and the Lady of the Stars, an affection I fancied to be as true a love as any man and woman could be happy and fortunate enough to find on Kregen.

They loved each other. Whether or not Gafard deserved the love of so fine a lady I cared not. She wanted him. He might want her; that did not count. What she wanted mattered.

The king must be an onker of onkers to imagine he could tame so free and fiery a spirit as hers!

Chapter Seventeen

"It is him! I know! Pur Dray, the Lord of Strombor!"

I, Gadak the Renegade, spat juicily on my harness and laid into it with a will with the best polishing cloth. Tack and gear lay spread about on the old sturm-wood table. Others of the men in the loyal squadron likewise polished and spat, spat and polished. We all felt we needed to look smart when the hired kidnappers of the king came calling.

Gafard had smiled that smile of his that was nowhere ironic but all grinning leem-grin.

"So you come to me, Gadak, knowing the king very likely can send you to the galleys?"

"If that is to be Grodno's will, that is to—"

"Aye, aye! And how do I know you have not made another bargain with the king's man—this Nodgen the Faithful?" Here Gafard curled his fist in contempt. "The conceit of the rast. He gives himself a name that is an anagram of the king's. Truly, he must he faithful, the cramph."

"I made the bargain I have told you of. I am to do as poor foolish Genal the Freckles did. To put poison in the wine of the guards and to open all doors."

Gafard's fist made a circle in the air.

"And so ten of my best men are dead, poisoned, and Genal the onker is slain."

"And they will stand a better guard this time and it will be at the mid-time, when no guard changes take place."

As I spat and polished I thought of what Gafard had said, and I did not marvel that he had reached the position he had, Ghittawrer, King's Striker, Sea-Zhantil. For he had produced a plan that should be foolproof—for a time.

In essence it was simple and brutal.

163

I was to do all that the fat cramph Nodgen the Faithful commanded. Except, I was not to poison the guards; they would feign sleep and death. But I was to open the doors and then stand well clear.

"You will have men hidden, to slay the black-masks?"

"No." He was enjoying himself. Had the stakes not been my Lady of the Stars, then I know for certain that Gafard would have enjoyed this game of stealth and wits with his king as much as Genod clearly did. "Oh, no! A slave wench will be bought from the barracoon, privately, before she is put on show for all to see. A beautiful shishi. A Zairian captive, no doubt. I shall treat her with great kindness. I shall call her my Lady of the Stars. She will think herself most fortunate to be thus chosen by the King's Striker."

I said, "And this girl will be taken by the king's men?"

"Yes. If she holds firm to her story, and she is beautiful, the king will be happy. I do not hold it against him as a king, only as a man. He has the yrium, and what he does he does."

So I spat and polished and thought on about my part in this.

I must report in to Nodgen that all was ready for the day.

If there was room for any pity in my bleak old heart I do not think I spilled over much for the girl slave bought from the barracoon and taken straight up into the Tower of True Contentment. If all went well she would be the king's mistress. If she pleased him, who knew how high she might aim or what her influence might be? Certainly, she would be far better treated than in many of the dumps and dives she might have been bought into.

Of course, if she failed to act her part and the king flew into one of the tantrum rages of which he was so terribly capable she might be strangled out of hand. But then, that was a risk, the risk of death, that everyone runs.

Thinking these and other equally odiferous thoughts on the next day I made my way to the appointed rendezvous, a wineshop in the Alley of a Thousand Bangles. The gewgaws tinkled in the breeze off the sea, bright and sparkling, cheap and cheerful, and there were many women admiring the bangles and bartering for their purchase. The wineshop lay in a curve of the souk and I waited outside. If there was to be double treachery, I wanted a space to run and swing a sword.

Nodgen sent the same pack who had brought me to him.

They eyed me with evident desire to get their own back. I said, "It is all arranged. Give me the poison."

They handed over the vial and refused my request for more gold, repeated their threats, and so strode off, pushing the girls out of the way. I turned and went in the opposite direction out of disgust and so found myself crossing an open area I had scarcely ever visited before, where they sold calsanys. No one loves a calsany except for his stubborn strength in carrying burdens—oh, and, of course, for another calsany.

The animals were quite peaceful, which was useful for the salubriousness of the quarter, and I went quickly along past the auctioneers and the crowds of men—merchants, traders, caravan owners and drivers—making their bids in the quick, incomprehensible ways of auctioneers two worlds over. The whole scene was alive with the movement of commerce and the glitter of money changing hands. The breeze puffed a little dust into the air. I reached to pull up the white scarf.

A voice burst out from a crowd around an exceptionally large man flogging calsanys.

"By Grodno! It is him! I know! Pur Dray, the Lord of Strombor!"

I hauled the scarf up and took a running dive into the middle of a pack of calsanys.

It was damned unpleasant.

But in the hullabaloo, the shouting and yelling, the braying and honking, the dust flying up, and the general effluvium upon everything, I managed to get out the other side, knock over a stall covered with calsany brasses and bells, and disappear running up an alley. People turned to gawp. I yelled "Stop, thief!" and pointed and one or two turned out to run with me. Earth or Kregen—it is a useful ploy.

I may make this sound lighthearted, with calsanys doing what calsanys always do when frightened and pots and pans rolling and people yelling and running, but it was a deucedly serious business. By the Black Chunkrah, yes!

I did think that after fifty years people might forget what my ugly old face was like. But fifty years to a Kregan is not like fifty years to an Earthman. And some of those people had cause to remember Pur Dray, the most renowned Krozair upon the Eye of the World. It was not so surprising, after all. But it was most inconvenient. I think, also, that so many rumors of the return from the dead of Pur Dray had swept over Magdag that people's nerves were keyed up. Certainly, the very next day, the day before the plot was to go into operation, some poor devil was shouted up as Pur Dray and set on and stabbed to death in the Souk of Silks. When he was dragged out by the heels, his green tunic a mass of bloody stab wounds, inquiries revealed no one anxious to own to the first shout of alarm. A lesson had been learned there by all Magdag.

So the day dawned.

Gafard said to me, standing in his armory with the wink and glitter of his priceless collections of arms upon the bare walls, speaking harshly: "Is all prepared?"

"Aye, gernu. The poison has been poured down a drain. The guards know their parts. Grogor—"

"I will answer for his conduct this day. I do not wish to miss this charade. Perhaps, one day soon, the king will relish the telling at a party. He must one day realize the position and relinquish this pursuit of my Lady."

He didn't sound convinced.

"As for the greater news," he said, and he fired up at once, as he always did when he spoke of the notorious Krozair, "I believe Pur Dray to be in the city! It must be. He is a man who will be up and doing, always scheming, working for Zair."

How mean and small he made me feel!

"I must meet him. Somehow it must be arranged. There is a matter between us."

Nowadays I would have been reminded of the famous if fatuous walk up the High Street at noon. As it was, he reminded me of a bull chunkrah pawing the ground and tossing his horns, ready to face the challenge of who was to be top chunkrah of the herd.

I said, and not altogether to goad him, "You as a Ghittawrer, gernu, have the lustre now. All the accolades won by Pur Dray lie in the past, sere and shriveled. There have been no great Jikais done by him since he returned from the dead."

He stared at me.

"You speak of things you do not understand, Gadak. You do not understand. Pur Dray was the greatest Krozair of the Eye of the World. No one doubts that or seeks to challenge it. And, today, I am the greatest Ghittawrer of the Eye of the World. Any who seek to dispute that will feel my heavy hand."

"Yet is one of the past and the other of today."

He clapped me on the back, at which I forced my hands to remain clamped at my sides.

"You mean well, Gadak. You mean well. Yet there are matters of honor that are past your comprehension."

If he meant he wanted a good ding-dong with Pur Dray to prove who was the better man, I understood that. But I was beginning to think it was not as simple as that. There was more to it than a straightforward confrontation. Gafard was fighting a legend. That is always more difficult than fighting a flesh-and-blood opponent.

So, in my cleverness, I worked it all out.

Stupid onker, Gadak the Renegade!

If only . . .

But, then, we'd all be rich and happy on *if onlies.*

Looking back as I do speaking to you into the microphone of this little machine here in the Antipodes, I try to visualize it all with calmness. I try to maintain a balance. I blamed myself bitterly for many and many a year afterward. I took the guilt. I did not luxuriate in guilt, as some weak people do. And yet, today, I know I was not to blame, not really, not when the situation was as it was.

Gafard had no doubts.

"The king is a wonderful man, Gadak. He is built in a different mold from Pur Dray and myself. He has the true genius for war, the yrium, the power over us all. Yet he has this weakness, this fault—which is not a fault for has he not the yrium, and does not that excuse all?"

If ever there was a man trying to make excuses to himself for some other cramph, there he was now, talking to me.

"Gernu," I said. I spoke with seriousness, for the answer to my question intrigued me. This man revealed more of himself to me than he realized. And, I did not forget that he was loved by the Lady of the Stars. "Gernu. What do you think would happen were the king and Pur Dray to meet, face to face?"

He did not let me finish. A little shiver marked his shoulders and he put a hand to his face. Then he rallied. "It would be in the manner of their meeting. Were it blade to blade, or sectrix to sectrix, or in council chamber, or wherever it might be, I—" He pulled down his moustaches, for, like the Zairian moustaches they were, they insisted on growing upward and jutting out arrogantly, like mine. "I would give everything I own both to be there and yet never to have to witness that confrontation."

Around about then he remembered he was a rog and the King's Striker and a great overlord of Magdag, and I was a mere renegade looking to him for everything. He bade me clear off and make sure my Genodder was sharp for the night, just in case.

My orders were simple, for I was to open the doors and then make myself scarce. Gafard knew as well as I that the king's kidnappers might seek to slay me to silence me. My own plans called for a somewhat more ambitious program. That plan, however, would go into operation only if the king himself came with his men. There was little chance of that, but this Genod was a man of mettle, even if he was an evil rast, and the adventure would appeal to him.

Stealth and secrecy and wild midnight journeyings by the light of the seven moons of Kregen—yes, they have all been my lot on that wonderful world. I had spied in Hamal. I had made friends of Rees and Chido. Now they had left in an argenter, going back to Queen Thyllis with a story of the inefficiency of King Genod's guards, no doubt, and I regretted I had not plucked up the strength of will to confront them and so joy in a reunion I felt they would relish as much as I. This night might see me once again in action, taking a king and his favorite back to Zy.

The emerald and ruby fires of Antares slipped below the horizon past the jumbled roofs of Magdag, casting enormous, elongated shadows from the megaliths across the plain. The guard details changed as usual. The life of the Jade Palace went on normally. The thought of Rees and Chido calmly setting sail and leaving the Eye of the World, sailing back around the world to Hamal, filled me with the kind of baffled fury the prey of the Bichakker must feel when he unavailingly tries to climb the sloping sandy sides of the cone, and slips down into the hideous jaws waiting for him below. I was not sure who had created the sandy slopes that kept me imprisoned in the inner sea. But imprisoned I was. Any argenter in which I sailed would never pass through the Grand Canal, never reach the Dam of Days.

Gafard remained aloft with his beloved when the king's men came. The doors were open. I watched them through a chink in the inner door and saw them carry their logs and wedges to hold within any guards I had not poisoned thoroughly. This time there were no less than ten of them. Five remained to guard the escape; five went aloft. They returned very quickly bearing the shishi wrapped in a black cloak. She had ceased struggling. I saw with relief that no one carried a bloodied sword; all the blades remained in their scabbards. Silently, the black-cloaked men fled into the moon-shot darkness.

After a time Grogor came down and opened the door for us, kicking the logs and wedges away.

"It is done," he said. The evil smile on his face made me think of him in a much warmer light.

So we went back to our regular guard duties, for there were many other perils in Magdag besides the lusts of the genius king Genod.

The next day I went along to the rendezvous to pick up the balance of my pay, the other forty golden oars. No one turned up. I waited some time and then, with a fold of green cloth over my face, went back to the Jade Palace.

Nodgen the Faithful had proved himself damned faithless, the cramph.

Chapter Eighteen

At the Zhantil's Lair

Of course, it had been obvious from the first that King Genod would not do his own dirty work. He would never descend to padding about one of his nobles' palaces snuffing out a girl for himself. He was the king. He had the yrium. He would never come to me. So I had to go to him.

That was settled.

I am sure I have not adequately conveyed my feelings of desperation and frustration during this time when I was Gadak the Renegade. My heart felt sore and bruised. My mind shrieked for me to be free of this evil place and to leave the Eye of the World and return to Valka and race up the long flight of steps from the Kyro of the Tridents and so burst shouting joyously into my fortress palace of Esser Rarioch and once more clasp my Delia in my arms, my Delia of the Blue Mountains, my Delia of Delphond.

Before that devoutly longed-for resurrection could take place I must once more be accepted as a member of the Krozairs of Zy.

A High Jikai seemed to me to be the only way.

Truth to tell, as the days passed in Magdag and suns arched across the heavens and the duties came and went, I felt I cared little for the Krzy. I wished merely to use them to escape.

If this is brutal, callous, mean, and vengeful, then this is also me, to my shame.

Sometimes I would see my Lady of the Stars riding in the grassy park expanse, for the Jade Palace is large and sprawling among the buildings and palaces of Magdag, and she would graciously incline her head as I stood respectfully looking at her. She invariably wore the green veil.

Then I would feel the tiny gold and enamel valkavol on its golden chain about my neck. I detest chains and strings and beads. They give a foeman a chance to grip and twist and so drag your head down ready to receive the final chop.

I wore the little valkavol, except when on duty, for then danger and instant action might occur at any moment.

Occasionally Gafard would foin with me in the exercise yard. He was very good. He was a skilled man with the shortsword, and his Genodder work made me use all my skill to let me lose to him gracefully.

Although it seemed to me in my frustration and misery the time sped by superhumanly fast, as time is measured on Kregen very little elapsed before the announcement of the excursion was made and busy preparations immediately got under way.

We were to form a happy holiday party and visit Guamelga, Gafard's enormous estates up the River Dag forming his rognate.

I said to Gafard that if he could spare me I would wish not to travel with the party. It was not that I was reluctant for a holiday. Truth was I wanted to stay in Magdag and work on my plans to take this evil king Genod and pitch him facedown in the muck and so, binding and gagging him, lug him off to a safe place. Then, I fancied, it would be comparatively simple to do the same to Gafard.

"What, Gadak the Renegade! Lose the chance of a holiday!"

"If it please you, gernu."

"It does not please me. My Lady of the Stars will go with us. She travels as she has before. But I need all my loyal men. Has Shagash got at your guts, and you are sluggish and bilious?"

So there was nothing for it. I decided I would have to take Gafard and then see about the king. It would be more difficult that way around.

One thing I felt sure of. This time there would be no Chido and Rees to halt me in my tracks.

Although at the time of our taking of the one-pastang flier I'd felt annoyed we'd missed the little two-place voller, now I saw the enormous benefit of that. The small flier remained in Magdag. Once I had the king I'd put the voller to good use. It would carry the three of us. I'd make it damn well carry the three of us. Its lifting and propulsive power, carried in the two silver boxes, would be ample. If necessary I'd hang the two devils in straps from the outside and let them freeze in the slipstream. . . .

With that decided I put a bold face on the matter. I would have to act as a man delighting in the excursion, the picnics and the hunting parties. Everyone meant to enjoy every moment. We all surmised this was a last holiday before Gafard, the King's Striker, was dispatched on new missions for his master the king.

Before we left Magdag I carried out the last of my reconnaissances of the king's palaces. He possessed many residences in Magdag, the largest and most gorgeous of which, the Palace of Grodno the All-Wise, he used the least. This was reserved for official functions and contained the reception chamber where I had been received as a Grodnim. Two things must coincide for my plans to work right. The voller was seen over the city from time to time and people would look up and shout and no doubt think how mighty and powerful was their king. Sometimes a green-clad arm would wave. I had been unable to discover at which palace the damned thing was kept.

If it was moved about, then that made my arrangements just a little more difficult, for—by Krun!—they were difficult enough as it was. The voller and the king must be in the same place at the same time. Anything less would be not only suicidal, but downright stupid.

This genius king was very highly security conscious. I knew that after he had successfully won his battle against the overlords of Magdag and taken over here there had been plots against him. The overlords are a malignant lot. But he had weathered the troubled times and now kept his apparatus of guards and watches and sentinels and werstings in full order, for his genius, no doubt, told him this was a prudent course.

The next palace I reconnoitered, the Palace of Masks, looked promising. It was small, or at least small as any building of a palatial kind could ever be in Magdag of the megaliths. It hugged the crest of a hill to the east of the city just within the walls, built of yellow stone and yellow bricks. I say that it looked a charming spot, and I say that genuinely. There were more flowers and blossoming trees here than is usual in bare Magdag. I hung about looking at the guard posts and the sentry boxes, eyeing the roof with an evil glint, figuring angles and possible places for climbing and descent. If voller and king coincided here, I would strike.

Walking back to Gafard's Jade Palace I found myself

wondering how that little shishi was faring with the king. If she kept her head—and I meant that figuratively, although it had as much force literally—and maintained the fiction that she had been with Gafard for some time as his Lady of the Stars, she might become a person of extraordinary importance in Magdag. Even the princess Susheeng might have to look very carefully before she struck back.

As for Susheeng—if I never saw her again on Kregen it would be too soon.

That night all was bustle and laughing preparation within the Jade Palace. Opaz knows, the overlords of Magdag were a vile, villainous bunch; but even for them, and more particularly their women, a holiday ranked as a capital time to slough off all cares. We, the men of the loyal squadron, would ride our sectrixes fully armed, armored, and accoutered. I had had a small piece of good fortune one day in the Souk of Trophies, one of the open-air markets that should, by rights, have been called the Souk of Loot. Here the stalls were heaped with booty from Zairian prizes. I recalled when I had bought a piece of cut chemzite, a handsome trinket, to take to Vallia, and the princess Susheeng had thought it for her, and of my dark knowledge later that when she discovered it was not for her the scene had saved my life. Well, I found there not a piece of jewelry but a South Zairian hlamek, a wind-and-sand mask used by the people living on the skirts of the vast South Turismond deserts. It consisted of a metal skull, a finely crafted piece of hammered iron, well-padded with soft humespack, to which were appended four long and wide white humespack panels. From the upper side of the left-hand panel a broad square of silk was hinged in such a fashion that the left hand might take the top corner and hook it to the right side. It would cover all the face below the eyes, crossing the bridge of the nose. As a protection against wind and sand it was first rate, loose and soft enough to keep the wearer comfortable. All the brave scarlet stitching had been stripped away, but the basic fastenings remained intact.

As a facemask it offered opportunities I could not refuse.

So the hlamek went into the saddlebag along with my toilet necessities, the book I was reading (*How the Ghittawrer Gogol Gan Gorstar Conquered Ten Kingdoms of Zair to the Glory of Grodno*), my eating irons, and the golden drinking cup, one of the set presented to all those who had rescued her by the Lady of the Stars. We drank deep and long to her health in her golden drinking cups, for she had had the forethought to include a notable quantity of wine with her gift.

In a glittering procession we rode out of Magdag early on the following morning only murs after Zim and Genodras cleared the eastern battlements of the city. Each sectrix had been rubbed down, its mane curled and decorated with green ribbons, its hooves polished. The harness burned in the light. Green banners fluttered. Following the lord came his staff and retinue, his aides, his loyal squadron. The overlords who owed him allegiance rode with their wives and families. Following after came the long lines of wagons stuffed with good things, their krahniks in the shafts and hauling on the traces as scrubbed and shining as the sectrixes and hebras of the escort. After them came the calsanys, loaded down with enormous swaying baggage packs, linked head to tail by caravan ropes dyed green.

Yes, we made a goodly spectacle as we rode out of evil Magdag.

Although the slow-moving River Mag was perfectly suitable for river navigation, Gafard had chosen to ride. We could cut across the vast lazy curves of the river and cross by the ferry services provided on this, the direct route to the north. Once free of the delta we could swing to the northwest and so leave the river entirely and march through fertile country, past the chains of factory farms run in so meticulous a fashion by the overlords of the second class and journey on until we reached Guamelga in its loop of the river.

Hikdar Nath ti Hagon received special permission to leave us to ride to the east to his home town for a visit. He would rejoin us at Guamelga later.

Among our bright company there rode the Lady of the Stars, accoutered like a warrior. Gafard rarely left her side where they jogged on at the head of the column. Perforce, I was left to trundle along in the ranks and meditate on my plans.

A hunting party of a similar kind in Havilfar, if they did not fly by voller, would have flown astride any of the marvelous saddle birds or animals of that continent. With a mirvol under me, or a fluttclepper, I could have breasted into the breeze and the slipstream would have blown the cobwebs from my mind. I do not think, as I have said, I would choose a zhyan, for all that Zena Iztar had appeared to me astride one of those snow-white birds. Best of all is the flutduin in my opinion, the flyer of my warrior Djangs, and a magnificent flying creature I had introduced into Valka. It seemed to me, jogging along toward Guamelga and a holiday that would be a farce, that King Genod would very soon receive another consignment of vollers to replace the ones I had smashed up in the tide released from the Dam of Days. If the empress Thyllis meant to do a thing, she did it come hell or high water—and she'd had the high water, by Vox! So I would have to provide the hell. That, in my mood, seemed a singularly pleasant prospect.

Still and all, during my enforced imprisonment on Earth I had missed the high enjoyment of sweeping through the sky astride a giant flying mount. Even a fluttrell with its ridiculous headvane would have been like water in a desert to me then.

The city of Guamelga itself was small, gabled of roof, of no particular distinction, walled—for it was near enough the lands of the Ugas for raids to be counted on—and dominated by the harsh stone bulk of the castle, the Goytering. We did not stay in the castle or the city for long, Gafard being anxious to get away from all cares, and so we went deeper into the countryside away from the cultivated areas to one of the hunting lodges he kept up. The one he chose was the Zhantil's Lair. A comfortable enough place set in woodlands with wide-open prospects of tall grasses beyond, it would not accommodate all his people and of those he kept with him I was one. I was pleased about this. I wanted the rogue under my eye.

Days of hunting followed. There was all manner of game, and there were leems and chavonths and, once, a pair of hunting lairgodonts. The hunting party was in sufficient strength to dispose of them. The trophies were brought back in triumph.

The Magdaggians do not go in greatly for singing. Oh, yes, they do sing, of course, and we had a few sessions around the fires of an evening. It is an odd fact that the Magdaggian swods when they sing on the march habitually bellow out only two or three songs, not caring for many others. Of these the most common is a song I find tiresome, going as it does with the beat of the studded marching sandals—"Ob! Dwa! So!"—One! Two! Three!—followed by a doggerel verse about Genodras or Goyt or Gyphimedes or Grodno. *Ob, dwa, so,* as intellectual subject matter for a song, seems to me somewhat below what is necessary. Still, it takes all kinds to make a world, particularly the world of

Kregen. As was to be expected, this song was known as the "Obdwa Song."

When some idiot started up this song in the wood-paneled dining room I stood up, swaying a little to color my appearance of fuddlement. "Ob, dwa so," they sang. "We're a bloodthirsty lot, as Gashil is our witness. Ley, waso, shiv, we'll slit throats and empty purses. Shebov, ord—"

I wandered out into the paneled hall and made my way to the kitchens in search of a drink of fresh water from the pump.

The room was brilliantly lit at the far end, down by the ovens and the preparation tables, but where I had come in to get at the hand-cranked pump shadows fell. I heard a noise and instantly, for the noise was a slither, I put my hand on my shortsword and padded forward silently. I heard a low voice, a very low voice, singing a song I knew.

It is impossible to translate the song as a poem from the Kregish to the English, as I have already mentioned. But the meaning of the words was something like: "If your swifter's got a kink, my lads, your swifter's got a kink. You'll go around in circles, boys, in circles around you'll go. Your ram will pierce your stern, old son, your ram will pierce your stern. You'll vanish like a sea-ghost, dom, a sea-ghost you'll become—"

At this point the soft singing stopped and I heard the evil scrape of steel on steel as a blade cleared scabbard.

A harsh voice, kept low and penetrating, bit out: "Weng da!"

At the formal challenge of *Weng da* I said, "It is only Gadak the Renegade."

For I knew who this was and I knew the next words of the song, that famous old Zairian song, "The Swifter with the Kink," were highly uncomplimentary to the Green of Grodnim and most satisfyingly urbane about the Red of Zair.

I stepped forward into the light.

If Gafard wanted to make an issue of this, well, now was a time I would not have chosen; but it was a time I would make serve. I saw the silver glitter run up and down his blade.

"Gadak! You heard?"

"I heard 'Ob, dwa, so,' gernu. That is all."

The reflections of the blade shimmered and then were engulfed in that scabbarding screech.

"Make it so." The slur in his voice was barely noticeable.

I made no formal bellow of loyalty.

I said, "But, all the same, it is hard."

He did not bite.

Instead he answered me in a way that showed he had thought about this thing and had reconciled himself.

"I am Gafard, Rog of Guamelga, the King's Striker, the Sea-Zhantil. Few men carry the honor I command. You would do well to think of who your just masters are, Gadak the Renegade."

My hand rested limp and relaxed, ready to whip the Genodder out in a blur of steel.

"You told me, gernu, that no overlord would treat me as you have done. This I believe. I think had you been an ordinary overlord of Magdag one of us would be dead by now."

He stepped into the light and smiled. He was not quite perfectly composed. "If that were so, I think it would be you who lay stretched in his own blood on the kitchen floor."

"Yet you did not strike."

"My Lady has said—it is a thing I marvel at—" He put something of his old imperiousness into his words. "She has taken a fancy to you, Gadak. For that alone many an overlord would have you done away with."

"Yet this business with the king—it is a worry."

He lost his smile and scowled.

"I have said before, this is no matter for you to concern yourself with. I am the King's Striker! The king has the yrium! That is all there needs to be said."

"That is all—until the next time."

"You step dangerously near the bounds of impudence, of insubordination. If one of us accused the other of singing 'The Swifter with the Kink,' who do you think the overlords would believe? Riddle me that, Gadak!"

"You are secure in your power, gernu. Yet—" I stopped.

"Yes. Yet?"

"I will say no more. I serve you and my Lady. You know that to be sooth."

"I know it is sooth now. Let it remain sooth."

If I clouted him over the head now I'd have the devil of a job hauling him back to Magdag and then of taking the king and the voller. Better by far to grab the king first, with the voller, as I planned, and then bundle up this Gafard after. Yes, far better.

As I stood there with him in the kitchen I thought how

dark and dangerous and powerful a man he was. I would then and there have joyed in hand-strokes with him, for he was a doughty fighter. But I let the opportunity pass.

"When, gernu, do we return to Magdag?"

"You are tired of this holiday? Aye, it palls." He stretched and yawned. "Give me the thrust of a swifter, to stand as prijiker in the bows, to bear down in the shock of the ram—aye! That is living."

"It is," I said. I believed the words as I spoke them.

"We will roam the Eye of the World, Gadak! We will create many a High Jikai! Soon all men will forget that Pur Dray existed—he will be a name, lost and forgotten with Pur Zydeng, the greatest Krozair of five centuries past. Dead with the great Ghittawrer Gamba the Rapacious, who went to the Ice Floes of Sicce these thousand seasons gone. Aye!"

"And yet, gernu, you speak always of the Lord of Strombor. I know you have no fear of him. But your interest interests me. I am fascinated not by Pur Dray but by your fascination."

He had forgotten to be imperious. His eyes held a long-lost look of a man sinking in a death-race of the sea.

"The Lord of Strombor was the greatest Krozair of his time. Greater than any Ghittawrer of Magdag. I would prove I am his match—and there is more. For this matter between us—and I speak to you like this only because my Lady smiles on you. I shall be sorry, tomorrow, and you may tremble lest I have your head off for it." He was, I could see, more than a little fuddled with wine. He was not drunk. I never saw him drunk or incapable. But he had had his tongue loosened.

Irritation at his petty problems flooded me. Perhaps I might have flamed out, in my stupid, prideful arrogance: "Sink me! You stupid onker! I am Pur Dray and what is this matter between us you prate so of?"

But I did not. I do not think, had I done so, it would have made any difference.

He probably would not have believed me, anyway, then.

He pulled himself erect and slapped his left hand down on his longsword hilt. "Enough of this kitchen talk! I came here to—to vent a little spleen. I want no more of them in there this night. Attend me to my room."

"Aye, gernu."

We went up the back stair to his suite of chambers in the Zhantil's Lair. They were lavish and expensive, as one would expect, hung about with trophies of the chase. A lounge had been furnished by a man's hand. But through the inner doors lay the apartments of my Lady of the Stars.

He slumped down in a chair and bellowed for wine.

"You, Gadak the Renegade. Have you ever been outside the Eye of the World? Out to the unknown, improbable lands there?"

I poured him his wine and pondered the question.

"Yes, gernu."

"Ah!" He took the wine. The shadows of the room clustered against the samphron oil lamps' gleam. "You have never seen my Lady—before you met me?"

"No. I swear it." This could be dangerous. "I respect her deeply. I feel I have proved that, yet I would not in honor speak of it."

"Yes, yes, you have served. And you swear?"

"I swear."

"And she is very tender of you. She was much impressed when you slew the lairgodonts. That was a jikai. You trespass where no man has trespassed before—and lived."

"I am an ordinary man. I know my Lady has the most tender affection for you. Do you think I would—?"

"What you, Gadak?" He drank the wine off, and laughed, and hurled the glass to smash against the wall, splattering a leem-skin hung there with dregs and glass, shining in the light. "No, Gadak, for I recognize you. You are the upright, the correct, the loyal man. You know which side your bread's buttered. With me you have the chance of a glittering career. You may be made Ghittawrer soon."

"If the king's man, this Nodgen the Faithful, does not have my head for the king."

"No. No chance of that. The king and I—we play this game, but for him it is a game. For me the stakes are too high. I do not know what I would do if my Lady was taken from me—" He bellowed for fresh wine then, to cover his words.

"She must not fall into the king's hands." He drank deeply. I had never seen him drunk; he was in a fair way to showing me that interesting phenomenon for the first time. "She must not! He would do what I should do—should do— and, by Green Grodno, cannot, will not—will never!"

I saw clearly that some oppressive matter weighed on his mind. As a renegade he was not fully accepted by the overlords. He believed in the king and yet in this matter he could not talk to the king. He desperately wished to confide in someone, as is a common practice among people, I have noticed. If he decided to tell me, I wondered if that would make my position more secure or destroy me utterly. I rather thought it would be the latter. Yet this man fascinated me. I could feel the strong attraction he exerted despite the evil of him. He was a mere man, as was I. He would pay for his crimes. Was the changing of allegiance from Red to Green so great a matter anywhere but on the inner sea? I found it hard to condemn him as I knew him now, as I had found it easy to condemn him when I did not know him.

"Riddle me this, Gadak. Which is more important, the good of your lady or the good of your country?"

"That has had many facile answers, and every case is different."

"But if it was you—you! Your answer?"

"No man can answer until he has faced the situation and the question."

"Do you know that my Lady of the Stars and I are married? No—only a very few know. Grogor knows. We married permanently. Not in the rites of Grodno—" He picked up his glass and spilled most of it. He barely noticed.

"Then the king would honor a legal and sanctified marriage."

"Fambly! He has the yrium. And the rites were not the rites of Grodno." He chuckled. "Even though there were two ceremonies, neither was that of Grodno." And he drank and let the glass slip through his fingers.

I felt a prod might bring him back to reason. For so strong and powerful a personality he was letting go of his will, was allowing this matter that tormented him to undermine all the strength he possessed, and so I knew this was no ordinary matter that so obsessed him. I spoke carefully.

"If the king succeeded in taking my Lady, would your men fight to regain her? If the fact was over and done, would they risk treason against the king? In that situation would not their loyalty to the king transcend their loyalty to you?"

He struggled to rise and slumped back, panting.

"So that is how you answer the question of loyalty to your lady and loyalty to your country!"

"You should know better—if this is the case you present, then—"

"It is the case! Grogor would go up against the king for

me, I know! And I picked you, for I thought you would be loyal—even if I could not, for the king has the yrium, even if I could not—you—"

If that was his problem I fancied the stab of an emergency would quickly make up his mind for him.

As though Drig himself had heard me and mocked me, on that thought the door opened and Grogor burst in. He looked ghastly. Both Gafard and I knew, at once, almost word for word what he would say. Gafard lumbered up, screeching, drawing his sword. Swords would be useless for a space, I fancied.

"Gernu! She is taken! Stikitches—real assassins in metal faces, professionals. . . . They ride toward the Volgodonts' Aerie!"

The Volgodonts' Aerie, another hunting lodge like the Zhantil's Lair, stood some three burs' ride away in the woods. That, we could not have foreseen.

Gafard's face appeared both shrunken and bloated. His eyes glared. All the drink he had taken made his face enormous and yet the horror of the moment shriveled him. He gasped and struggled to breathe. I caught him and lowered him into his chair. Grogor stood, half bent, expecting an avalanche of invective. Gafard croaked words, vicious, harsh words like bolts from a crossbow.

"We must ride, Grogor! Have the sectrixes saddled up. Gather the men. We must ride like Zhuannar of the Storm!"

"Rather, master, call on Grakki-Grodno—"

I knew what he meant. Grakki-Grodno was the sky-god of draft-beasts of Magdag. So for all his brave talk, he had failed the test.

But Grogor said, "The king has taken my Lady and she is now his. He is the king and he has the yrium. The men would have fought for you—*have* fought for you, master— when she was rightfully yours. Now she is rightfully the king's. No man will raise his hand against the king." Then, this bulky, sweaty man, a renegade, drew himself up. "I would ride, my lord. Would you have me ride alone against the king?"

He had a powerful point. Gafard looked crushed. The strength and power oozed out of him. I felt a crushing sorrow for the Lady of the Stars. Evidently the little shishi had failed to convince the king. Spies had done the rest. There were those in Gafard's household who did not love him, that was certain, and we had made a splendid spectacle riding out of Magdag. There was no point in my offering to ride. If Gafard roused himself, if Grogor rode, that would be three of us against a band of professional stikitches. The assassins of Kregen are an efficient bunch of rasts when they have to be, and on a task of kidnapping they are no less ruthless. No, sorrowful though this made me, I would have to go with the majority.

My own concerns for my Delia must come first. My Delia—ah! How I longed for her then. . . . How could a pretty girl, even a girl with the fire and spirit and charm of the Lady of the Stars, stand for a moment in my thoughts against my Delia!

The shadows in the corner of that masculine room—with the harsh trophies of the hunt upon the walls, the stands of arms, the pieces of harness and mail, the tall motionless drapes—all breathed to me of softer, sweeter things: of Delia's laugh, the sight of her as we swam together in Esser Rarioch, the love we had for our children, all the intimate details that make of a man and a woman, make of a marriage, a single and indivisible oneness.

No, I would not throw away my Delia's happiness for my Lady of the Stars.

Gafard was breathing in hoarse, rattling gasps. The drink, the shock, the fuddlement, had left him bereft of that incisive command. He had been stricken down.

"The men will not ride!" He shook his head, hardly able to believe and yet knowing the stark truth of it. He turned to me and stretched out a hand. "And you, Gadak the Renegade, the man I chose and pampered—will you, Gadak, ride for me this night?"

"No," I said.

He fell back in the chair. His face sagged. He looked distraught, wild, near-insane.

Then he proved himself.

"Then to Sicce with you all! I will ride myself, alone, for I know well what my Lord of Strombor will say!"

I felt no shock, only puzzlement.

He staggered up, waving his arms, casting about for his mail. I gripped his arm and Grogor jumped. I said, "What is this of the Lord of Strombor?"

Gafard swung a wild, sweaty face upon me. The sweat clung to his dark, clustered curls and dripped down his face. The lines in that face were etched deep. His beard bristled.

"You onker! If the king takes my Lady—Pur Dray is in the city! He has been seen in Magdag, it is very sure." He spoke down from that high screech, as a man explaining a simple problem to a child. He put a hand on my hand. "Let me go, Gadak, traitor, ingrate! I will save my Lady for Pur Dray and then I will deal with you."

I held him. Grogor moved and I swung my head and glared at him. "Stand, Grogor, as you value your life!" I shook Gafard, the King's Striker. "Listen to me, Gafard! You prate of Pur Dray, the Lord of Strombor. What has he to do with this matter? Tell me the matter that lies between you, Gafard! Tell me! What has the Lord of Strombor to do with the Lady of the Stars?"

Some semblance of sanity returned to him. He was Gafard, the Sea-Zhantil, and he was not to be shaken by a mere mercenary, a renegade, a man he had made!

"You cramph!" he said. He spoke thickly. "You are a dead man—for you sit and let my Lady go to certain death—hideous death—death by torture for what she knows, and, before that, to humiliation and the baiting of a trap."

"Tell me, Gafard, you nurdling great onker! *Tell me!*"

He shrieked as my fingers bit into the bones of his arm.

He twisted and glared up, his fierce, predatory face close to mine and so like my own, so like my own.

"You fool! Pur Dray, the greatest Krozair of the Eye of the World, is here, in Magdag. And King Genod takes the Lady of the Stars! When he finds out, as he will find out— for he has the yrium, he will find out—then—and then—"

I shook him again. I bore down on him, all the hateful ferocity in my face overmatching his own. Grogor took another step and I said "Grogor!" and he stopped stock still.

"When the king finds out what, Gafard? What is this trap? Tell me or I will break your arm off!"

He shrieked again and foam sprang to his lips. He tried to pull away and Grogor moved once more so I swung Gafard, the King's Striker, about, prepared to hurl him at Grogor. I could feel his bones grinding under my fingers.

"Now, Gafard, now!"

"You are a dead man, Gadak! For King Genod has taken Velia, who is the daughter of Pur Dray, the Lord of Strombor."

Chapter Nineteen

Stricken by genius

Gafard screamed it out, foaming, as I hurled him into the chair.

"The king has taken Velia, Princess Velia, daughter to Pur Dray, the Lord of Strombor, Prince Majister of Vallia!"

Everything blurred.

I remember colliding with Grogor on my way to the door and knocking him flying. There were stairs. There were people shouting and milling. Men stood in my way and were suddenly not there. There were softnesses under my feet. The air was suddenly cool and fresh. Stars blazed. The moons were up, gliding silently through the starfields. The sectrix stalls lay shrouded in darkness. Harness—no time, no time—bareback! A sectrix beneath me. A vicious kick, more vicious kicks. The lolloping six-legged gait. Hard, merciless kicks, the flat of my sword, then sharper, more urgent bounding. The dark flicker of tree branches overhead. The dazzlement of the moons. The harsh, jolting ride, the clamor of hooves, the rush of wind, the pain, the agony, the remorse—

Velia!

My little Velia!

Fragments, I remember, of that night ride with the horror gibbering and clawing at me, the ghastly specters obscenely taunting me, mocking me—

I knew what this kleesh of a King Genod would do when he discovered he held in his hands the daughter of Dray Prescot, the Lord of Strombor, the notorious and dreaded Krozair of Zy.

I would consign all the Krzy to Sicce to save my daughter. What would Delia say? What would be her agony?

184

I galloped and galloped and I galloped as a man who has no heart, has never had a heart, and is never likely to find a heart in this wicked world.

Velia . . . Velia. . . . The sectrix hooves beat out her name on the hard forest paths, over the rippling grasslands silver and pink and gold beneath the moons, the breeze swaying them as a breeze ruffles the inner sea.

Years and years ago I had last seen her. I had not recognized her, and she had not recognized me.

Yet—was not that strange feeling I had suffered now explained, the weird compulsion in me to do nothing to destroy the happiness of the Lady of the Stars? Now I knew why Gafard, the King's Striker, was not bundled in a blanket and safely in the hands of the Krozairs upon the fortress isle of Zy.

If we had not recognized each other's faces, and our names had been strange and false, had not the blood called, one to the other? Oh, maybe that is sentimental nonsense, maybe it is mere wishful thinking; but there *had* been some deep psychological force drawing and binding me to my daughter. Perhaps the racial unconscious, if there be such a thing, is most pronounced and powerful in relatives, and the only bond as powerful as that of a father to his daughter is that of a mother to her son.

The sectrix's hoofbeats echoed in my ears, a strange triple echo. I twisted about. In that streaming moonlight a second sectrix followed me, bounding along, its rider's cape flaring in the golden light. The man rode like a maniac. He rode as I rode.

I recognized Grogor.

I smashed at my mount again and he responded. We flew out into a clearing of the tall grasses and splashed across a stream. On and on—the stikitches would take my daughter to the king at the Volgodonts' Aerie. There was every chance he would have flown here in the little two-place airboat. If he had I would take his voller. Somehow I did not think I would bother to take him back to Zy.

Looking back now, as that mad ride brought me raving across the wild country to the Volgodonts' Aerie, I recognize my headlong foolishness. I had been denied many of the best years in which a father may see his children growing up. Velia had been three when the damned Star Lords had whirled me back to Earth for a miserable twenty-one years; she would be twenty-five now. What had her life been like?

Fragments, impressions, the jolting of the sectrix, the blustering of the wind, the pain in my jaws, and over all the moonshine, streaming gold and pink and glorious upon the nighted face of Kregen, mocking the blackness upon me. For every moon shone in the sky, full and gleaming, in that tiny period when the three smaller moons in their hurtling passages coincide and form with the Maiden with the Many Smiles, and the Twins, and She of the Veils; that magic time of the Scarf of Our Lady Monafeyom.

Brilliant the light, brilliant and yet soft with the exquisite delicacy of moonlight.

The land lay as though enchanted.

And through that magic midnight splendor I rode with the devils gibbering at me and ghastly phantasms tormenting my mind, for I knew that this genius king planned no pleasure for my Velia.

Through a screen of trees I flung the sectrix, striking away branches and leaves, silver and gold and rose in the radiance, and bore out onto a meadow where a stream ran, liquid bronze under the moons of Kregen—and there lifted the Volgodonts' Aerie.

Stark and many pinnacled, it rose against the stars like a stretched and piercing claw of a volgodont itself.

The sectrix was not as fine a mount as Grogor's. Now Gafard's second in command was up with me. The two animals galloped neck and neck. I did not speak. I could not speak. I stared ahead as a leem stares, entirely vicious and feral, without mercy.

Grogor shouted. "We will never save her—only us two! The lord follows. Gadak, this is madness!"

I did not answer him, but hit my failing beast with the flat of the sword.

"The lord bid me say he would forgive you, Gadak, only if you humble yourself to him—he follows—Gadak!"

Still I did not answer. We raced on. I feel sure that you who listen to my story will long ago have realized who the Lady of the Stars was, that she was my daughter. Now, with hindsight, it seemed obvious. But, to me, plain Dray Prescot who had so little experience of daughters to go on, how could that stunning truth possibly be easy? I had not known, had had no remotest idea. How could I?

Sectrix riders trotted out into the clearing to front us.

I saw their green cloaks, weird in the moons' radiances, and the blackness of their clothes. Pinkly golden glitter reflected from their steel facemasks. They wore mail.

Grogor saw and cursed.

I did not halt the laboring sectrix. The animal lunged straight ahead, gasping in convulsive effort, the steam jetting from his nostrils. The stikitches lifted their swords. There were six of them, I believe. I did not count. I recollect the jar of blade on blade, the quick and deadly cut, and the vicious thrust. I lopped and chopped. I spitted. The facemasks splintered in shards of flying metal. I whirled that Ghittawrer weapon and I sliced those damned assassins, and there was no real time or reason in it beyond the swirling madness in my brain, the crazy viciousness of insanity driving me on.

The six of them, if there were six of them, lay sprawled upon the grass of the meadow, their black and shining blood dribbling in pools from their mutilated bodies. I did not spare a single look, but hit the sectrix and galloped on.

I did hear Grogor screaming: "You are a devil!"

That was true. Why remark on it?

"We are too late!" Grogor was yelling and hauling his beast up. He almost collided with me, the six-legged animals struggling together and staggering sideways.

"Get out of my way, rast!" I said, hauling my mount up, driving it to stand and run although it was almost done.

"Look!" Grogor pointed. He pointed up.

I looked. If the king was away in the voller it would be over.

A great winged shape lofted from the top tower of the Volgodonts' Aerie. Against the radiance of the moons the fluttrell soared up, his wide pinions beating in that long, effortless rhythm of the saddle bird.

Grogor yelled in openmouthed disbelief. The truth was plain. More argenters had arrived from Hamal and as well as vollers they carried saddle birds. The fluttrell was the most common saddle-mount of Havilfar. Thyllis had spared a few to please the whim of King Genod and he had mastered the knack of flying and had come here, in person, to show off his prowess to his new conquest, the Lady of the Stars, who had once been the lady of Gafard, the King's Striker, and was now the lady of the king—for a time.

"The devil from the bat-caves!" yelled Grogor. My sectrix staggered with exhaustion. Grogor hauled out his bow, drew and nocked an arrow, lifted and let fly. I reached out to him, dropping the blood-choked Ghittawrer sword. But his fingers released the string and the shaft flew.

If he hit Velia . . . !

The fluttrell winged up, its pinions beating. I did not see the arrow strike. I saw those wings suddenly flap limply; they beat off-rhythm; and the bird swerved in the air.

Grogor's arrow had wounded the fluttrell, yet it could still fly. I saw it curve around in a mazy, sweeping circle. It was dropping. The wings beat erratically. The bird extended its legs, talons spread wide.

Grogor hauled out his sword. He yelled, high and fierce. He sent his mount charging for the point where the bird would land. I could see two figures on the fluttrell's back, abaft the wide headvane. Two figures, struggling. I held my breath.

The king must have newly learned the art of flying a saddlebird. I guessed my Velia—my Velia! My daughter! —would be an expert in the air, trained by my Djangs astride flutduins. She would not thus foolishly struggle as a bird planed in for a landing.

Grogor's sword blurred in the mingled light of the Scarf of Our Lady Monafeyom.

The king saw us below him. I saw his face, a pale blur in the light, saw it lift and stare past that other face so near his hateful features, stare and look past me. I turned. A body of men rode in the shadows of the trees. It was difficult to distinguish them, save for the green and the mail and the glitter of weapons and war harness. I did not think they rode on behalf of Gafard. But they might. Gafard, himself, might ride at their head.

This is what the king thought.

I swung back. Grogor was bellowing and shaking his sword.

The bird made a last effort. It beat its wings and tried to rise. The two faces up there were close together as the bird tried to lift and fly in obedience to the frenzied flogging from Genod's goad. It tried to beat its pinions and rise up, and could not. I saw those two faces—then there was one face only above the fluttrell's back and a white-clad form pitching headlong from the air.

King Genod, the genius, had thrown my daughter from the fluttrell, thrown her to the ground beneath.

Relieved of the extra weight the fluttrell beat more powerfully and rose. Its wings thrashed the air. It lifted and soared up. Grogor's second shot fell far too short.

I saw all that from the corner of my eye, not heeding.

I saw the spinning form of Velia, her white dress swirling

out, pitch down through the empty air. She fell. She fell to the ground. She fell. She fell on the ground.

I was riding hard.

How often I had picked up little Velia as she tottered on her chubby little legs, there on the high terrace of Esser Rarioch, learning to walk, determined, clambering up and trying again, to tumble down again in a sprawl of her short white dress.

I rode on.

An arrow whipped in past Grogor's ear. He swung his mount about, yelled, high: "Overlords! We are dead men! We must run!"

He stuck in his spurs and was away, the sectrix hurtling along low over the ground, its shadows spreading about it, undulating eerie blobs of half-darkness.

The overlords of Magdag trotted over the meadow toward me.

I galloped and I did not care what the damned overlords did.

The six legs of my beast skidded and splayed as I reined it up. I was off its bare back. It just stood, waiting for me to remount.

I knelt.

She lay crumpled, her white dress spread out, with no sign of blood anywhere. Her eyes were open, those beautiful brown eyes I could see now were those of a Vallian; beautiful brown eyes like my Delia's. Her glowing brown hair was dyed black and artificially curled, in imitation of a Zairian. That was so.

"Velia," I said, and I choked.

"Why, Gadak," she said. "You know my name." As she spoke a tiny line of blood trickled from the corner of her mouth. "I—I like that, Gadak, for I have always been fond of you."

"Velia—" I took her hand in mine as I knelt. It was cold. "Velia—I am not Gadak. That is not my name."

She smiled up. Now I could see my Delia in her face—my glorious Delia reborn in a subtly different way, as glorious, as wonderful—and thrown callously through the air by a genius.

"You will look after me, Gadak? And my lord? He is safe?"

"He is safe, my heart. Listen—I love your mother as no man has loved a woman. There in Esser Rarioch we were happy, and we joyed in our twins, Segnik and Velia—"

She stared at me, her soft mouth curling in puzzlement, for she felt no pain.

"What do you say, Gadak? What of—Esser Rarioch, and Valka? And—my mother—you—I have no father. He is gone away, a long way away, a long time ago."

Those Star Lords! If I'd had one under my hands then, he would never more play cruel tricks on plain men.

"Yes, Velia, you are my dear daughter, for I am your father, and I have sinned—it is all my fault—and—"

"Father . . . ?"

"Yes."

I did not know what she would do. Had she cursed and reviled me I would know she was right.

She said, "Gadak—you do not say this—to please me? Where is my lord? Has he told you to say this?"

I held her hand and it was cold. I touched her lips with a silk kerchief and wiped away the blood. I smoothed her hair. We spoke, then, and I told her little things, things that she would understand Dray Prescot, the Strom of Valka, would understand. She could not move. She smiled and I saw in her face that she forgave me. I did not deserve that, but she forgave me. We talked—and I took her into my arms and held her and smoothed her hair and looked down upon her face. Her pallor gave her an ethereal beauty there in the light of the moons of Kregen as the Scarf of Our Lady Monafeyom gleamed in pure brilliance against the stars.

"Father?" She understood I spoke the truth. "I wish my lord were here. We are married. In the rites of Zair and Opaz. He is a fierce man, proud and brave, but very gentle. He means well."

She moved her head slowly to one side, and then back, nestling in my arms, and looked at me. "There is a child. My little Didi. Gafard—my lord, my beloved—keeps her well hidden. She will love her new grandfather."

I had to close my mouth. I could not speak.

"I came with Zeg to the Eye of the World. He is a great Krozair, Father, a famous Krozair of Zy. And—and I was taken. I fought them with my dagger as Mother knew I would. The Sisters of the Rose . . . but it was Gafard, my lord. I knew, even then, and he knew, too." She breathed a long, shuddering sigh and I looked down on her, but she went on speaking in that small girl's voice through the gathering darkness about her. "The king—Genod—is evil, Father. Drak and Zeg have told me. Now he has vollers and birds. The overlords—they laughed when the king flew off with me. If only Gafard—"

The mists were closing down over her eyes. She stared up, trying to see me clearly. "Father—where is Mother? Where is my lord?"

"They will soon be here, Velia, my heart. You will soon see them. And little Didi."

Now I could hear the trampling of sectrixes and the clatter of harness. The overlords of Magdag were riding up for me. A strong party galloped in pursuit of Grogor. They left their comrades to deal with the willful girl and this uncouth man of Gafard's. They approached slowly, confident in their might. My sectrix still stood, head drooping, reins dangling, waiting for me to mount up and ride.

I held my Velia in my arms, her head against my breast, and I would not move.

"It is very dark, Father. Is this the night of Notor Zan?"

"Yes, Velia. The Scarf of Our Lady Monafeyom is all rolled up and put away, and the dark cloak of Notor Zan is unfolded. You will sleep for a while. Then Mother and Drak and Lela and Segnik and your Didi will come to see you."

"I long to see them again, and Jaidur and Dayra and—" Her soft whispering voice gathered strength. "And my lord?" She tried to move in my arms. "And my lord Gafard? He will come to see me. He is safe—Father! He is safe?"

"Yes, Velia my daughter, Gafard is safe."

"You will like him, Father. I wished you could have known him. He is a very good man and he loves me so." Her eyes were wide open, not seeing me. "It is very dark. When will Mother come to see me? And Gafard . . ."

The overlords of Magdag trampled nearer in their iron and their might.

I, Dray Prescot, with a host of stupid titles, sat and held my daughter Velia in my arms.

Shadows fell across the bright faces of the moons.

Toward the end her sight cleared. She looked up as I held her cradled and she saw the tiny gold and enamel valkavol she had given me.

"The valkavol!" she said, and the dark blood ran down her white chin, thick and thicker. "Father—it will be all right. . . ."

I did not care if the whole of Kregen heard her. The overlords meant nothing. The metallic rattle of their war harness sounded loudly now, the stamp of sectrix hooves iron-hard on the turf.

She lost that brief spurt of luminous reason. She lay back in my arms, as she had when I had first held her, looking up from her tiny face to the glory of my Delia beyond, smiling. Her hands and her face were ice-cold.

"My lord . . ." she whispered. "My love . . ."

She was slipping from me.

"Mother," she said. "Here is Father."

The pallor of her face, the coldness of her, and that ugly red dribble from her mouth . . .

"Father—" she said again. And then: "Gafard." She spoke his name three or four times. At the end she said, "Oh, to be home in Val—"

The overlords of Magdag rode up to take me.

I sat on the ground holding the broken body of my daughter in my arms as they came for me—as my Velia died.